BROKEN FATES

SEVERED FLAMES
BOOK THREE

ANNIE ANDERSON

BROKEN FATES

Severed Flames Book Three

Annie Anderson

Published by Annie Anderson

Copyright © 2025 Annie Anderson

Edited by: Angela Sanders

Cover Art by: Tattered Quill Designs

All rights reserved.

Paperback ISBN: 978-1-960315-78-6

Hardcover ISBN: 978-1-960315-80-9

SEVILAVA

PERDER LUCEM

DIREVEIL

GIROVIA

TARRASCA

FESTIA

THE CONTINENT OF
CREDOUR

For all my girlies who know that love, in all its forms, can change your stars. Here's to writing our own endings and refusing to bow to the whims of Fate.

You were wild once. Don't let them tame you.

— ISADORA DUNCAN

CHAPTER 1

VALE

The night threatened to swallow me whole.

Like the great maw of the gorge under the mountain, the void yawned wide, waiting to consume me. Each step felt like a gamble, like I was back on that stone staircase, the weight of unseen eyes pressing down on me, waiting for me to fall.

But it wasn't the darkness that frightened me.

No, it was the stillness.

Not even the whisper of wind stirred the branches. No rustling leaves. No distant hoot of an owl or chirp of a night insect. Just silence—thick, absolute, and *wrong*.

I forced my breath to stay steady, each inhale sharp and thin in the winter air. My lungs burned, raw from running too hard, too fast, for too long. The ache in my ribs was a constant reminder that my body had limits, but I ignored it. I had to.

My cloak snagged on the jagged branches, the brittle twigs clawing at the fabric like fingers of the dead. I jerked it free, not stopping. Not looking back.

I'd really done it.

I'd left.

I'd left *them*.

A sharp ache lanced through my chest, but I shoved it down. Kian. Xavier. Idris. They didn't need me anymore. They had gotten exactly what they'd always wanted—the return of magic, the unbinding of their King.

Idris was whole. His dragon was no longer caged. The balance had been restored. And I'd had to betray them to do it.

I still felt the pulse of Rune's hot blood flowing over my fingers, his resonate voice in my head begging me to help, pleading with me to save Idris. I swallowed hard, rubbing at the empty space over my heart as I forced my tears down.

Rune was gone now—dead. Everything he was now lie inside Idris, and even though we'd won, I still felt like I'd been the one to lose.

Rune.

My mates.

In every way I could fail, I'd managed it.

The bonds with my mates weren't gone exactly, but they were—damaged. Fractured. I could still feel them if I let myself.

Kian's warmth—golden and steady, but distant.

Xavier's presence—cooler, coiled tight, unreadable.

Idris—silent. A wall of steel between us.

I didn't reach for them. I couldn't. Instead, I focused on putting one foot in front of the other. One more step. And another. And another—until I reached Nyrah.

I'd failed them, but I couldn't fail her.

The castle was behind me, hidden beyond the towering trees of the forest—its spires, and fragile wards nothing but a memory now. I hadn't let myself wallow. Hadn't let myself feel the pull of the bond, the sharp edges of guilt clawing at my heart.

If I thought too long, I'd hesitate.

And hesitation meant death.

That was just as true here as it was underneath the mountain.

My steps faltered as exhaustion gnawed at my bones. I had been walking for hours—maybe longer.

My legs ached, and a deep, burning throb settled in my chest from running too hard, too fast. I didn't know when I had last stopped to breathe. When I had last drunk water.

I was dry to the bone, my throat a raw ache, but I didn't dare stop. I couldn't. The moment I slowed, I felt it. A pressure against the edges of my mind. A weight pressing at my skin.

No.

I clenched my jaw, pushing forward. If I stopped, I would hear them. The whispers. The laughter. The soft, lilting voice of a thing I could not see—but felt.

Zamarra.

She was waiting. Lurking just beyond my reach, her presence curling through the dark like a patient spider spinning its web.

Dream, little Luxa.

My breath hitched. The voice wasn't real.

Come to me.

I squeezed my eyes shut. It wasn't real.

She wanted me to sleep. She wanted me to step into her world.

Clenching my jaw, I tried to shake the unease slithering down my spine. I would not dream—not tonight—not until I had no other choice. Because she was there, lurking in the shadows of my mind, waiting to strike.

Ahead, a flicker of light cut through the trees. I froze, my breath stalling in my throat.

Lanterns.

Not the cold, unnatural glow of mage light. Not the eerie glint of grave magic. Actual lanterns—the kind carried by people. My heart picked up speed as I swallowed down the urge to run the other way.

It was a village—small, tucked away at the edge of the forest. I forced my feet forward, suppressing the instinct to turn back. The Girovian mages had attacked the castle, but had they reached the town? Had they burned it to the ground like so many other places left in the wake of their destruction?

I stepped closer, my heart hammering.

The lights glimmered, warm and steady. The buildings stood, untouched. Relief flooded my chest so fast it almost knocked me to my knees. They hadn't destroyed the town. They hadn't burned it, hadn't slaughtered its people. The Girovian mages had only come for us.

Only for Idris.

Only for me.

I clenched my fists.

Good.

At least that meant the people here were safe. At least this wasn't another ruin in the wreckage of our war. At least it wasn't another failure. But that didn't mean I was safe here. Lirael's words drifted through my mind, as soft as the golden light she'd pressed into my chest.

You are more than you realize.

I swallowed hard, adjusting the strap of the satchel over my shoulder. The book inside pressed against my torso—a weight both comforting and damning.

You must go back to the book.

I hadn't understood what she meant. Not then, and not now. But I would.

I pulled my hood lower over my face and moved toward the stables. I needed a horse. I needed to keep moving. And I needed to do it before they noticed me.

The stables smelled of damp hay, warm leather, and sweat, the earthy scent of animals settling thick in the air. I moved cautiously, keeping my steps light, my breath shallow as I scanned the rows of stalls.

I'd stolen a lot over the years, but nothing bigger than a brick or two of rations. Stealing a horse was more than a little outside my wheelhouse. Hell, I had barely ridden one, and even then, Kian and Xavier were leading the way.

But this isn't the first time you've stolen a horse.

The bite of grief gnawed at my insides as I remembered Rune's voice in my head when he guided me to the castle—to Idris.

Now? I was all alone.

I clenched my jaw, my fingers twitching as I peered into the stalls. Most of the horses were too large, too muscled—built for work, not speed. My best bet was something leaner, something fast.

A sleek, black mare caught my eye at the far end of the stable. She was restless, shifting in her stall, her ears flicking as she sensed my presence. She was perfect. I just had to figure out how to get on her without breaking my neck.

You must go back to the book.

Lirael's words whispered through my thoughts again, her presence lingering in the depths of my mind like a fading ember. I didn't have time to decode riddles or question prophecies. Nyrah was out there, and I was wasting time worrying about my stupid heart and my stupid guilt.

Zamarra was hunting.

Unlatching the stall with more confidence than I felt, my fingers fumbled slightly as I reached for the saddle hanging nearby. After two tries, I managed to pull it from the hook. Body drained from the trek and lack of sleep, I staggered under the weight as I tried to toss it over the horse's back.

Finally, I draped the saddle over the mare's back, muttering curses under my breath as the stirrups clanked awkwardly against her side. I didn't even know if I was doing this right—what straps went where, what needed to be tightened. The mare huffed and stomped her hoof, shifting uneasily.

I flinched, yanking back my boot before one of those hooves crushed me.

"I get it. You don't like this any more than I do," I muttered, fumbling with the strap around her middle. I'd watched Kian and Xavier do this before —loosely remembering what pieces went where— but my hands were clumsy. The buckles were stiff, and my breath came too fast, my hands shaking.

Hurry. Hurry. Hurry.

The mare snorted and shifted again, tossing her head as she made her displeasure known. My heart slammed into my ribs. She was going to make noise. She was going to give me away.

I grabbed the bridle, hesitating for a split second before forcing it over her head. The leather straps dug into my hands as I struggled to fit the bit into her mouth. She tossed her head again, resisting.

"Please," I murmured. "I know you're tired, but I need you to work with me."

The mare snapped her teeth, and I yanked my hand back, narrowly avoiding a bite. My pulse pounded in my skull, frustration burning at my edges. I didn't have time for this—I needed to get on her and go.

Finally, the bit settled into place, and I tightened the last strap, praying I had done it correctly.

I reached for the stirrup, only to realize I couldn't get on. The only time I'd ever been on a horse, Kian or Xavier had helped me, and I had no idea how to mount her. I tried to remember how Xavier or Kian had done it.

My foot in the stirrup, I latched onto the saddle and hauled myself up, but the moment I tried to kick my leg over, my boot caught the edge of the saddle, my balance tipping dangerously.

The mare jolted sideways, and I let out a strangled curse, nearly face-planting into the stable wall.

My heart hammered. I could hear my own breath, ragged and too loud in the empty space. I would get caught if I didn't get my shit together.

Then, I heard the sound of footfalls. "That's not your horse."

Fuck.

On instinct, I spun, reaching for a weapon I didn't have and magic that refused to come. A stable hand stood blocking the exit, his silhouette barely visible in the flickering lantern glow. He was young —maybe eighteen or nineteen—and all too aware of the situation.

His eyes shifted from me to the horse, to the awkward mess I had made of the tack. His brow furrowed, his lips parting.

And then his gaze landed on my face before darting down to the ring I still wore, the pulsing onyx stone a dead giveaway. Recognition dawned as his breath hitched.

"Y-you're the queen."

Shit. Shit. Shit.

Panic surged through me—a wild, electric spike of fear. I didn't think. I moved.

My hand flicked up, the magic that had refused to come earlier, now sparking at my fingertips before fanning out in small bolts of light. The lanterns hanging along the beams exploded, plunging the stable into complete darkness. The stable hand stumbled back, cursing as the horse jolted in alarm.

I used the moment to scramble onto the mare's back, gripping the saddle for dear life. She reared slightly, startled by the explosion, her muscles coiling as I dug my heels in.

"Stop! Thief," he yelled, his voice lifting in alarm, calling for help.

I had maybe seconds before my escape flew away like a puff of smoke. Without another moment to think about it, I kicked, and the mare lunged forward, nearly throwing me as she bolted into the night. I had no reins, no real control. I gripped anything I could—mane, saddle, whatever kept me upright.

The wind tore at my cloak as we sprung from the stable, racing down the cobbled lane as the village behind me stirred, voices rising.

I didn't look back. I just held on and rode.

And deep inside my chest, the bond pulsed.

Kian.

Xavier.

They were stirring. They would notice my absence soon if they hadn't already.

Would they come for me? Would Idris? Did I want them to?

My heart pounded as pain lanced through me, the memory of Idris' stoney expression—his disgust—tearing at my insides like a wild animal.

What had he said? *Chasing ghosts won't help anyone.*

No, they wouldn't come for me—*he* wouldn't—and that was just fine. I'd survived without them before, and I'd do it again.

I just had to keep riding.

CHAPTER 2

KIAN

The candlelight flickered, or maybe my vision was just going to shit.

My sight blurred as I stared at the battle maps, the border lines melding together as I tried to figure out where Girovia might hit us next. Idris was counting on my centuries as his top general to make this call, and I was no closer to an answer.

The coming dawn meant it had been two gods-damned days since the battle.

Since everything changed.

Since Vale had stopped breathing.

Since the mages had torn through the castle.

Since she'd broken the curse.

And still, it felt like we were missing a step—

some vital signal from the gods that we were on the right course.

I dragged a hand down my face, the scrape of stubble against my palm, a jarring reminder of how long I'd been awake. My body ached, my muscles tight with exhaustion, but none of it mattered. Sleep hadn't been an option. Not when the bond was frayed, flickering like a falling star, too quiet for too long.

My chest ached as I remembered Vale walking into the war room, her voice steady despite the weight pressing against all of us. How many hours had it been? Five? Ten?

She'd looked me in the eye and begged for us to listen to her, and what had we done?

I clenched my fists against the wood of the war table, breathing through the sharp sting in my chest. She was avoiding us—that's what I told myself. That's what made the most sense.

After everything that had happened—who could blame her?

Vale's sister was the only thing she'd cared about—the only thing that kept her going—and Idris had shot her pleas down without even bothering to listen...

He'd been so cold, distant, blaming her for

something I doubt she had even an ounce of control over. Xavier had tried to meet her halfway, but there was too much left unsaid between all of us.

And me?

I'd let her leave.

I'd just sat there and watched her go. I didn't fight for her. I didn't stand up to Idris. I didn't even ask her to stay.

I'd let her walk away, even when I knew she was fraying at the edges. Even when I wanted nothing more than to reach for her. To tell her that I knew. That I saw the way she was unraveling, breaking apart right in front of us.

But I hadn't done a damn thing, and now I was suffering the consequences.

I'd given her space. Too much space.

And now—

The bond lurched, and I froze. Not silence, not shielding. No, this was different.

This was *absence*.

A sharp, searing emptiness ripped through my chest, and I shoved up from my seat so fast the chair scraped against the stone. The world tilted, my pulse roaring in my ears as I reached for her in my mind. The bond, honed by distance, should have given me a sense of where she was. The closer she was to me, the stronger it was. But right then?

The tenuous thread was barely there.

She wasn't avoiding us. She wasn't hiding. Vale was gone.

Cold slammed into my ribs. I had felt her in the bond yesterday—frayed, wavering, but still there. Still connected. But this?

I was already moving before I had a thought to stop myself, my feet pounding against the stone floor as I barreled through the halls, past the guards, too exhausted to do more than blink at me. I followed the fading thread of her scent, my breath coming too fast, too shallow.

No. No. No.

I shoved the doors open to Idris' chambers, half-expecting to see her curled up somewhere, half-expecting my own idiocy to slap me in the face.

The icy air hit me like a blow.

The fire had long since burned out. The bed sat untouched, the linens—while rumpled—were cold from disuse. The room still smelled like her, but it was fading fast.

And the bond—

It was frayed, thin, stretched so far, I could barely feel it.

No.

My gaze swept the room, frantic, landing on the bedside table and the jeweled dagger—the one I'd given her what seemed like ages ago. It gleamed in the dim light.

The breath punched from my lungs.

I stared at the weapon, my pulse hammering in my skull. She'd once told me it was the nicest gift she'd ever been given—the only gift—and she'd left it behind.

My throat tightened as I reached for it, the cool metal biting against my palm.

She'd left it behind.

She *left*.

She *fucking* left.

The weight of it crashed into me, searing through every fiber of my being. The bonds weren't just distant now. They were all but cut. Not gone. Not broken. But damaged enough that they might as well be.

I braced a hand against the doorframe, my claws digging into the wood as I tried to pull air into my lungs.

She was alone. Unprotected.

Why would she do this?

Because we didn't listen.

I squeezed my eyes shut, the last image I had of her flashing behind my lids. Vale standing in the war room, her shoulders squared, her voice steady, even as her hands curled into fists at her sides.

"You think I don't know that? You think I don't feel the weight of it every second?"

I should have said something to Idris—should have stopped her. Instead, I had let her walk out of that room, and now she was gone.

A door slammed—sharp and abrupt—cutting through the buzzing in my skull.

Xavier.

I pushed off the frame, moving before I even made the conscious decision. The others were about to realize what I already knew. And when they did?

Gods help us all.

The room was too damn quiet. Even with the guards patrolling, the torches flickering, the distant murmur of the wounded being tended to, there was an unnatural stillness that crawled under my skin.

Or maybe that was just the absence of her.

The dagger in my grip felt heavier than it should. The sharp facets of the gemstones bit into my palm, grounding me in a way that did nothing to dull the ache in my chest. She had left it. Left us.

Left me.

I hadn't slept. None of us had. And now, all of it —the exhaustion, the frustration, the fucking guilt —was boiling over inside me, coiling so tight I could barely breathe.

And then I heard his footsteps.

Xavier was moving fast, his boot falls sharp against the stone floor. He wasn't quite running, but there was urgency in the way he carried himself. The moment he turned the corner, his icy gaze locked onto mine, and I knew. He felt it, too.

His expression twisted in confusion, in the first spark of realization. "Kian?" His voice was rough, strained. He'd barely spoken since the battle. "What the fuck—?"

"She's gone." The words were bitter in my mouth, and they landed like a punch.

Xavier stopped short, the tension snapping tight between us. His brows drew together, his whole body going still. "What do you mean she's gone?"

"I mean she left." I threw the dagger onto the nearby table, the clatter of metal echoing through the corridor. "She's not in the castle. She's not in the fucking wards. And that bond?" I thumped my fist against my chest, my voice shaking with anger. "It's barely there."

His pupils flared, the faintest crackle of his

magic snapping in the air. "No," he murmured, his head shaking slightly. "She wouldn't—"

"She did." My voice was sharper than I intended, but gods, I couldn't hold it in. "She walked out of here alone, and none of us noticed until now."

Xavier's jaw clenched, the muscle ticking as his breathing turned shallow. His hands curled into fists at his sides, tension locking his body in place.

No. Not just tension. Panic.

Because it was sinking in now. The bond. The absence. The fucking truth.

His chest rose and fell too fast, his usually unreadable expression shifting between rage and something worse—fear.

He felt it now. That yawning emptiness splitting his chest wide open.

His ice-blue eyes darkened, his nostrils flaring as the flames of his power licked up his arms. "How the fuck did this happen?"

I let out a bitter laugh. "How?" I took a step forward, my own control slipping as scales danced over my flesh. "Because we let her walk away in that godsdamned war room. Because none of us said the right fucking thing. Because she thinks she's alone in this—again. And instead of fixing it, we let her suffer in silence."

Again.

Gulping, I squeezed my eyes shut, the memory of her breaths dying, her bloody and broken in my arms.

Xavier shook his head, taking a step back, his hands raking through his silver-streaked hair. "No. No, we would have noticed—"

"Would we?" I cut him off, stepping closer. "We've been so caught up in this fucking war, in Idris' rage, in our own godsdamn guilt, that we let her slip right through our fingers."

His breaths were coming shorter now, faster. Shit.

I exhaled hard, raking a hand down my face as the weight of it all pressed down on me. Xavier and I had always been the ones closest to her. The ones to notice when things were off. To fucking protect her.

And we failed.

His lips parted like he wanted to say something, but no sound came out. His gaze flicked to the dagger, then back to me. His fists trembled at his sides.

"How long?" His voice was quieter now, rough and hoarse.

I swallowed the lump in my throat. "I don't

know. A few hours. Maybe more. She could have left the second she walked out that door."

Xavier swore under his breath, turning sharply, his magic crackling in the air as he moved—not pacing, not aimless, but calculating. His mind was already working through the details, the possibilities.

"She doesn't know how to travel alone," he said, almost to himself. "She's barely been outside the castle without us."

I nodded, my jaw tightening. "She'll need supplies. A horse. We need to check the surrounding villages—"

Xavier's head snapped up, his eyes flashing. "She would have gone for Nyrah."

The words cut through me like a blade. That fucking mage filling her head with fear.

The chains are breaking, little queen. Every realm trembles because of what you've done.

I hadn't understood at the time, but he'd been talking about Zamarra. Zamarra was breaking free, and Vale told us exactly what her priority was. She hadn't been lying or bluffing. Vale knew what was coming, and she still left.

The knowledge struck deep, leaving me reeling.

"She thinks she has to do this alone," I said, my voice tight, my heart withering.

Xavier let out a slow breath, but it did nothing to settle him. "Then we find her."

I nodded once. "We find her."

But first, I'd need to put my fist in Idris' stupid fucking face.

My stomach twisted.

Xavier met my gaze, the same grim understanding passing between us.

This was going to be bad.

THE WAR ROOM WAS TOO DAMN QUIET.

Not the good kind of quiet—the kind that came after a battle when the dead were counted, and the survivors took their first breath. No, this was the thick, suffocating kind that settled over a place right before it burned to the ground.

And Idris was standing in the middle of it.

I should have known he wouldn't react the way we did. Should have known that when I stormed in here, when I said the words that tore me apart —"Vale is gone"—he wouldn't even fucking flinch.

I'd spent the last two days drowning in exhaustion, running myself ragged trying to piece together our defenses, trying to breathe around the frayed edges of the bond I still had with her. I'd felt her slipping away—an inch, then a mile, and I had done nothing.

I'd convinced myself she needed space. That after everything that had happened, we all did.

And now?

Now she was gone.

And Idris knew.

Not just now—not when I'd burst into the war room, shoving the words down his throat like a fucking dagger.

No, he had *known*, and he hadn't said a godsdamned word.

The chair scraped against the stone as I shoved back from the table, my claws flexing at my sides as I tried to breathe through the fury tightening my chest.

"Look at me, you fucking coward. I just told you that your Queen, your wife, your mate is gone, and you're not going to even acknowledge me? She's gone, Idris." The words tasted like ash. "She fucking *left*."

The silence pressed in on me as I stared at my King.

The fucker couldn't even bother to lift his head from that godsdamned map.

I moved before I even had a thought to stop myself. My fist connected with his jaw, snapping his head to the side with a sharp *crack*.

Xavier didn't move to stop me—didn't even fucking blink—because he felt it, too. The raw, searing ache in our bond, stretched so far it was barely there.

Idris righted himself, slightly rolling his head on his shoulders. He flexed his jaw, testing the damage, but he still didn't look at me.

He just exhaled slowly, finally—finally— meeting my gaze. "I know she's gone."

He knew?

The fury inside me cracked wide open.

"Gods damn you, Idris!" I roared, the words clawing their way out of my throat. "You knew and you didn't say a fucking thing?"

A muscle in his jaw ticked. "She made her choice."

I fought off the urge to pummel him until he was

mincemeat. The only thing that stopped me was the fact that I needed him conscious to fix this.

"She made her *choice*?" I echoed, my voice sharp, edged with something dangerously close to breaking. "You pushed her to that choice."

His golden eyes burned, but they were empty. No rage. No fight.

Just steel. Just cold.

"We let her walk away," Xavier said, his voice quieter, more controlled than I ever could have managed. He was standing still, hands at his sides, his magic crackling in the air like a frozen storm. "We let her think she had to do this alone."

"We abandoned her." The words felt like shattered glass in my mouth.

And it was our fucking fault.

All of it.

We let her stand there in that godsdamned war room, pleading with us to listen, and we let her walk out alone. And now she was gone.

I could still feel her if I focused, but it was faint, a flicker at the edges of my mind. She wasn't shielding herself from us—not entirely.

She was far, and if we didn't leave now, she'd be too far to reach.

"Why aren't you doing anything?" I demanded,

moving closer to Idris. "Why the fuck are you just sitting there?"

He squared his shoulders, his expression unreadable. "What would you have me do, Kian?" His voice was dangerously calm. "Tear through the continent after her like a reckless fool? She knew what she was doing when she left."

The words landed like a blow, stealing my breath, but not from anger—from fucking disbelief.

"Is that what you think?" My voice was hoarse. "You think she left because she wanted to? Because she planned this?"

He didn't answer—didn't need to. I saw it in his face.

The doubt.

The hesitation.

The guilt.

Xavier took a slow, controlled breath. "She thinks she's protecting us," he murmured. "That's what she does. That's what she's always done."

"Even when it's killing her," I added bitterly.

Idris closed his eyes, bowing his head. He'd watched her take those final breaths, too— the ones so agonizing, we'd known there was no way to put her back together again. He'd begged her not to, but she'd put him—*us*—first.

She'd been willing and ready to die for us, and he'd just let her leave.

A long, heavy pause filled the air with all the things none of us wanted to say. Then Idris rose from his chair, his fingers pressing into the table like he was steadying himself.

"Get the horses."

I exhaled sharply. "So, you actually do give a shit. Fantastic."

His jaw clenched. "She's my queen."

I let out a bitter laugh. "Oh, yeah? Maybe it's time you fucking acted like it."

I expected Idris to snap back—expected him to hit me the way I'd hit him.

But he didn't.

And maybe that was worse. Because this version of Idris? The one who wasn't fighting? That scared me more than anything else.

I turned sharply, my magic sparking against my fingertips as I moved for the doors.

Xavier followed.

The bond still flickered in the back of my mind, and I clung to that, clung to her, because if we were fast enough, if we moved now—

Maybe we could still bring her back.

Before it was too late.

Before she was truly lost to us.

CHAPTER 3
VALE

The mare refused to take another step.

Her muscles coiled beneath me as she dug her hooves into the snow, snorting as I tugged at the reins, urging her forward.

But she didn't move. Not an inch.

Frustration clawed up my throat. "Come on," I whispered. "We don't have time for this."

She flicked an ear back but stayed rooted to the spot, nostrils flaring. A warning. My stomach twisted. Was she sensing something I couldn't? Or was she just as exhausted as I was?

Probably both.

I exhaled sharply, loosening my grip as I shoved wayward strands of hair from my face. *Fine.*

If she wanted to stop, she could stop. If I pushed

her too hard, she'd collapse, and then I'd be stranded. I didn't know much about horses, but even I knew that much.

A faint trickle of water reached my ears.

The mare tossed her head, pulling toward the sound, and I—knowing better than to fight a creature ten times my weight—let her go. The small stream cut through the forest, a thin ribbon of clear water, barely more than three feet wide. The mare lowered her head instantly, drinking deep.

I exhaled, rubbing a hand down my face.

"Guess it's not just me that's beat," I muttered.

I swung my aching legs over the saddle and nearly collapsed under my own weight. Gods, I was exhausted. My body felt like it was made of stone—too heavy, too stiff. Two days of running, no food, no rest. My stubbornness had carried me this far, but even that had limits.

The forest pressed in around us, thick and dark, but the steady trickle of water against the rocks was soothing. A moment's peace. A dangerous thing.

Crouching beside the stream, I scooped water into my palms and drank. The icy chill burned against my raw throat, shocking me awake for a moment before fading into a dull ache.

My stomach clenched as I reached into my

satchel, my fingers brushing against my meager rations—bread, dried meat, an apple. It was a hell of a lot more than I'd ever had under the mountain, but still not enough. I should have planned this better— should have thought it through.

I rolled the apple in my palm, staring at it for a long moment. My first instinct was to ration it out, to save it for later.

The mare shifted beside me, ears twitching.

With a quiet sigh, I held out the apple.

She flicked an ear, sniffed, then took it from my palm with a sharp *crunch*.

I shook my head. "You better be worth the trouble."

The mare just chewed, utterly indifferent. A familiar kind of indifference. Rune had looked at me like that, once.

That thought hit like a dagger to the gut. What I wouldn't give to hear his voice in my head telling me what to do.

What I wouldn't give to know I wasn't alone.

And then I felt it—a spark of something in the back of my mind. Not the mate bonds. Not the lingering pull of Kian's warmth, or Xavier's sharp focus, or even Idris' cold, distant steel.

This was different.

A whisper. A ripple of magic threading through my chest.

I swallowed hard, reaching for my satchel with trembling hands. The book sat inside, pressed against my ribs like a heartbeat.

Go back to the book.

Lirael's voice echoed through my mind. She was so insistent that the stupid thing had answers, but all it had ever given me was more questions. Reluctantly, I pulled it free, my breath coming too fast as I flipped through its brittle pages. I had no idea what I was looking for. No concrete lead, no plan—just a whisper from a goddess I barely understood.

Go back to the book.

I'd read it before—but just barely—the faint skimming of someone too afraid to learn her own history. Every faded word, every crumbling edge of the pages held something else I never wanted to know. It was a piece of my parents—the only thing I had left of them.

My fingers skimmed over the parchment, but the words blurred together, shifting like ink spilled in water. The ink shimmered, bleeding at the edges, rearranging themselves like the pages were alive.

I blinked hard.

The letters refused to stay still, and a spike of

pain lanced through my head as my stomach churned. I pressed the heel of my palm against my eye, breathing deeply.

Focus. This is important.

The mare was still drinking, her ears flicking lazily as she lapped at the water. Each sip echoed in the quiet, the only sound in the vast emptiness of the forest.

I leaned heavily against my pack, the book still in my lap, its worn edges rough beneath my fingers. My limbs felt leaden, the weight of exhaustion pressing down harder than before. I needed to move. I needed to keep going.

But my body had other ideas.

The mare let out a slow breath, her warm exhale curling against the night air. Then, with a deep sigh, she shifted. I barely registered it at first, my vision blurring at the edges, but then—the sound of a quiet rustle and a heavy *thump* touched my ears. She lowered herself to the ground beside me.

I blinked, sluggish and dazed, watching as she tucked her legs beneath her, her massive body settling onto the snow-dusted earth. She shifted her weight, adjusted, then stilled—her warmth radiating outward, a solid presence against the biting cold.

A soft huff of breath stirred my hair.

She was close. Close enough that if I leaned just a little to the side, I'd be resting against her.

I swallowed against the tightness in my throat.

She should have been skittish, wary of me after I'd stolen her from that stable. But here she was, choosing to stay, settling down beside me as if she understood. As if she knew I needed her.

As if she knew I was alone.

A lump formed in my throat, too thick to breathe around. I let my fingers drift over her shoulder, barely skimming the coarse hair. She didn't flinch. I exhaled slowly, the tension in my body unraveling just a fraction.

"Guess you're stuck with me now, huh?" I murmured, my voice hoarse, barely above a whisper.

She didn't answer, of course, but she didn't move away, either. Her warmth seeped into my frozen limbs, a quiet comfort against the endless dark.

I tried to fight it. Tried to stay alert, tried to keep my grip on the book.

But the letters swam, warped by my own exhaustion. The edges of my vision darkened. Sleep pulled at every limb, weighing me down.

Not yet. Not yet. Not yet—

The last thing I felt was the steady rise and fall of her breath against my side. Then, the world faded. The book slipped from my hands, and I fell.

Not physically—my body remained slumped against the mare's flank, the frigid air snaking around me like ghostly fingers. But inside, something yanked me down, deeper than sleep, deeper than anything I could control.

The world twisted, folding in on itself, and when I opened my eyes—

I stood in ruins.

A temple—half-buried in overgrowth, its stone walls cracked and broken. Vines curled around towering columns, roots splitting through ancient carvings. Snow clung to the jagged edges of stone, filling the gaps between shattered pews.

The wind howled through gaping windows, shaking brittle branches and sending dead leaves skittering across the floor. Above me, the sky was golden, glowing, filled with stars that pulsed like living things.

I knew this place.

I had seen it before.

A whisper—soft as wind over water.

"Go to the temple." The voice drifted through the ruins, curling around the broken stones, seeping into the cracks of the earth itself.

I turned, searching. Shadows stretched unnaturally long, creeping across the floor in jagged, twisting shapes. The weight of unseen eyes pressed against my skin, sending a shiver racing down my spine.

No one was here.

And yet—

A figure moved in the corner of my vision.

I snapped my head toward it, but the space was empty.

The wind shifted.

A blonde girl—just a flicker, just a glimpse— vanished through the ruined archway.

I inhaled sharply, my pulse hammering in my chest. I'd seen her before. Here, in this very place, when Idris had found me in the Dreaming. A flash of golden hair, a pale face disappearing into the ruins, just a breath too fast for me to catch.

Was it Nyrah?

I took a step forward. Then another. My boots scraped against the stone, the sound unnervingly loud in the vast, ruined space. The air smelled of cold ash, of something old and waiting.

Another whisper—everywhere and nowhere at the same time. "Find me. Hurry."

I stumbled, my breath catching as the air itself seemed to shift. The golden glow above wavered, turning darker, bleeding into the sky like a whisper unraveling into the bones of the wind.

And then I felt it.

A pulse of something dark. Watching. Waiting.

The shadows slithered, stretching toward me like grasping hands.

No.

I staggered back, but the world around me lurched. The temple's walls trembled, the stone groaning under an unseen weight. The ground beneath my feet buckled, warping, twisting—

I was being pulled under.

A sharp, searing cold wrapped around my throat, dragging me back into wakefulness.

My body jerked upright before I even knew why —heart pounding, breath sharp, a scream trapped behind my teeth. The cold air burned my throat.

Snow? Trees? My pulse hammered in my chest.

Still in the forest. Not the temple. *Not the Dreaming.*

My gaze snapped downward. The book lay open on my lap. To the temple. A rendering, detailed and precise—exactly what I had seen in the Dreaming. A sharp shudder racked my spine. My fingers trembled as I ran them over the aged parchment.

The Dreaming clung to me like frostbite, the whisper still echoing through my mind.

Go to the temple.

This wasn't coincidence. This wasn't my imagination twisting a nightmare into something real. Lirael had led me here.

But why?

Before I could think too hard about it, hoofbeats thudded against the frozen ground, their echoes freezing the very breath in my lungs. Then came the low rumble of voices.

That sound wasn't from the Dreaming, not some figment of my exhausted mind. This was real.

The mare stiffened beside me, ears flicking sharply toward the sound. I twisted, barely breathing. Through the trees, four mounted figures emerged, gliding between the trunks like specters. My sluggish mind lagged behind my body, too slow, too exhausted before I finally registered the danger.

A Girovian patrol.

My pulse slammed into my throat.

Too close.

Panic flared through me. I slid low against the ground, pressing into the thick shadows. The mare barely moved. Her breath fogged the air, her sides heaving from exhaustion—but she didn't bolt. She didn't snort or shift.

Smart girl.

The men were speaking in clipped tones, too far for me to make out the words. Yet. One of them let out a sharp, barking laugh before it died a swift death. The loud one stopped, scanning the trees.

"What are you doing? It's freezing out here," one complained, his horse shuddering as if to drive his point home.

"Thought I heard something."

A fresh wave of ice rolled through my veins. I pressed myself lower, fingers curling into the dirt. *Please keep moving. Please—*

"Probably a deer or something. Keep moving. The sooner this patrol is done, the sooner I can get some sleep."

"Sure, you're probably right."

The first voice didn't sound too convinced. The hooves shuffled, pausing, shifting as every muscle in my body locked. I counted heartbeats, forcing myself not to breathe.

One.

The hoofbeats resumed, but still, I didn't so much as breathe.

Two.

The voices grew fainter, trailing off in the other direction.

Three.

The patrol moved on, their voices swallowed by the trees, and I exhaled.

Finally.

Relief hit too fast. Too hard. I slumped forward against the cold, my muscles unclenching. Gently, slowly, I closed the book and stowed it in my satchel. Without making a sound, I put my arms through the straps.

It's fine. I'll wait another minute, then—

Cold fingers clamped around my wrist, strong and unyielding. A scream clawed its way up my throat, but the stranger's grip tightened, crushing. I nearly yelped in pain, but I couldn't give my position away.

"Thought you were clever, didn't you?" a voice hissed against my ear.

Yanking myself free, I whirled, bracing for a fight as he stepped from the shadows, a smirk curving his lips. His violet eyes skimmed over me—calculating and, amused. My veins were made of ice as I realized just how screwed I was. The fifth soldier—the one I hadn't seen—wasn't a soldier at all.

No, he was a Girovian mage.

I had been hiding from the wrong fucking patrol.

"What's the matter, little queen? Lose your kingdom?"

Magic crackled at his fingertips as a bolt of energy streaked toward me.

Move. Move. Move.

I threw myself sideways as the mare jolted to her feet. The blast seared past my cheek, burning hot before slamming into the tree right next to the horse. *Too close.*

Hitting the frozen earth, I rolled. I had seconds —if that.

My limbs felt like lead, sluggish and slow, but I reached for my belt, anyway—

Nothing.

No steel, no weapon. But I didn't need steel. My power answered before I even thought to call it. The blade of light formed, pulsing in my grip.

Move. Now.

The mage twisted—the blade of light grazing his shoulder instead of his throat. He hissed, staggering back, magic sparking wildly. He flicked his arm and the detritus on the forest floor rose in the air. Rocks, branches, and the like surged toward me, but I didn't let him finish.

Rushing forward, I slammed into him, knocking

him off balance. We hit the ground hard, rolling, but I came out on top. The mage cursed as he grabbed for my throat, his blackened fingers cutting into my skin as I faked left.

Then I drove my dagger up, beneath his ribs.

Blood flowed over my hands as his eyes widened in what had to be shock. And then, I twisted the blade.

My ears rang as I scrambled to my feet, panting. My hands shook, my skin burned, the world blurred at the edges.

Then voices registered past my wheezing breaths and galloping heart.

More soldiers—they'd heard the fight, and now I was well and truly fucked.

Panic seized my chest as I grabbed the reins, vaulting onto the mare's back.

Then I dug my heels in—hard—fleeing into the trees.

I needed to find that temple, yes.

But first, I needed to live.

CHAPTER 4
XAVIER

We'd been tracking Vale for hours.

Wind howled through the trees, shaking loose drifts of snow from their branches. The night stretched on, vast and unyielding, the world suffocating beneath the weight of winter that seemed to stretch on forever. The moon, pale and hollow, hung high in the sky, casting long shadows through the dense woods.

But there was no sign of her—only fading tracks, half-faded ghosts of movement left behind in the snow. A hoofprint here, a scuffed boot mark there. Each sign of her presence fading by the second, the trail disappearing beneath the snowfall, getting harder to follow with each passing mile.

Kian rode ahead of me, his jaw tight, his body a

coiled wire ready to snap. Idris rode behind, silent as the grave.

And I...

I couldn't breathe around the weight in my chest.

She was alone. Too far ahead. And we were still wasting time.

We'd left the kingdom on the edge of a blade.

Freya—a thousand-year-old vampire with the temperament of a battle-ax—had been the only choice to leave behind. She had no patience for politics but more loyalty than most of the nobles combined. If anyone could keep the council from fracturing while we were gone, it would be her.

But the kingdom was on the brink of civil war.

Half the noble houses wanted war—a retaliation against Girovia, a display of power so ruthless that no one would ever think to challenge us again. The other half wanted Idris dead for letting Vale ascend the throne in the first place.

It didn't matter that the curse had been lifted. It didn't matter that their magic was finally whole again. They wanted blood, and we were one wrong move away from collapse.

And here we were—three of the most powerful

figures in the kingdom—riding into the cold, leaving it all behind.

For her.

I ran a hand down my face, fighting off the bone-deep urge to shift. It would have been faster. So much faster.

But speed meant nothing if we lost her in the trees. The Girovian forests were vast—too dense, too dark, too tangled in shadows. If we took to the skies, we'd lose her. She could be a mile ahead or ten, but from the air, she would be invisible.

And worse—Girovia was watching. Malvor and his ilk might have been on their own, but Girovia and Festia had been at war since the curse started. Mages were stationed at every border, waiting for an excuse to drag Idris down.

If we shifted, we'd be seen, and if we were seen, we'd be hunted.

Girovian battle mages specialized in grounding dragons. We were powerful, but not invincible. If they caught us mid-flight, they'd rip us from the sky like birds shot from the heavens.

So we tracked her the only way we could—on horseback—and we were running out of time.

A sharp gust of wind cut through the trees, stir-ring loose snow from the branches. The cold bit at my exposed skin, but I barely felt it. I kept scanning the ground, looking for any sign—a trail, a broken branch, something.

And then I saw it.

The faint impression of hoofprints leading toward a frozen stream.

I pulled back on the reins, slowing my stallion to a halt. Kian did the same, both of us scanning the clearing, tension coiling thick in the air.

The world had gone silent.

The trees stood like watching sentinels, their frostbitten branches weighed with snow. The only sound was the distant trickle of water—a frozen stream, fractured and broken. Kian pulled up beside me, eyes narrowing. We both dismounted in one fluid motion.

The moment my boots hit the ground, I knew.

She'd been here.

The air still carried the faintest trace of her scent —burning embers, a blooming rose, and something else uniquely Vale. The scent was fading, but it was here.

Kian crouched, running his gloved fingers over the indentations in the snow.

"Not more than half a day ago." His voice

sounded as if it had been dragged over hot coals, the desperation like a knife in my gut.

"She stopped here," I muttered. "To rest."

I tried not to think about how exhausted she must have been. How little time she'd had to breathe since she left. I hadn't managed to sleep since we'd been apart, and as far as she'd gotten, she'd barely had time to breathe, let alone rest.

Kian stood, eyes scanning the tree line. "Then why the hell did she leave in such a hurry?"

The thin ribbon of water in front of us had begun to freeze over, but near the edge, the ice had been disturbed—like she'd left fast, without time to cover her tracks.

My gut twisted at the thought.

That was bad. That was very fucking bad.

And then Kian stiffened. "Shit."

I turned and saw it—a body. Half-frozen, stiff with ice, dark robes barely visible beneath the snowfall. The only reason I didn't lose it right there and then was because he was far too big to be Vale. Kian crouched first, pressing two fingers to the man's throat.

"Dead?" I asked, my voice low, my magic crawling over my skin, reaching for the ice around me.

Kian shook his head as he reached for the sword at his belt. "Not yet."

I stepped closer. That was when I saw the blackened veins crawling up his neck. The hollow look in his half-lidded violet eyes. This wasn't just any soldier. No, he was a mage. Vale had almost killed a Girovian mage.

A glimmer of pride cut through the bitter worry clawing up my throat. Good.

I knelt beside him, gripping the front of his robes, pressing just a bit of healing magic into him to get him to speak. "What happened?"

The mage's bloody lips cracked into something too close to a smile.

"She's already..." His voice rasped against the wind, "...too late."

Kian and I locked eyes.

I gritted my teeth, shaking him, the desire to rip him limb from limb nearly overtaking my brain. "Too late for what?"

His mouth opened, but no sound came out.

"Answer me," I ordered, shoving more magic into him to keep him talking.

A shudder racked his body as his eyes rolled in his head. "You think you can save her?" He let out a breathy chuckle. "She might have ended me, but she's dead already. She just doesn't know it yet."

Then, he convulsed, the breath rattling in his chest. His fingers twitched once, twice, and then stilled. A fresh gust of wind cut through the trees, and I felt it—a whisper of something unseen. A pulse of magic.

Not Vale's.

Not even Idris'.

Something else. Something dark.

The sensation slithered against my skin—watching, waiting, pressing at the edges of the clearing, and then it was gone, and the mage was dead.

A long silence stretched between us as I tried and failed to reach for Vale through the bond. All I felt was the faint flicker of her fear coiling like a snake in my belly.

She was terrified.

And she was alone.

Wind howled through the trees, shaking loose the last remnants of snowfall clinging to the branches. The forest had gone eerily still, watching, waiting—as if the very land knew that something was about to break.

Then Idris' voice cut through the tense miasma curling around us.

"She wouldn't have done this unless she had to."

His words were quiet—too quiet. Not broken. Not regretful. Just stated like a fact, as if that made it better.

I dropped my hold on the mage, watching dispassionately as his body flopped limply in the snow. My fingers curled into fists, the cold biting into my skin as rage boiled in my gut.

"Is that all you have to say?"

Idris finally lifted his head. His golden gaze met mine, unreadable, but something about it set my teeth on edge.

"You want me to tell you she was running?" His voice was level, a thread of something sharp woven beneath the steel. "That she's afraid? That she regrets leaving?"

He exhaled slowly. His jaw tightened.

"That's nothing you don't already know, and I don't think she does. If she regretted it, she'd be headed back to us—not running off again."

That broke something inside me.

The cold, detached way he said it—like it didn't gut him to admit it. Like he wasn't fucking dying inside. Like the mate bond wasn't stretched so thin it felt like thorned vines wound through my whole fucking body.

He wasn't even angry. He wasn't desperate like Kian and I were. He was just—*nothing*. Like he'd already accepted life without her. Like he'd already given up.

It was the last fucking straw.

I moved before I thought, the distance between us vanishing in an instant. My fist collided with his jaw, snapping his head to the side.

Kian didn't lift a finger to stop me. Didn't even flinch.

Because he knew.

Idris staggered back but didn't fall. His breath left him in a sharp exhale, his magic crackling beneath his skin. His gaze snapped back to mine— and for half a second, something flickered.

Something raw. Something so close to breaking. But then—

He locked it down. He *always* locked it down. This was exactly why she'd left.

Before I could think, I grabbed him by the collar, slamming him into the nearest tree. The bark splintered behind him, brittle from the cold, cracking under his weight. Snow dusted from the branches, shaking loose like dying stars.

"If you're the reason she won't take us back," I

snarled, my voice razor-sharp, "I will fucking end you."

Kian didn't move—didn't breathe. Neither did Idris. His jaw clenched, his throat working around words that never came.

I pressed in closer, lowering my voice to something lethal. Something final. "I swear to all the gods and goddesses, on all the blood in my veins, on the fucking air in my lungs—if she won't return to us because of your bullshit, I will rip you limb from limb. Do you hear me?"

His breath hitched.

For a fraction of a second, he almost looked away. Almost let himself feel it.

Then, his mouth parted. "I—"

"*No*," I growled, cutting him off. My grip tightened on his collar, my claws digging into the fabric. The only thing keeping me from tearing him apart was the fact that I needed him breathing long enough to find her.

"If I lose her because you can't get your head out of your ass long enough to realize she sacrificed herself to save us all—that she loved you enough to fucking die for you—you won't have to worry about Zamarra or Arden."

The next words left me like a death sentence. "I'll kill you myself."

Something inside him fractured. Betrayal, hurt, fury—all crossed his expression as his golden eyes burned. I'd warned him the day she'd waltzed into the kingdom that I would not watch her die. He'd already made me a liar once. He wouldn't do it a second time.

Idris didn't argue, didn't fight back.

Because he knew I was right—we both knew it.

I let him go and stepped back. The silence burned between us. Thick. Tangled. Poisoned.

He just stood there. His hands balled into fists at his sides, shaking just slightly. His jaw was still tight, his breathing slow and controlled—but his magic flared, spinning out from his body in a great golden arch.

For the first time, the cracks were forming beneath his armor, and I had to wonder if he was just as close to breaking as we were.

But then he swallowed it all down, just like he always did. He exhaled sharply, rubbing his jaw, rolling his shoulders like he was shaking it off.

"We're wasting time."

For once, I didn't argue.

I turned toward my horse.

Kian mounted first, still watching Idris like he was waiting for him to shatter.

I swung onto the saddle, my knuckles still burning from the hit, my chest still coiled so tight it hurt to breathe.

And the mage's last words haunted me.

She's already too late.

Vale was still ahead—still alone.

I didn't know what she'd found or if she was safe, but I knew one thing.

If we didn't get to her in time, there wouldn't be a kingdom left to save.

CHAPTER 5
VALE

I urged the horse forward, my thighs tightening around her heaving sides. The frigid air burned through my throat, each inhale sharp and thin, every breath stolen by the wind.

Behind me, the Girovian patrol was closing in. Hoofbeats pounded against the frozen ground, mingling with the sharp crack of breaking branches as the soldiers crashed through the underbrush.

Too close. Too fast.

I gritted my teeth, leaning low over the mare's neck, my fingers clenched tight around the reins. The trees blurred past, their reedy branches clawing at me like skeletal fingers. One whipped my face, the only warmth coming from the blood trickling down my cheek.

I had no plan—just move, run.

But the forest was too thick, the trees pressing in from all sides. The deeper we went, the more the shadows tangled, making it impossible to see more than a few feet ahead.

The horse skidded, hooves sliding on an icy patch, her body lurching sideways and nearly throwing me off her back. My heart slammed against my ribs as I clutched at her mane, forcing her back on track.

That was close. Too close.

If she went down, we were done.

I gritted my teeth. *We can't keep running like this. They'll corner us.*

I needed another way. Then, through the tangled trees ahead, the land disappeared, and my stomach dropped. The ground fell away in a steep, jagged slope, the trees thinning along the edge. The drop wasn't sheer, but it was close—too steep for a horse to take at a full gallop without breaking a leg.

I yanked her to a stop, my breath heaving, my brain racing. There was no way forward and no way back. Behind me, a shout rang out—sharp and commanding—and my blood turned to ice. They were right behind me.

I didn't hesitate.

The moment I heard a soldier bark an order— "There! She's stopped!"—I nudged the horse forward. She hesitated only for a breath, and then she jumped. We plunged down the embankment, sliding through snow and ice, my fingers fisted in her mane as I braced myself.

Her hooves fought for purchase, her body lurching left.

Don't fall—don't fall—

Then we hit the bottom.

Hard.

The impact ripped me from the saddle, pain lancing up my side as I slammed into the frozen ground. My shoulder crashed against ice so hard that white-hot agony exploded through my entire right side. My vision blurred at the edges, my pulse faltering in my ears. A strangled gasp wrenched from my throat as I skidded to a stop, the cold biting deep, stealing my breath.

For a moment, I just lay there. The earth beneath me felt too solid, too still, while everything inside spun like a top. Everything hurt. My pulse thumped unevenly, my limbs trembling, my entire body tight with exhaustion. Above me, I heard the patrol halt. They'd seen me go down.

One soldier's voice drifted from the top of the ravine. "She fell. Loop around. We'll cut her off at the next crossing."

I barely managed to roll onto my side, my muscles burning, my breaths coming too fast, too shallow. A warm breath huffed against my face.

The mare. She'd stayed.

Somehow, through sheer instinct or loyalty I hadn't earned, she had stayed.

A lump lodged in my throat as I pressed my forehead against her shoulder, my breath trembling. "You stupid, stubborn girl."

Letting out a shaky exhale, I forced myself upright. My shoulder throbbed, my fingers nearly numb as I grabbed the reins. I had to move, had to keep going.

Stumbling through the underbrush, I nudged the horse forward, pressing deeper into the ravine. The shadows thickened, swallowing the pale moonlight— even the wind seemed quieter here. I forced myself to focus, one breath at a time. My chest ached, my skin burned from the cold, but stopping wasn't an option.

Then, through the tangled branches—I saw it. A

hunter's lodge, half-buried in snow. Small, isolated, and best of all: hidden.

I didn't think. I just guided the horse forward, lurching toward the door. The hinges groaned in protest, the wood splintering beneath my weight as I forced it open.

Inside, the air was stale, thick with dust and old wood.

It wasn't much.

But it was shelter.

I pulled her inside behind me, forcing the door shut, wedging an old chair against it. Then I grabbed the threadbare blanket from my satchel, stuffing it along the base of the door to block out the wind. My hands wouldn't stop shaking.

I was so damn tired, and so was the horse. As soon as the door closed, she lowered herself to the floor, tucking her legs under her as her head rested on the rough planked wood. She was the only thing keeping me tethered, keeping me grounded.

She wasn't just a stolen horse anymore. She was mine.

A breath shuddered out of me. My knees buckled. The exhaustion I'd been outrunning finally caught up.

Then I collapsed as the darkness I'd been fighting swallowed me whole.

The first thing I felt was warmth.

It wrapped around me, swirling beneath my skin, melting the bone-deep ache that had settled in my limbs. For the first time in days, I wasn't shivering, wasn't running. I was safe.

A sharp inhale caught in my throat, my breath stuttering on a sob. The scent of fire filled my lungs—spiced smoke and sunbaked stone, molten gold, and scorched earth.

Familiar.

Home.

No...

My heart stumbled, my chest tightening as my fingers curled against the warmth beneath me.

It couldn't be—

A low, thunderous rumble echoed through the air. A sound I knew in my bones.

A shadow moved beyond the ruined temple walls.

My breath hitched.

Slowly—so slowly—I turned.

And there he was.

A beast of flame and fury, his massive body stretching across the temple floor. His scales burned a deep, crimson red, like the last embers of a dying star, rippling with each breath. The sharp ridge of his spine, the lethal curve of his talons, the great arch of his wings —he was too big for this world, too ancient, too monstrous to be contained by anything but the sky.

My vision blurred. My body crumpled beneath the weight of relief. I'd thought I'd lost him forever. Malvor had told me he'd died.

Swallowing down tears, I choked out his name. "Rune—"

His giant head snapped toward me, and suddenly, I wasn't warm anymore. Because his molten eyes—the color of blood and fire—were furious.

"What took you so long? I've been waiting for you."

The words slammed into me, knocking the air from my lungs. I choked on a breath, my relief twisting into confusion. "What?"

Rune moved—powerful, predatory—his massive form shifting as he turned fully toward me.

"I waited for days." His voice rumbled, the earth quaking beneath us. "And you didn't come."

My hands shook as I pushed myself to my feet. "That's not—Rune, I tried. I—"

His tail lashed, shattering what little remained of the temple's altar. "You should have finished it."

Finished it?

My stomach twisted. I staggered back, shaking my head. "I—I did. I broke the curse. Idris can shift. He—"

Rune snarled, the sound splitting the sky. "No."

His wings flared wide, casting long, burning shadows across the ruined stone. His voice wasn't cruel, wasn't cold—but it shook with something deeper. Something raw. Something broken.

"You didn't merge me with him."

I froze.

Rune's chest heaved, smoke curling from his nostrils. "You left me like this."

My pulse stuttered. My breath shook. "I—I don't—"

"You died," Rune growled, "before you could finish it. You tore the curse apart, you freed him, but you left me behind."

The breath in my chest shattered as my body swayed, my legs buckling.

Oh, gods...

I hadn't saved him.

A ragged sob clawed up my throat. My hands trembled as I staggered toward him, reaching—needing—to feel him. Needing to know he was real. Rune let me come. Let me press my hands against the scalding heat of his snout. His scales were solid, real, burning beneath my palms.

And then my forehead dropped against him, my

fingers fisting in the smooth ridges of his face. A broken breath racked through me as I sank into him.

"I failed you. I'm so sorry." My voice cracked, a whisper of grief, of guilt so sharp it felt like I was bleeding from the inside out.

Rune didn't speak. His massive form shifted, a low sound rumbling deep in his chest. Not anger. Not rage. But something aching. Something almost... gentle. For a moment—just a moment—he leaned into me.

Just a little.

Just enough.

Then—the ground shuddered.

Rune's body tensed, his molten eyes snapping up, and the warmth vanished. I sucked in a sharp breath as the world darkened.

"Vale." Rune's voice dropped, low and urgent, his wings flaring wide.

Protective. Shielding.

A shadow crept along the temple walls, stretching toward us like a hand reaching from the abyss. My blood turned to ice. Something was coming.

The Dreaming trembled.

Rune's fire lit the sky, the temple crumbling around us.

And then—his voice—ripped and raw—filled my mind.

"You have to find me. Find me and finish what you started. But first, you have to wake up. Now."

The world slammed back into focus like a dagger to the heart.

I gasped awake, my body wrenching forward, my lungs seizing as though I'd been drowning and only just breached the surface. Ice-cold air burned down my throat, sharp as razors, sending a violent shudder through my body.

My heart thundered in my chest, Rune's voice still ringing in my ears.

You didn't finish it.

A fresh tremor racked my frame. I pressed a hand over my chest, as if I could hold myself together, as if I could keep from shattering beneath the weight of it. I wanted to go back. Gods, I wanted to go back.

To stay in that dream. To feel Rune's warmth. To let myself believe—just for a moment—that he was still real.

But he wasn't.

Not really.

I had broken the curse, torn the chains that bound Idris' dragon half in place, freed the power that had been caged for centuries. Idris could shift. Rune should have been whole. He should have remained with Idris.

And yet...

A choked breath scraped my throat as I pressed the heel of my palm against my forehead, forcing back the burn of hot, stinging tears. I hadn't finished it.

Not because I hadn't wanted to—because I physically *couldn't*. My body had given out before the merge had been complete. Before I could fully bind Rune and Idris into a single soul again. And now Rune was trapped in the Dreaming, a massive red dragon still tethered to the world of gods and ghosts.

I wasn't strong enough.

Swallowing back my tears, I tried to ignore my thundering pulse.

I had to keep moving.

The mare huffed beside me, her breath billowing white against the cold. She flicked her ears, watching me with dark, intelligent eyes, sensing the turmoil bleeding from me like an open wound. I reached out, pressing a hand to her warm, solid neck, grounding myself.

I was still here, still breathing, and I wasn't alone.

Not entirely.

"Guess I should call you something, huh?" My

voice came out hoarse, raw from sleep and too many swallowed screams.

The mare twitched an ear but didn't move away.

I closed my eyes, thinking. A name.

I hadn't even realized how much I'd been holding back. Afraid to claim something as mine. Afraid to lose it. But I'd lost Rune. I'd lost my mates. I'd lost my sister. I'd lost everything.

And the mare had stayed.

A shaky breath left me as I hesitated for just a moment. Naming her seemed so final, so lasting.

"What about Vetra?" I whispered.

She let out a slow, soft exhale, blinking up at me.

It was a name from the old stories—one Rune had told so I wouldn't be so scared to fall asleep alone on my first night in the castle. Vetra had been a legendary mare, swift as the wind, stubborn as the gods.

I ran my palm along Vetra's neck, nodding to myself. It fit. Then the wind shifted. A sharp, unnatural gust whirled through the cabin, rattling the frost-covered branches against the patchy roof.

I froze.

That wasn't wind. That was something else.

A hum beneath my skin, an electric vibration in

the air, a shadow pressing against the edges of my mind, a presence. Not Rune, not the Dreaming.

Something older.

Something hungry.

Zamarra.

It wasn't a voice. It wasn't a shadow or a body. But it was watching.

My hands tightened around Vetra's mane, my heart hammering against the confines of my chest. I forced myself to move, to pull her from the cabin and myself onto the saddle, even though every muscle ached, and exhaustion still clung to me like chains.

I guided Vetra forward, my fingers tightening around the reins as we moved through the dense underbrush.

And then—through the tangle of trees—I saw it.

The temple.

A massive, crumbling ruin, half-buried beneath centuries of frost and overgrowth. Its once-proud columns stood split with cracks, vines choking the broken stones, the ancient steps half-collapsed.

I exhaled sharply, my breath billowing in the frigid air.

It was exactly as I had seen it in the Dreaming.

A pulse of recognition hummed through me, a

whisper threading through my blood, urging me forward. I didn't know why, only that I had to get there.

It was a safe haven, a piece of the past. A place where I might finally find answers. I nudged Vetra into a gallop, the relief of being so close thrumming through my veins.

Then I heard it.

A man's shout. Metal shifting.

My stomach dropped as I jerked the reins, twisting in the saddle, my breath seizing in my lungs.

They were behind me. Not whispers this time. Not shadows. Real voices. Real men.

They know where I'm going.

They know I'm here.

If I don't get there first, I won't get there at all.

I gritted my teeth, kicking Vetra harder, faster. The trees blurred past as we rode, my breath burning, every muscle screaming. The temple was so close, but so were they.

A bowstring twanged seconds before a bolt of searing blue light streaked past my shoulder, slamming into the dirt inches from Vetra's hooves. She jerked sideways, nearly throwing me from the saddle.

Not a patrol of regular guards. Mages.

I swore, clenching my thighs, forcing Vetra onward.

Come on, come on, come on—

I hit the temple steps, yanking Vetra to a sharp stop, my breath coming in ragged, heaving gasps. I didn't know what safety I'd expected, but it wasn't there.

I twisted as they emerged from the trees, weapons drawn, cutting off every escape route.

Three. Four. Six. Ten.

Their faces were hidden beneath their hoods, but their glowing violet eyes proved me right. I swallowed as I watched their magic crackle at their fingertips.

Vetra stamped the ground, ears pinned back, nostrils flaring.

The temple loomed behind me, its entrance dark, gaping, and waiting. There was nowhere to run, no choices left. My hands clenched into fists as I let go of the reins.

My magic flared, bright as a burning star. I wasn't giving up. I wasn't running.

Not this time.

A figure stepped forward, his hood shadowing

his face—but the smirk, the way he tilted his head, sent a fresh wave of fire through my veins.

His magic crackled at his fingertips as he studied me. "Give it up, little queen. You can't fight us all."

I smiled. Sharp. Ruthless. "Watch me."

They wanted a fight? Well, they'd fucking get one.

And if I went down, I'd take every last one of them down with me.

CHAPTER 6
VALE

The mages closed in, violet eyes flaring beneath their hoods, eerie halos of light flickering in the snowfall.

Their power slithered through the air—an unnatural, festering thing, thick with hunger and coiling around me like smoke.

I'd barely survived one mage, and now I faced a damn army of them. Their magic burned, but it wasn't mine. It wasn't the searing fire of Rune, nor the sharp-edged blade of Xavier's flames. It was different—twisted, predatory, hungry.

My pulse hammered in my chest, so loud they could probably hear it. I curled my fingers around the reins, my breath sharp and fast. Magic burned under my skin, twisting at my fingertips, aching to break free. I refused to wait. If I hesitated, I'd die.

And if I was going down, I would take as many of them with me as I could.

The first bolt of magic shot toward me, a jagged spike of violet light. I twisted in the saddle, throwing up a shield of my own. My power met theirs in a clash of force, the impact rattling through my bones.

Another mage lunged.

Lashing out in a searing arc of light, fiery power burst from my palm, crackling through the frost-thickened air. It slammed into the closest mage's chest. The blast sent him flying backward, his cloak igniting as he crashed into the snow, his body limp, unmoving.

I barely had time to see if he was dead before two more rushed me. No hesitation. No fear.

Vetra reared, hooves striking out. A sickening crunch echoed in the night. A mage crumpled, his bones shattering from the force. I twisted my body, gripping the reins with one hand while throwing out a second blast of magic with the other.

One went down screaming. The other—faster than I expected—dodged and retaliated with a flick of his wrist. Something thin, dark, and needle-sharp sliced through the night, aimed at my chest. A bolt of searing magic punched through flesh as white-hot pain ripped through my upper arm.

Vetra screeched with rage, rearing higher. I clenched my thighs, holding on for dear life as agony dug deep into my bones. It wasn't a normal wound. The magic burrowed into my flesh as my muscles seized.

Shit.

I bit down hard, fighting back against the invasive power, shoving it out, rejecting it as I called for my own. I couldn't let it take root, but that arm was useless, the reins falling from my limp fingertips. I tossed out a feeble arch of light, but another bolt came.

A second.

A third.

I dodged the first, deflected the second with my dying magic, but the third hit home. Pain exploded in my ribs, knocking the breath from my lungs as it flung me from my seat. I hit the temple steps hard, the impact rattling my entire body as I tried and failed to suck in air.

No. No. Not like this.

Vetra reared with a furious bellow, lashing out

again as she did her best to protect me, but I felt it. The mages were closing in.

A putrid wave of violet magic wrapped around my wrists like thorned ropes, cutting into my flesh. Magic burned through my skin, constricting, squeezing—

My fingers locked as it wrapped up my arms, around my shoulders and down my torso. A scream tore up my throat when my power wouldn't rise, but before I could let it out, it was cut off by a boot in my damaged ribs.

Breathe. Gods, breathe.

Vetra's cry shattered the night, the mare lashing out as her front hooves struck the nearest mage. Bone crunched. A man hit the ground, shrieking as his leg bent the wrong way.

She wasn't running.

She was fighting for me.

"Hold the damn horse!" someone snarled.

Another mage threw out his hands. A lash of violet magic snapped through the air, wrapping around Vetra's neck like a leash. She reared violently, fighting the restraint, her muscles bunching beneath her coat.

She shrieked—a sound of rage, of fear.

"Easy now, beast," the mage sneered, digging

the spell deeper. "We'll take you, too. A little gift for the king."

No, no, no.

A mage loomed above me, taller than the rest, power curling from his hands in putrid ribbons as he let out a low, satisfied chuckle.

"There we go," he murmured, his voice a slick, oily thing, slipping under my skin like poison.

He tilted his head, studying me like a cat would a wounded bird.

"You both put up a fight. I'll give you that."

Vetra let out a strangled cry. She jerked against the spell, her muscles trembling, hooves tearing at the ground as she tried to break free.

But the magic tightened.

The leash yanked her down.

She hit her knees, panting, violet bands digging into her flesh.

He crouched, the glow of his eyes searing against the dark. "But really—did you think you'd win?"

I bared my teeth, straining against the magic pinning me down.

The mage's grin widened. "Don't bother, little queen." He gave the binding a sharp tug—the magic burned deeper, locking me down. "You're out of tricks. And out of time."

Another soldier stalked forward, sneering. "All that trouble to get here—just to get dragged right back."

My stomach clenched. They weren't going to kill me. They were going to take me.

The first mage ran a finger along my cheek, his touch leaving a trail of static in its wake. "Our King will be pleased. He thought you'd make this harder, but in the end..."

His fingers clenched around my jaw, forcing me to look up.

"You're just another stupid little girl who thought she could play queen."

Rage flashed hot and wild in my chest, and I did the only thing I could. I spat in his face. His eyes flared, violet magic snapping around him like a living thing before the bastard backhanded me.

Pain exploded across my cheekbone, my head snapping to the side.

"I was going to be gentle," he said, mock disappointment dripping from his voice. "I figured—maybe you weren't as foolish as they said."

His fingers dug into my throat. "But now?"

He smiled. A cruel, bloodthirsty thing. "I think I'll break you first."

His magic snaked up my throat, twisting like vines around my neck. The air vanished as I choked.

Vision blurring, lungs burning, the violet light tightened—

Then the air changed.

The wind died, and the snow stilled midair. Vetra stiffened, her ears pricking forward. The mages froze, their glowing eyes snapping up, nostrils flaring. One of them barked a warning, but the words barely left his mouth before a shadow blurred across the field.

Not a shadow—a nightmare.

The first mage vanished. No scream. No body. Just *gone*.

Magic crashed through the clearing like a tidal wave as the temperature plummeted. Frost crept along the stone, the air turning razor-sharp with ice. And then fire swept over everything.

But not red.

Not orange.

Blue.

Xavier.

His magic unleashed like a storm, erupting from his hands in an inferno of frost. The blue fire swallowed the first wave of soldiers, freezing their armor, locking them in place as shards of ice dug into them like knives.

One stumbled, but Xavier was already there. His blade sliced through the air, and ice crystallized along the wound before the man even hit the ground. And when he did, the mage's body shattered into a thousand pieces.

Xavier's magic was different—it felt different. Sharper. Stronger. The curse was gone, and now his power was something so much more than it had been before.

The mage nearby turned, his eyes going wide—seeing something I couldn't. He froze, stumbling back, shaking his head. It was only when I saw Kian reveal himself from the shadows that I understood.

The mage was under one of Kian's illusions. Kian's magic twisted around him, wrapping the soldier in a waking nightmare. His breathing hitched, hands clawing at his throat—then Kian was on him.

One strike from his sword, quick and final, and then the mage's head was on the ground.

Then there was Idris.

I didn't see him, but I could *feel* him. Magic poured from him like a broken dam, thick as smoke, too heavy to breathe. Then he strode from the trees as the earth cracked beneath his feet. The ice shattered, the trees splintered, and it was as if Hell itself had opened wide and the devil sauntered out.

The remaining mages stumbled, clutching their chests like their magic was being ripped from their bodies.

One dropped to his knees as his violet magic was yanked from his body. Then another fell and another —their power withering in his presence. The noose around my neck loosened as their power died, and I finally understood.

Idris didn't wield magic.

He *was* magic.

The golden glow flowed from his hands, his skin, his mouth—too bright, too raw. I'd never seen anything like it. Neither had the Girovians. But the last mage didn't fall like the others. He resisted, bracing himself against the pulsing waves of golden light pouring from Idris' body.

"You think you're a god?" he scoffed.

The words barely left his lips before Idris lifted a single hand.

A pull. A breath.

The mage's body locked up, violet magic bleeding from his pores, screaming as it was ripped from his chest.

I hadn't so much as moved, but my body still shook as I sucked in glorious air, pain and exhaustion hitting me full force as the adrenaline flooded from my body.

Magic still lingered in the air—thick, crackling, electric.

It clung to my skin, wormed through my veins, gripping my bones like unseen chains. Not the enemy's magic. Theirs.

Idris. Kian. Xavier.

I could feel them.

Their power rolled over me, sharp and hungry, like a storm ready to break. It coiled through the clearing, stilling the air, pressing into my skin, into my mind. The mate bond pulsed—too strong, too raw, too close.

My stomach twisted. I tried to shove them out, to lock them away, but the bond had other ideas. It crashed through my defenses, searing through my ribs, my heart, my mind.

They were here. They were furious. And they were trying to get in.

"Vale." Idris' voice burned through the link, low and ragged, edged with something sharp. *"Vale—look at me."*

I clenched my teeth, swallowing the sharp sting

of nausea. *"No."*

I didn't want to look at him. Didn't want to feel him.

Didn't want to feel any of them.

Xavier's magic was still crawling over my skin, healing my wounds, even as my body screamed in protest. My cheek throbbed, my ribs ached, but it was the bond—the connection—that hurt the most.

My fists clenched against the frozen ground. They were too close. Too much. Xavier's warm hand brushed my cheek. I jerked away, rolling onto my side, dragging in ragged, shaking breaths.

His voice was soft, yet pained. "Vale—"

"Don't," I rasped.

Silence stretched as I curled my knees to my chest, trying to gather the courage to stand.

"We need to get you out of here, little witch," Kian murmured as his rough, calloused hand pressed to my jaw, forcing my gaze to meet his.

Kian's amber eyes scanned over me, his pupils dilated with adrenaline, his expression carved from something dangerous. But he wasn't touching me like I was fragile. He knew better.

I forced myself to sit up, my ribs protesting the movement. My limbs trembled, exhaustion dragging at every muscle.

Then I felt him.

Idris.

Still standing. Still watching. Still waiting.

The bond thrashed within me, desperate to close the space between us. It reached for him without my permission, without my control, and I slammed it down hard enough that pain ricocheted through my skull.

No.

I wouldn't let him in. His magic pulsed—an ocean pressing against a breaking dam. He stepped closer.

I dragged in a breath. "Don't." That single word came out raw, a threadbare whisper.

Idris froze. For a heartbeat, no one moved. The temple loomed behind us, its crumbling walls whispering with the weight of history, of power, of ghosts.

Kian's grip tightened, his thumb brushing absently over my cheek. "You're hurt."

"I'm fine."

"You're not." Xavier's voice was quiet but threaded with steel.

Idris exhaled sharply. "Vale—"

I flinched.

It was small—barely there—but he saw it. They

all did. Something flashed across Idris' face—something dangerous, something shattering. Then it was gone, and I hated that I still knew him well enough to see the way he locked it down.

My throat burned. "You weren't supposed to come."

Xavier scoffed. "Do you really think we'd let you go?"

I lifted my gaze, my fury cracking through the exhaustion. "I didn't ask for your permission."

Kian's jaw tightened. "No, you didn't. You just left."

The weight of their anger pressed against me, but it was Idris I felt the most. His magic coiled around my bones, slow and deliberate, and I realized—he was still trying to reach me—to touch me through the bond. I gritted my teeth, shoving back against him.

Hard.

A muscle ticked in his jaw, but he didn't stop. "Vale."

I laughed. It was harsh, bitter, and broken. And then I said it—the words I knew would cut the deepest. "I'm fixing what I broke, remember?"

He worked his jaw but said nothing. The air

cracked like a living thing, magic shifting between us, pressing too tight, too thick.

A warning.

His power flared—reflexive, raw—but then he forced it down.

The words had landed. I knew they had.

Knew the moment his golden eyes darkened, the moment his hands closed into fists at his sides. Knew because that was exactly what he had said to me in the war room back when I had still been naïve enough to think we were whole.

I was too tired to take it back and too hurt to care.

For a moment, just a breath, Idris didn't move, and then—he did.

Slow. Controlled. Careful.

He crouched beside me, close enough that the bond shivered between us, desperate to mend what I wouldn't.

"Is that what this is?" His voice was too soft, too careful.

I didn't answer.

His gaze locked onto mine, unblinking. "If you're fixing what you broke, then why do you still look like you're falling apart?"

The breath in my chest stilled. Something inside

me cracked—too small to see, too deep to reach. I hated him for knowing me too well. For saying it out loud.

Kian shifted closer, grasping my wrist—not to hold me, but to ground me.

Xavier's magic whispered over my skin, his healing touch careful, but still there.

And Idris...

He didn't touch me. He didn't force it. Didn't even move. He just waited.

Because he was right.

I hated that some part of me was still waiting, too. And that, more than anything, made me feel like I was drowning.

CHAPTER 7

IDRIS

The moment Vale shoved herself to her feet, I knew I'd lost control of the situation.

Blood streaked her cheek, her hair a tangled mess, her clothes torn from the fight. The wound on her arm, the one Xavier had barely finished healing, still glowed faintly with the remnants of magic. Her breaths came sharp and ragged, but she didn't slow, didn't pause, except to let her fingers trail briefly down the mare's flank—a silent reassurance, a tether.

Then she moved on.

As if she hadn't nearly died minutes ago.

As if she wasn't still shaking.

As if she wasn't breaking before my eyes.

The temple loomed, cold and waiting. It felt different now. The crumbling stone had been standing for centuries, yet it felt alive, like it was holding its breath. Something about it reached for her, a pull in the air, an invisible thread winding between them. The moment Vale turned toward it, something shifted.

Magic, ancient and thick, curled through the ruins, responding to her—to *us*.

A shiver of power pulsed outward from the foundation, nearly imperceptible, like the temple had just recognized its queen.

She didn't seem to notice. Or if she did, she didn't care. She stumbled once, her body betraying her exhaustion, but she caught herself before I could reach for her. Then she kept moving—marching straight toward the entrance like a woman with a war to win.

I clenched my jaw, forcing my feet to move, but Kian caught my arm, yanking me to a stop.

"Give her a second," he murmured. His grip was firm, a silent command, not a request.

I turned, staring him down. I wasn't in the mood to be handled—not anymore. I'd let him hit me in the war room because I'd earned it. I wasn't going to let him hold me back from her now.

Kian sighed, his amber eyes sharp with the roiling tension tightening his shoulders. "She just fought for her life. She's pissed. Let her be pissed."

I exhaled through my nose, ripping my arm from his grip. "She's hurt."

Xavier stood just behind Kian, his eyes locked on Vale's retreating back. His fingers twitched at his sides like he wanted to reach for her, but he didn't. Instead, he said, "At least she's alive."

I knew what they weren't saying.

We'd all watched her die once.

Once was enough.

Still, I forced my magic down, forced myself to hold back as Vale reached the temple steps. She lifted a hand toward the crumbling stone, paused, then balled her fingers into a fist and let it fall back to her side.

And for the first time since we arrived, she hesitated.

I took a step forward, but before Kian or Xavier could follow, I turned to them.

"Stay here."

Xavier's brows slammed together. "What?"

I held his gaze, my voice low and firm. "We don't know what else is in those woods. If anything comes for us, I need you two guarding the entrance."

That wasn't the only reason.

This confrontation had been coming since the moment Vale walked away from me. If they followed me inside, she wouldn't lay into me like I knew she wanted to. And I needed to hear it. Even if it killed me.

Kian's lips parted like he wanted to argue, but something in my expression must have stopped him. He exhaled sharply, his jaw tight. Xavier looked like he wanted to strangle me, but in the end, neither of them fought me on it.

Not out loud, at least.

With one last glance at them, I followed Vale.

Vale's shoulders stiffened. She didn't turn, but I knew she could feel me there. The mate bond pulsed between us, slow and aching. A silent war neither of us wanted to acknowledge.

Then, her voice—quiet, sharp, exhausted—cut through the thick air between us.

"What is this place to you?"

The words hit harder than they should have.

Not "What is this place?" Not "What is this temple?"

What is this place to you?

She was right to ask. I'd brought her here before in the Dreaming. This wasn't just a ruin. It wasn't just an abandoned temple buried in the snow. It meant something.

I just didn't know what.

The memory flickered—dreams of stone halls swallowed by time, of whispers in the dark, of power humming beneath my skin. It was power, but not mine.

I exhaled slowly, my fingers curling into fists. The cold bit deep, but it wasn't the cold making my chest tighten. "I don't know."

That was the truth, and from the sharp inhale Vale took, she didn't like it.

Her head snapped toward me, her green eyes flashing in the low light. "Bullshit."

I held her gaze. "Vale—"

"No. No, you don't get to do that. You don't get to stand there and pretend this place isn't familiar to you." She took a step closer, her voice rising. "You brought me here, Idris. You showed me this place before I even knew it existed. Don't tell me you don't know what it is."

The temple *sighed* around us—like it had been waiting for her to say it. The walls trembled, dust shifting from the carvings like an exhale. I barely resisted the urge to reach for her. To steady her. To steady *myself*. I'd brought her here before, but I hadn't known why. And now we were standing in it —and I still didn't know.

Her hands tightened into fists at her sides. "So either you were lying then, or you're lying now."

Gods.

I knew that look in her eyes—the exhaustion, the anger, the desperation. She wasn't just demanding answers. She *needed* them. But I didn't have any—not yet—and that was the problem.

Trying to calm myself, I took a slow breath. "If I knew, I would tell you."

She didn't believe me. I could see it in the tight set of her jaw, the way her shoulders bunched like she was bracing for a fight.

Her voice lowered, rough around the edges. "I don't trust you."

It shouldn't have stung, but it did, anyway.

I forced my magic decper, locking it down, trying to ignore the ache in my heart where the bond twisted tighter. "Then don't."

Something cracked in her expression. Not just anger. Not just hurt. Something worse. But before I could reach for it, she turned on her heel and stepped through the temple's entrance.

And just like that, the air changed again.

The temple *recognized her.*

A low hum reverberated through the walls, ancient magic stirring awake. The air thickened, pressing against my skin like a second heartbeat. The shadows deepened, shifting in the dim light. A sharp gust of wind coiled through the temple, rattling the ancient carvings—like a door had just unlocked.

The faintest echo of something old rippled through the air—something I recognized.

I didn't hesitate. I followed her inside.

Because whether she trusted me or not, I wasn't letting her do this alone.

The moment I stepped past the threshold, I felt the magic. It wasn't just humming beneath the stone—it was woven into it. Twisting through the walls, whipping through the air, pressing against my skin. It recognized me. It recognized *her*.

And it was watching.

Vale barely hesitated. Her boots scuffed against the dust-laden floor, her breath unfurling in ghostly tendrils. She didn't flinch when the shadows shifted, when the air pulsed with something ancient.

She'd seen this place before. In her dreams. In the pieces of my soul that had leaked into the bond, showing her memories I hadn't known I had.

And gods help me, I was terrified of what we'd find.

Vale's touch ghosted over the nearest column, tracing the faint markings carved into the stone. Not words. Symbols.

She stilled.

I felt it the moment recognition passed across her expression. Her fingers clenched, her breath catching.

I stepped closer, my voice low. "Vale?"

She didn't look at me. Didn't stop tracing the symbol—a small, etched insignia near the base of the column. A runic carving etched deep into the stone, with jagged lines cutting through its center.

"I've seen this before," she murmured.

The silence stretched between us, building into an almost tangible wall. Then she turned, eyes locking onto mine. "In the book."

My stomach dropped.

The Luxa history book her parents had stolen decades ago. Of course it wasn't just a book. It had never been just a book.

I moved forward, reaching for the carving, my fingers brushing the stone just beneath Vale's. The moment my skin made contact, the magic in the room shifted.

A pulse. A flicker of power, old and hungry.

Vale jerked back. "What the fuck was that?"

I didn't answer. Because I didn't know. The weight of the temple pressed against my lungs. The walls were listening, waiting. It wanted something, and I didn't like it one bit.

Vale exhaled sharply, rubbing a hand over her face. "She never made it here," she muttered, her voice rough as if she were swallowing a sob. "Of course that dream meant nothing. Of course the answers are just out of reach. Of course this was just a waste of time."

The exhaustion in her voice, the raw edge of frustration—it set something off inside me.

Because she wasn't wrong.

She had clawed her way here. She had fought through hell to get to this place, and still, nothing was easy. And gods help me, but I wanted to make it easy for her.

Just once.

I took a step toward her, not thinking, not stopping myself.

"Vale—"

"Don't." The word cut between us like a blade.

Her gaze snapped up, green eyes burning, her

chest heaving with barely leashed anger. Not at the temple. Not at the book.

At me.

I didn't stop. I couldn't.

"Vale," I tried again, quieter this time.

She shook her head, shoving her fingers through her tangled hair. "I don't want your pity, Idris."

Pity?

A sharp, bitter laugh tore from my throat before I could stop it. "Pity?" Something raw cracked through my voice. "Is that what you think this is?"

She bared her teeth. "What else would it be?" Her breathing was sharp, ragged. "You didn't want me to stay, but you chased me down, anyway. And now what? You want to fix me? Put me up on my pretty little throne and pretend I didn't just die for you?"

My pulse hammered. "Vale—"

"You abandoned me."

The words landed like a blade, clean and deep. I sucked in a sharp breath, but there was no air to take. I exhaled sharply, shaking my head. "I didn't—"

"You *did*." Her voice cracked. "You shut me out, Idris. You shut me out when I was the one who died for you."

I flinched. She saw it, and it only made her angrier.

"I gave everything for you." Her voice shook. "And you let me walk away."

I clenched my jaw, a sharp, aching heat blooming in my chest. "You left."

She let out a sharp, humorless laugh. "Because you made it clear there was nothing left for me to stay for."

I couldn't stop myself. "I begged you, Vale. I begged you not to and you did it, anyway."

Tears pooled in her eyes. "You think I don't know what I've done?"

Her voice cracked. And that was what shattered me. Because I'd spent days pretending she hadn't broken me, and here she was, splintering right in front of me.

"I killed him," she whispered, voice shaking. "He begged me to save you—said there was no other way. So I killed him. I knew when I did it that I couldn't handle that much power, but I loved you all so much that I had to save you—save *them*. I thought with that one act, I could fix everything, and instead, I broke it. I broke all of it. And I left because I thought—" She sucked in a sharp breath, shaking her head. "I thought if I could just fix one fucking thing—"

She stopped like the words had gotten caught somewhere deep inside her. Like saying them would make them real.

I took another step toward her.

She squeezed her eyes shut. "I don't—"

I didn't stop myself this time. I reached for her, and again, she flinched. And gods help me, that hurt more than anything.

She forced herself to still, her throat working around a sharp inhale, but I'd already seen it. Already felt the hesitation crawl up my spine. She didn't trust me to touch her. I swallowed against the raw, gnawing ache inside my chest.

"Do you think I don't know what that felt like?" I asked, my voice lower, rougher. "Watching you die? Knowing you did it for me?"

Her breath hitched.

I stepped closer, my magic curling at my finger-tips. "Do you think I don't know what it's like to hold you in my arms and feel you slip away?"

Vale trembled, but I didn't stop—couldn't stop.

"You think you failed?" My voice was a whisper, dark and razor-sharp. "You think you broke everything? Gods, Vale, I would have set the world on fire if it meant you never dying for me."

She shuddered, her lips parting, but no sound came out. My magic crackled at my fingertips, fire licking beneath my skin. Not to hurt. Not to cage. Just to reach her.

"I shut you out because I thought I'd lost you," I murmured. "I shut you out because when you died, I broke, too."

Her fingers curled into fists as the temple hummed around us. The walls seemed to pull tighter, the magic shifting, waiting, watching.

Vale took a shaky step back, her shoulders rigid. "I don't—I can't—"

I forced myself to let her go.

"Fine," I murmured. "Then let's find out what this place wants from us."

She swallowed hard, nodding once.

I turned toward the wall, toward the carving.

The symbol seemed to pulse, and as she reached out, fingers grazing the stone once more, the temple responded.

A whisper of something ancient.

And then—the stone shifted.

A pulse, like a heartbeat, rippled outward from the carving, shaking the temple's foundation. Runes flared to life across the walls, the columns, the floor—searing symbols burning into existence, glowing like embers before settling into a slow, steady pulse.

I gasped and jerked my hand back.

My heel caught on a broken slab of stone, my balance tipping. I crashed into something solid— Idris.

His arms came around me instinctively, his body heat wrapping around me like a shield. Scales rippled along his skin, the scent of smoke curling in the air as his dragon flared in response. His grip was firm, possessive, his stance set between me and the temple.

His growl rumbled against my back. "What the fuck did you do?"

"I—" My pulse hammered. "I don't know."

The runes were still glowing—still breathing. The whole temple felt alive. A slow, creeping awareness crawled over my skin, like something unseen was watching, waiting. I swallowed hard and fumbled with the straps on my pack, my fingers trembling as I yanked out the Luxa book.

"Vale," Idris warned, his voice a low snarl. "We need to get the fuck out of here."

But I continued flipping through brittle pages, frantically searching for the symbol now carved into my mind.

"I did not almost die for this to leave now. I was led here, dammit, and I—"

Then I found it.

It was barely noticeable, small, and faded in the corner of a page. A footnote, almost an afterthought, but the text beneath it made my breath catch.

A Luxa stronghold. A sanctuary hidden even from the Waking. Sealed with the blood of the Lighted Ones.

The "lighted ones" had to be Luxa. The symbol

was sealed in our blood, which meant the only way to unseal it was...

Idris stiffened behind me. His breathing sharpened, his body coiling tight as a bowstring. I felt him reading the words over my shoulder, felt the exact moment his entire being rejected what I was thinking.

"No," he growled.

I turned, my breath fogging in the cold. "Idris—"

"*No*." His voice was sharp. Final. "We don't know what the fuck this is or what you'll unlock."

But I knew I was supposed to find this place. *I knew it*. It had called me here.

I swallowed, glancing back at the carving. "There's only one way to find out."

"Vale—"

Before he could stop me, I moved. A sharp sting bit through my hand as I dragged my fingertip along a jagged splinter of a broken pew. A single bead of crimson welled up, and I pressed it to the stone.

The temple inhaled, a soundless rush of power sucked at my lungs, the pressure mounting in my skull. A thunderous *crack* split the air before the runes exploded with light. A shockwave slammed into me, into Idris, sending us both stumbling back.

The walls trembled, the air thickened, and gravity warped.

The runes flared hotter, the glow turning molten, and for a second, I swore the temple woke up and stared right at me. A rush of air twined around my ankles, the deep pull of something ancient and unseen, like fingers curling around my ribs. It wasn't just awake. It was aware.

And then—

I was falling.

No gentle transition. No slow descent. Just a violent, merciless drop into the abyss. The temple ripped away from me, the stone dissolving into darkness.

A roar tore through the void—Idris' voice, ragged and desperate. "*Vale!*"

But I was already gone.

I tried to scream, but there was no sound.

I crashed into something soft. A frigid bite tore through me, my hands sinking into thick, powdery snow. But the moment I touched it, I knew.

This wasn't real.

Staggering to my feet, my breath wisped in the frozen air. The temple stood before me—whole. No cracks, no ruins—just pristine white stone, towering spires stretching toward a too-dark sky.

Everything felt... wrong.

The air was too still. The silence too deep. And then came the whispers.

Not words, just sounds like icy breaths on the back of my neck. My stomach knotted. I turned, searching—

And the temple shifted.

Figures flickered in and out of existence, clad in golden robes with white veils. Moving through the halls, their voices distant echoes.

Luxa witches.

Their faces were blurred, distorted. I reached for one, fingers outstretched—they passed right through. A vision maybe or an echo of the past.

Or a warning.

A low, musical laugh whipped through the temple, slithering through the walls. "Look at you."

I spun, my pulse spiking because I knew that voice. Zamarra wasn't visible, but she was here.

"Once again stepping into places you don't belong."

I clenched my fists, fire licking beneath my skin. "Show yourself."

Another laugh. "Oh, little queen, I don't think you really want that."

The air shifted, a dark wind curling through the hall, knocking into my chest, making me stumble.

Zamarra hummed in glee. "Your parents were pathetic fools."

My breath hitched. What the hell did she know about my parents?

"They begged the Dreaming for salvation." Her voice slithered through the darkness, too close, everywhere and nowhere. "Asking the very power they should have feared for help. They should have left it alone. Now where are they? Dead and gone with nothing to show for it except for playing right into my hands."

I forced my voice steady. "You're full of shit."

Zamarra chuckled, her voice getting closer, even though she stayed hidden. "Am I? What about now?"

The shadows coiled tighter, and then the world around me changed.

Nyrah sat bound and unconscious on a high-backed chair, the ropes biting into her flesh. A dagger hovered over her heart, held by an invisible hand.

I froze, my lungs seizing.

Zamarra tsked. "You think I want you?"

I swallowed hard, not knowing what to do.

"I don't." Her voice was silk and venom. "I already have a vessel all trussed up and waiting for me."

Ice crawled up my spine as the blade pressed into Nyrah's filthy tunic.

"She's young," Zamarra mused, her form flickering in and out of view. "Not as powerful as you—not yet. But she will be."

The dagger dragged higher, slicing into the fabric as it reached for her throat.

"And if you won't kneel for me..." Zamarra sighed. "Perhaps you'll kneel for her."

Something inside me snapped. I screamed, my magic surging outward, shattering the vision—

But the laughter didn't stop.

"You'll break before the end," Zamarra purred, her form solidifying for just a moment. "You'll give in."

Then her shadows swallowed me as the ground shook. A deep, earth-splitting roar sliced through the Dreaming. Heat blazed at my back, scorching hot, but I knew it as well as I knew my own soul. My heart stammered as a wall of red scales blocked my path.

Rune.

He stood, colossal, furious, his golden eyes burning. His wings stretched, his fire curling from his nostrils as his flames held the shadows at bay. His fire tore through the darkness, ripping the nightmare apart.

"Get up, my Queen," he ordered, the command rumbling through my chest. His voice wasn't soft—it never had been. It was fire and fury, molten and ancient. "You can't stay here. I can't hold her back forever."

His jaw snapped, teeth bared. "You have to wake up."

It was as if a hook had yanked me from the depths, and I violently slammed back into my body. The cold stone bit into my back as I sucked in a breath. Idris was above me, gripping my shoulders, shaking me.

"Vale." His voice was hoarse—pleading—the worry in it palpable.

I sucked in a sharp breath, my chest burning, the mate bonds screaming through my body. Somehow, I was still in the temple, still on the floor, but the carving beneath my hand was different now.

A new inscription—written in my own blood— seemed engraved in the stone. I blinked, my vision swimming as I tried to focus. The symbols pulsed, shifted, rearranged—

Then the words revealed themselves:

THE BLOOD OF THE FIRST WILL SHOW THE WAY. SEEK THE ONE LOST TO THE DREAMING.

Idris stiffened beside me, his voice quiet. Dark.

"What the fuck does that mean?" he growled, sending shivers down my spine.

I gulped down air, trying to get my bearings. I had no idea what those words meant, but I did know one thing. Somewhere, deep inside the Dreaming, "the First" was waiting.

I just didn't know who that meant.

And I was afraid to find out.

The moment I stood, the ground rumbled. A low, warning tremor, deep as a heartbeat.

Then the temple doors burst open, slamming into the stone with a force that sent dust billowing through the chamber. Sunlight knifed through the dim, spilling across the glowing runes as two hulking figures stormed inside.

Kian and Xavier.

Weapons drawn, breath heaving, their eyes wild and searching.

"What the fuck is going on?" Kian demanded, his voice rough, his gaze locking onto me.

"We heard you scream," Xavier added, his gaze sweeping the chamber as if he expected something to lunge from the shadows.

I opened my mouth—to explain, to reassure—but Idris was already moving.

He stepped between us, his stance coiled and protective. I could feel the heat of his magic wrapping around him, the sharp bite of his power barely restrained. His jaw was tight, unreadable.

Then the temple shifted—not the floor. Not the walls. It was something deeper.

A cold pressure twined around my ribs, sinking into my bones. The air thickened, pressing in, and then they appeared—spectral figures emerging from the walls.

Not quite ghosts.

Not quite alive.

They moved like smoke, clad in golden Luxa robes, their faces blurred, hollow. Whispers flowed through the chamber—not words, not yet—just sounds, drifting like wind through dead trees.

My breath hitched as one stepped forward. The others stilled, waiting as it glided toward me. It lifted its ghostly hand but didn't touch me—didn't need to. Her empty gaze burned into mine, and in a voice reminiscent of fractured wind, it spoke, pressing into my mind.

"The blood awakens. The Dreaming calls."

A shiver of unease raced down the length of my spine.

Idris snarled.

His magic surged hot, fire licking over his skin as he shifted forward, his stance braced between me and the figure, shielding me, but the Luxa didn't attack. They simply watched.

A moment stretched—tense and charged. Then, one by one, they flickered, their robes rippling as their forms dimmed, like shadows retreating from the light.

All but one.

It lingered, watching me. Not like the others. This one knew me.

A pressure built in my chest, heavy and ancient, as if my ribs were forced together with a vise. It wasn't just looking at me—it was seeing me.

"Blood of the First..."

A sharp jolt of magic ripped through me, searing hot. I gasped, stumbling back as power coiled beneath my skin, gathering like a second heartbeat. Idris moved instantly, his magic flaring in response. Fire licked at the air, heat radiating from his skin as he grabbed my wrist.

"Vale!" His voice was sharp, grounding. But I barely heard him.

"You are the key..."

The words slammed into me, but they weren't whole. Like an echo of something unfinished. The figure's edges frayed, flickering like a candle guttering out. And then the temple groaned. The walls shuddered. Dust rained from above. The columns sighed, their runes shifting, rearranging, as if reacting to the words just spoken.

Kian's curse sliced through the thickening air. "What the fuck is happening?"

He and Xavier were still tense, weapons drawn, preparing to fight the figures that seemed no more solid than ghosts. But I wasn't looking at them. The pressure twisting around my ribs was deepening. Something else was shifting. Something waiting.

The spectral figure wasn't gone. Not yet.

Her hollow eyes stayed locked onto mine, and in a voice like a shattered whisper, she gave me an ominous warning.

"Find the lost... before the dreamer wakes."

A sharp chill ran down my spine, and then it was gone. The temple fell silent. The air stilled.

My palm burned where I'd touched the carving. And when I looked down—a faint glow pulsed just beneath my skin.

Kian's voice cut through the silence, his tone dark and unreadable. "Vale?"

I swallowed hard, my voice tight. "Yeah?"

His jaw tensed. His gaze darted between the runes on the wall, the faded spirits, and finally, my glowing hand. "What the fuck does that mean?"

I exhaled slowly. My head still spun, my pulse still thundering. I didn't have an answer. But, I knew one thing. Somewhere, deep inside the Dreaming, "the lost" was waiting.

And I had a feeling we were already running out of time.

CHAPTER 9

KIAN

Vale was standing.

She was breathing.

She was whole.

But my body still hadn't caught up to that fact.

Because for a moment—for one fucking moment —I had felt what it would be like to lose her. *Again*. And I couldn't take it.

I moved before I could stop myself, closing the distance between us, grabbing her shoulders—not hard, not to hurt, just to feel that she was real, that she wasn't slipping through my fingers again.

"Again, what the fuck was that?" My voice came out rough, uneven.

She flinched—not from me, but from everything. Her green eyes were wide with something I didn't like—something like dread.

"I—I don't know."

Bullshit.

Xavier's voice cut through the thick tension, sharp and low. "You were frozen—unmoving. The temple was shaking, and Idris looked like he was about to rip a hole through the world trying to get you to react."

Vale swallowed hard. "I wasn't—" She stopped, shaking her head. "I was awake."

I let out a harsh, bitter laugh. "Yeah? Well, you sure as fuck weren't talking."

She opened her mouth, but I wasn't done. My hands slid down her arms, skimming over her wrists, checking for wounds—checking for anything.

I couldn't fucking stop myself.

Because the last time I had held her like this, she'd stopped breathing in my arms. The last time, I had to watch while she slipped through my fingers, helpless to do anything but scream her name and pray to gods who never fucking answered.

"Don't," I ground out, swallowing down my fear.

Her brows furrowed. "Don't what?"

I lifted my head, locking my gaze onto hers. "Don't ever fucking do that again."

Something flickered in her expression—guilt, defiance, something sharp enough to cut.

"I had to," she whispered.

I let go of her, stepping back like I'd been burned.

She had to? She had to nearly fucking die on me again?

A bitter, choked laugh ripped out of me. "Of course you did." I raked a hand through my hair, my pulse still a mess. "Of course you had to go alone, had to do this on your own—because why the fuck would you ever stop and think about the rest of us?"

She flinched.

Good.

I wasn't trying to hurt her, but gods—she had to understand. She had to know what it did to me. To Xavier. To Idris. To all of us every time she threw herself into danger like this.

Xavier exhaled sharply beside me. "We ran straight into a fucking warzone to find you, Vale." His jaw tightened, his voice dropping lower. "You don't get to do this alone. Not anymore."

Vale's throat bobbed, but her chin lifted—stubborn as always. "As much as I appreciate you saving my ass, I didn't ask you to. You have your kingdom to run and your war to fight, and I have mine. This is something I have to do."

I laughed again—hollow, rough, and a little unhinged. "Have to?" I echoed. "You have to walk into a temple full of unknown magic? Have to nearly get yourself killed by mages? Do you even hear yourself?"

"I didn't plan for that to happen!" she snapped, her voice cracking. "I didn't know—"

"No. You *never* know. You just run straight into the fire and hope you don't burn."

Her magic flared. I felt it crackle through the air, golden light dancing at her fingertips. And my own fire met it—heat sparking over my skin, deep and scorching, because I wasn't done.

She took a breath, steadying herself. "Everything I have ever done was for the people I love. I won't apologize for giving a shit about the only fucking family I have left."

Tears pooled in her eyes as her shoulder sagged. "I don't want to fight you."

I shook my head. "I don't want to fight you, either. I just want you to fucking *live*."

The words hit her, and for a second, I thought she might actually listen.

Then her hands curled into fists, her voice steady. "It's not like I did this on a whim. My sister is in danger, and I'm not leaving without her."

Fire still burned at the edges of my vision, but I forced myself to breathe.

Vale was alive, but she wasn't listening. She was still standing there, ready to fight me instead of facing reality.

"We need to keep moving." Her voice was sharp and unyielding. "Nyrah's out there, and if Zamarra has her—"

"Then charging in like an idiot will only get you killed." My voice was just as sharp.

Her mouth pressed into a thin line, but I didn't back down. We'd chased her across the fucking continent to find her. I was not letting her run off again.

Xavier exhaled through his nose, stepping forward. "Look. We do this together. No more running off." His pointed gaze shifted to Vale. "No more secrets. No more shutting us out."

Vale hesitated, but she nodded. "*Fine.*"

It wasn't enough—not for me. I rubbed a hand down my face, trying to force my heart rate back to normal. Xavier was right. We couldn't keep doing this, couldn't keep splitting apart every time shit got hard.

But it was damn near impossible when every instinct I had screamed at me to get her the fuck out of here.

Idris finally spoke: "Sevilava."

Vale blinked, turning to him. "What?"

He adjusted the strap of his scabbard, his jaw tight. "It's the closest place we can go that might have something—*anything*—on the Luxa. Old strongholds, records, history. At the very least, it's the only place we'll find shelter that isn't in hostile territory."

Vale frowned, hesitating. "Why would Sevilava have Luxa strongholds?"

Idris sighed. "Because the Luxa weren't just witches. They were people. They needed places to live, to train. They had temples, sanctuaries—places hidden away from the Waking. I don't know if any are still standing, but if there's even a chance they left something behind, Sevilava is the closest bet."

"And if there's nothing left?"

Idris' eyes darkened. "Then we figure out the next step after you get some fucking sleep."

Vale opened her mouth to argue, but I was already done.

I stepped in front of her, tilting my head down, voice low and rough. "You are not walking blind into whatever the fuck that was," I gritted out.

She folded her arms. "I wasn't alone. Even when I was pulled into the Dreaming, Rune was there."

I stilled.

"Rune?" My voice was sharp and cutting. "What do you mean Rune was there? Rune is dead."

Her smile was brittle. "Just another thing I failed at, Kian. He managed to pull me out before Zamarra could—"

Zamarra.

The name hit like a knife between the shoulder blades, and the entire room tensed at once. Xavier cursed. Idris went rigid.

I grabbed her wrist, voice low and rough. "Zamarra was in the Dreaming with you?"

Vale didn't flinch, but there was something in her eyes—something raw. "I think she might actually have Nyrah. She said she has plans for her. She wants her as a vessel—whatever the fuck that means."

A growl rumbled in my chest, my flames flaring. We were not letting Zamarra hurt her sister. Vale could see it in my face. I knew she could. But she was still standing there, ready to fight me instead of listening.

I ran a hand through my hair, trying to breathe, trying to think, but it was damn near impossible when every instinct I had screamed at me to get her the fuck out of here.

I needed her safe.

But she wasn't safe, not even with us. Not while she was still bleeding magic and still hell-bent on running herself into the ground.

And then she made it worse.

"I need to get Vetra," she said, like it was the simplest thing in the world.

I stared at her. "What?"

"Vetra," she repeated. "The horse. She saved my life. I'm not leaving her behind."

Gods. Of fucking course.

Vale would never just walk away from something she loved—not even when it would make all of our lives a hell of a lot easier. I exhaled sharply, forcing myself to think. The temple was on the border of Sevilava and Girovia. We were close.

Vale wanted her warhorse, I wanted her alive, and Idris wanted a fucking plan.

Fine.

We could work with that.

I turned to Xavier. "The horses?"

Xavier's gaze shifted toward the tree line. "They should still be where we left them. Getting them through the ruins won't be easy, but we can do it." His gaze flicked to Vale. "You're sure she can handle the trip?"

Vale bristled, her gaze darting from her horse and back to me. "Of course she can."

I huffed a bitter laugh. "He meant *you*, Vale."

She glared at me, fire flashing in her eyes, but I didn't fucking care. Because she was exhausted. Because she was still pale and shaking. Because I had just watched her almost die again, and I wasn't in the mood for her bullshit.

I moved closer, my voice dropping lower. "You need rest. And you need a plan. We all do."

Vale clenched her jaw, her mind still shutting me out, refusing to let me see her thoughts. Then, finally—*finally*—she nodded.

She wanted her damn warhorse? *Fine.* But she wasn't leaving without protection.

A few minutes later, the horses were retrieved, and I swung up onto my mount, muscles tight, every part of me still on edge. My hands flexed against the reins as I shot one last look at Vale.

She was still standing there like she was

thinking about fighting me on this, like she was plotting another path that left me—left us—behind.

Gods fucking help me.

I exhaled sharply, swinging my leg back over my mount before grabbing her by the waist and hauling her onto the horse she'd managed to steal from somewhere.

She let out a startled sound as I set her firmly in the saddle, but I didn't let go yet.

Instead, I crouched to tighten the straps, adjust the stirrups, and make damn sure the saddle was sitting right. She must have thrown it on in a hurry before running into that temple, because the girth was too loose, the angle slightly off.

The whole time, she didn't say a word.

Maybe she was too tired to fight me. Maybe she knew I needed to do something, anything, to keep from losing my fucking mind.

I finished adjusting the saddle, giving it a firm tug before finally stepping back. I met her eyes, holding them. And that's when it hit me.

We'd chased her across the fucking continent. Tracked her through hostile territory, through blood and smoke and war, through *everything*.

And she had still left.

She had still run.

And I'd let her.

My heart slammed against my ribcage, my vision blurring at the edges as fire licked at my skin, as every terrifying, agonizing moment of searching for her came crashing down all at once.

She had almost died on me. *Again.*

I couldn't do this.

I couldn't lose her again.

I moved before I could stop myself, fisting my hands in her cloak and yanking her down off the saddle, catching her as she stumbled.

She barely had a second to breathe before I crashed my mouth against hers.

Hard. Desperate.

Not gentle, not careful, because I wasn't fucking either of those things right then. Because I was breaking. Because I had spent hours picturing her cold, lifeless, *gone.*

And now she was here. Warm. Alive. *Mine.*

I felt the second she surrendered, her hands gripping my jacket, clutching me back just as hard. Her breath hitched against my lips, her whole body pressed against mine, caught in the same storm, the same fire.

Her magic flared. I tasted it on my tongue— bright and sharp and alive.

But when I finally pulled back, panting, shaking, feeling like I was about to tear apart from the inside out, I let my forehead rest against hers.

And gods help me, I whispered it: "Don't you fucking do that again."

Her fingers tightened against my chest. "Kian—"

I kissed her again. Softer this time, but still urgent. Still rough.

Because I needed this. I needed her. But I had to let go.

I forced myself to pull back, to lift her and settle her back onto the damn horse where she belonged. Where I could fucking see her.

She didn't fight me.

Maybe she finally understood.

I crouched, tightened the girth one last time, adjusted the straps, made damn sure the saddle was set right.

Then I looked up at her, at my mate, at the love of my life, at the woman who was going to fucking kill me one day. And I meant every damn word when I said:

"Because I swear to the gods, if you scare me like that again, Vale"—I narrowed my eyes, making her hear me—"I will tie you to the fucking horse myself."

CHAPTER 10
XAVIER

My hold tightened around the reins as we rode through the ruins, my teeth grinding with every breath I took.

I should have felt relief at seeing Vale alive and whole, but relief meant trust, and I didn't trust my mate. Not after she broke her promise.

Not after I'd felt our bond fray to the breaking point. Not after I'd spent hours chasing the ghost of her magic, gripping the reins so tight my hands had gone numb, waiting for the moment it would vanish completely.

For the moment *she* would vanish completely.

I blinked hard, shaking it off, but my hands still ached—like they were still holding nothing.

Vale was behind me—close enough that I could

hear the soft rhythm of her horse's hooves, but not close enough that I had to look at her. Because if I did, I didn't know whether I'd kiss her or start yelling, and I wasn't sure which would be worse.

She left me. She *chose* to leave.

I exhaled sharply, the rage coiling tighter inside me. I'd spent hours tracking her, hours wondering if she was alive or if I'd be too late. And now here she was, riding behind me like nothing had changed. Like she hadn't ripped my fucking heart out and taken it with her.

I couldn't speak—couldn't even look at her.

Because I knew if I opened my mouth, I wouldn't stop. And I wasn't sure she could handle what I had to say.

The air changed as we crossed the temple's ruins into Sevilava. The crumbling building stood on the border, but it wasn't a lone place of worship out in the middle of nowhere. Once upon a time it had been a city, a place for Luxa to live and breathe without fear of the Waking world.

But that was before Idris' curse and Zamarra's wrath.

Beaten buildings lay like burned out carcasses across the border, and we picked our way through them. It was slow going, but Vale's horse held up, carrying her over the detritus as if she'd been bred for the task.

Wind howled as we rode across the blackened ground, the ruins of the temple fading behind us. Vale now rode beside Kian, just close enough that I could see the tension in her shoulders, the way she kept sneaking glances at me when she thought I wasn't looking.

The bond between us still ached, raw and stretched thin after hours of silence. She had shut me out. Not just Idris. Not just Kian.

Me.

And gods, it hurt.

I'd thought I was finally part of something, part of them. But when it mattered most, she left.

I hadn't said much since we found her—not because I wasn't angry. Because I didn't know if I could say what I needed to without breaking something between us that we wouldn't be able to fix.

The air grew heavier the farther north we rode, the temperature shifting into something that wasn't exactly hot or cold—just searing.

Not from the sun. From the ground.

Volcanic rock stretched for miles, black and jagged, some places still glowing faintly red from lava that had cooled centuries ago. The wind carried the scent of ash and something metallic, but what struck me most was the sky.

It was like the world was on the edge of an eternal dusk, clouds thick and streaked with crimson fire from distant eruptions.

And as we approached Shavrik, the largest city in Sevilava, the red glow of the lava rivers running through the streets cast eerie shadows on the obsidian buildings. The people here didn't cower. They walked with purpose, with weapons strapped to their backs, with eyes that measured a threat before it could reach them.

A place of sharp ridges and red-hot rock that would split open beneath your feet if you stepped in the wrong place. It was a land that tested you—and if you weren't strong enough, it fucking devoured you.

And the people were no different.

Their faces were marked with ash-streaked tattoos, their clothes lined with woven fire-resistant threads. Some carried obsidian-bladed weapons strapped across their backs, others wore thick wraps to shield them from the heat that still pulsed from the ground.

And every single one of them looked like they could kill a man and keep right on walking.

It was not a welcoming place. But Idris—Idris fucking belonged here. He wasn't just comfortable, he was commanding. Like the fire in this land answered to him and only him. He rode ahead, barely sparing the city a glance.

We followed him through the twisting alleys, the lava-glow casting long shadows against the black stone buildings. The deeper we went, the less I liked it. Not because of the city—because of the eyes. People watched us.

Measuring.

Calculating.

It had been years since Idris had been here, and still, it was as if the city knew him. As if the heat in the stone itself bent toward him. People didn't bow, didn't greet him like a ruler. But they moved out of his path without question.

Kian rode close to Vale, his hand resting on his sword hilt. I kept my grip on my own weapon, scanning every darkened corner, every stall, every open window.

Idris turned sharply down an even narrower passage, leading us into what looked like a dead-end courtyard. But then, with a flick of his wrist, the rock groaned. A section of the wall shifted, revealing a hidden entrance.

A burst of hot air swept out as the door opened, exposing a cavernous stone stable inside the cooled lava ridge. It wasn't large, but it was fortified. The moment we stepped inside, I saw why.

Weapons lined the walls. A well-worn forge sat in the back. And the smell of ash and horse filled the air.

Not just a stable. A hidden armory.

Idris dismounted first, rubbing his horse's neck before leading it to an open stall.

I arched a brow. "You have your own fucking stable here?"

He didn't look at me. "I have a lot of things here."

Vale slid from her saddle, barely catching herself before she stumbled. Kian was there before I could move, gripping her elbow, steadying her.

She muttered something under her breath, her fingers brushing against Kian's arm for just a second longer than necessary before she pulled away. Not because she didn't want to hold on—because she wasn't sure she still could.

I swallowed hard and turned back to my horse, gripping the reins tight. Not the time. Not the place. But it still felt like something inside me had come loose.

The moment the last horse was settled, Idris was already moving. He didn't check the street. Didn't look back at us. Just strode to the far side of the stable, gripping the heavy metal door set into the stone wall.

He pressed his hand against it, his magic bleeding into the iron.

A low hum rippled through the room. The door's runes flared to life, shifting and rearranging as if the metal itself was breathing.

Vale stiffened beside me. She recognized that magic.

So did I.

The metal groaned. Locks clicked free. And then, the door swung open on its own.

Idris glanced back at us. "Inside. Now."

By the time Idris locked the door behind us, exhaustion weighed on all of us. No one had spoken since we crossed the threshold, but I could feel the tension buzzing under our skin, too sharp, too raw to ignore.

Vale stood near the center of the room, arms wrapped around herself like she was trying to hold herself together. She looked too damn pale, too damn small.

Kian leaned against the far wall, arms crossed,

eyes shadowed. He had been quiet since we got inside, and that wasn't like him. His usual easy humor, his snark—it was gone. A muscle in his jaw ticked, but he didn't move, didn't say anything. He just watched.

Idris finally broke the silence. "Eat. Now. And when you do, I want to hear everything you're not telling us."

Vale flinched, her lips parting like she was about to argue, but Idris was already pulling a bundle of wrapped food from his pack and tossing it onto the table.

She hesitated.

Kian pushed off the wall, grabbed a knife, and started cutting into the bread and dried meat with more force than necessary. His movements were sharp, controlled, like he needed something to do with his hands or he might lose it.

Vale sat down last, her movements slow, like her exhaustion had finally caught up with her. She reached for the bread, took a single bite, then stopped.

She wasn't going to eat. Not if someone didn't make her.

I clenched my jaw and shoved my portion toward her. "Eat it, Vale."

Her brows furrowed. "Xavier—"

"You're shaking." I cut her off. "You can barely keep your head up, and you're bleeding magic like a fucking beacon." I nudged the hunk of dried meat again, harder. "Eat. Or I swear to the gods, I will make you."

Silence stretched between us, and then, finally, she tore off another piece of bread, forced herself to chew, and swallowed.

Kian's gaze flicked toward me, something unreadable passing through his expression before he turned away. Usually I could read him, but I was at a loss.

Vale pushed her food away, barely half-finished. She didn't say anything, but her fingers clenched on her lap.

She was debating, holding something back. I knew the look, knew the way she curled into herself when she didn't want to speak—when she was afraid of the words once they were out.

The silence stretched too long.

Kian exhaled sharply, pushing his own food aside. "Vale—"

Her shoulders tensed. Then, finally, she spoke.

Slowly. Cautiously. Like saying it aloud made it real.

She told us about Rune—how she'd failed in merging him with Idris, how she'd died before it could be completed. About Zamarra—how she was looking for a vessel, how she seemed to lurk in every corner of Vale's mind.

Then she told us about Nyrah and what Zamarra planned to do with her. About how the Dreaming was pulling her in, dragging her deeper every time she closed her eyes.

How she didn't know if she'd wake up again.

Kian muttered a curse. Idris' jaw tightened. And me? I just listened. Because for all my anger, for all my fucking hurt—I saw what she was really afraid of. She wasn't just shutting us out. She was terrified at what she'd done. Her magic crackled at her fingertips, light pulsing weakly before flickering out.

"I don't want to fall asleep," she admitted, her voice barely there. "If I do... I don't know if I'll wake up."

The words hit like a fucking blade. The room went silent. Then Idris stepped forward, not hesitating for once. "Then I'll keep you here."

Vale looked up, startled.

He crossed his arms. Steady. Unshaken. Certain. "You forget, my brave one, what I said to you." His voice was soft, but final. "If you can't control your dreams, the only place you're dreaming is next to me. It's just another realm. I can keep you safe."

Vale's breath shuddered out of her. For the first time tonight, she looked relieved. And gods, I hated that she had been carrying that fear alone.

The silence stretched, thick but not uncomfortable. For once, there were no immediate threats. No fights. Just exhaustion pulling at every muscle, every frayed nerve.

"We rest here," Idris said finally. "Tomorrow, we decide our next move."

No one argued. There was nothing left to argue about.

Kian rolled his shoulders, tension still coiled tight in his frame. He reached into his pack and pulled something free—a dagger. *Her* dagger.

Vale's breath hitched.

"Figured you'd want this back."

Kian turned the dagger in his palm, the flickering firelight catching on the edge of the blade. Then, without hesitation, he held it out to her, jeweled hilt first. No words, just a quiet promise.

Vale sucked in a staggered breath as she took it, her fingers curling tight around the hilt—slow and reverent.

"Thank you," she whispered. She'd left it behind

when she ran. Now, Kian was giving it back—not as a warning, but as a promise.

Kian only nodded, his gaze steady. "Always."

Idris didn't wait for Vale to change her mind. He turned toward the far end of the safe house, toward the heaviest door—the one lined with reinforced metal. Without hesitation, he pressed his palm to the iron, his magic sinking into the locks.

A low hum rippled through the air. Runes flared along the doorframe, shifting and rearranging, unlocking something ancient, something unseen. The lock clicked free, and the door swung open.

The walls were obsidian, lined with shelves of books, weapons, and supplies. A single fireplace burned low in the corner, casting flickering light over the one massive bed in the center of the room, large enough to accommodate all of us. This wasn't a house meant for guests—only Idris.

Vale hesitated at the threshold.

"I told you," Idris murmured. "You don't dream unless you're next to me."

A muscle in her jaw ticked, but she didn't argue. She was fraying at the edges, her magic weak, her pulse too damn faint against the bond.

It took forever, but she finally peeled off her armor, every movement slow and deliberate. Kian handed her a damp cloth, and she used it to scrub the dirt and blood from her arms, her hands. A quiet ritual of survival.

No one spoke. Even Kian, normally the first to fill a silence, only stood nearby, watching.

I hated this—hated the way she curled in on herself, like she was still carrying something too heavy to share.

She rummaged through a trunk at the end of the bed, pulling free an oversized tunic—one of Idris' old shirts, probably. The moment she touched it, she hesitated, fingers tightening around the fabric.

She turned toward Idris, her voice quieter than I'd ever heard it. "You won't let me slip?"

It wasn't a question. It was a plea.

Idris—who had been watching her, silent and unreadable—exhaled softly. "Never."

Vale nodded once, then stepped away, retreating behind the dressing screen. The fire crackled low, filling the silence.

Kian rubbed a hand down his face, then turned, dragging one of the chairs closer to the bed before slumping onto it. "I'll take first watch."

Idris didn't argue. He sat on the edge of the bed, one boot resting on his knee, fingers tapping against his scabbard in quiet thought.

I paced. I couldn't sit. Couldn't sleep.

Because this—this quiet, this stillness—felt like the end of something I couldn't name.

When Vale finally reappeared, her face was scrubbed clean, her hair still damp from where she'd run wet fingers through it. She was drowning in Idris' tunic, the hem brushing her knees.

And gods help me, even like this—especially like this—she was still the most beautiful thing I had ever seen.

She didn't say anything. Just climbed into bed, her body giving out the second she hit the mattress. She exhaled once, long and slow, her fingers curling into the sheets like she was trying to keep herself anchored.

I couldn't look at her anymore.

I turned back toward the fire, raking a hand through my hair, my pulse still too fucking erratic, my thoughts a mess.

Time passed. The fire burned lower. The sound of Kian's chair creaked as he shifted.

Then, Vale whimpered.

A small, broken sound. Barely audible.

I let myself look. She was shifting in her sleep, her breath coming faster, fingers twitching against the blanket like she was reaching for something—someone—who wasn't there.

I turned to Idris, who sat at the edge of the bed, arms crossed, eyes shadowed with exhaustion.

"She in the Dreaming?" I asked, my voice rough.

He shook his head. "No." His gaze swung to Vale, lingering for a beat before he exhaled. "Just a regular nightmare."

That should have been enough to keep me where I was.

But it wasn't.

Vale shifted again, her breath uneven, her whole body curling in on itself, like she was trying to shield herself from something.

I gritted my teeth. My fingers balled into fists. I should've stayed exactly where I was—left her alone. But then she whimpered again—soft, broken, like she was drowning in something she couldn't escape.

Fuck. *Fuck.*

I moved before I could stop myself. In an instant, I was across the room, lowering onto the bed beside her. I didn't think, didn't hesitate. My body acted on its own, as if it had always known where I belonged.

I slid in behind her, curling around her, my arm

slipping over her waist. She was so damn small like this, fragile in a way I never let myself see.

She let out a long, shaky breath. Then her body melted into mine, the tension draining from her limbs as her breathing steadied. Like even in sleep, she knew me. Trusted me.

Like she still belonged to me—to *us*.

My throat tightened. I let my forehead rest against the back of her neck, my fingers clutching her tighter. Not enough to wake her. Just enough to hold her there.

She'd left, but gods help me—I couldn't leave her. Not even now.

I exhaled, my breath warm against her hair, and let my eyes close. I wasn't ready to forgive her— not yet.

But letting her go had never been an option.

CHAPTER II
VALE

A steady, unshakable heat pressed against my back, another wrapped around my waist, anchoring me to the bed—to *them*. My breath came slow, deep, my body cocooned between them, their scents wrapping around me like a memory I'd thought I'd lost.

Kian's arm was slung over my hip, his fingers curled into the sheets, anchoring me to him. He slept heavy, his presence grounding, even in unconsciousness. Xavier's grip was tighter. Protective. Possessive. His hand splayed against my stomach, his body lined up behind mine, his breath a slow, even exhale against the curve of my shoulder.

I should have felt trapped. Instead, I felt safe. For the first time in days, my body didn't ache. For the first time in days, I wasn't bleeding, breaking, or fighting for my life.

But my mind?

That was a graveyard, filled with all the ghosts I couldn't bury.

I inhaled slowly, pressing my lips together as my magic twitched beneath my skin. I should stay. I wanted to stay. But the moment I closed my eyes, I felt her.

Zamarra.

Her voice slithered into my skull, whispering through the cracks, twisting through and around my ribs like a vise.

You cannot escape me.

My breath hitched. I tried to push her out—tried to focus on the warmth of Kian's body, the solid weight of Xavier's arm, the quiet hush of their breathing. But the Dreaming still clung to me, sticky and unshakable—a spider's web I couldn't break free from.

In an instant, the safety was ripped away, her presence suffocating me as if her hand was closing around my throat. I needed air.

Slowly—so, so carefully—I uncurled from Xavier's grasp, shifting away from Kian's hold, inching my way out of bed. Neither stirred. Xavier mumbled something in his sleep but didn't wake.

The moment my bare feet touched the cold obsidian floor, a shiver ran up my spine as panic settled deep into my bones. I needed space. I needed to breathe. I needed to—

"Going somewhere?" The growl cut through the dim light like a blade.

I startled—only for a second—but it was enough.

Idris leaned against the far wall, arms crossed over his chest, golden eyes flickering in the firelight, glowing with censure. He'd been there the whole time.

Watching.

Waiting.

His presence filled the room, heat and stillness, silent, and yet unreadable.

I exhaled, rubbing a hand down my face. "I just needed a second."

Idris didn't move. "You never just need a second."

There was something too calm in his tone, something too sharp in his gaze.

My fingers twitched at my sides. "I wasn't running. I just needed some air."

His eyes flashed. "You know, I'd believe that if I hadn't just chased you into the middle of a war zone. Try again."

His words slammed into me like a battering ram, and yet, they cut so deep it was a wonder I wasn't bleeding. But Idris wasn't finished.

"You left." His voice was too quiet. Too final. "And you didn't just leave. You cut us off, shut us out."

My throat tightened. "I had to—"

"There's *always* a choice, Vale."

But there wasn't—not one that didn't leave someone bleeding. Kian and Xavier stirred, their hurt bombarding me through our bond, and that was the breaking point. He didn't understand— none of them did—how few choices I really had. Magic flared at my fingertips, a crackling heat curling in my lungs, pressing too tightly against my ribcage.

"You weren't there." My voice shook, the pain of the last few days crashing into me. "You didn't see. You didn't *feel* it—"

Idris stepped closer, his eyes burning, his rage filling every millimeter of the room until I could barely breathe under the weight of it. "Then show me. Show me why."

Idris' command sliced through my ribs like a blade, cutting past the walls I had been desperately trying to hold up. They didn't understand. How could they? They had only seen pieces, fragments. They had felt the loss, but I had lived it.

I had to make them *see*. For the first time since I'd woken on the cavern floor, I let go of the shields I'd clung to so tightly.

The bond between us exploded open, a flood of raw magic pouring from my mind into theirs. I didn't just show them—I dragged them into my memories, drowning them in everything I had seen, felt, and suffered.

I felt Kian's breath hitch as the memory yanked him under. Xavier cursed, the sound barely a whisper. Idris... Idris didn't breathe at all.

They didn't just watch. No, they were there, seeing it from my eyes. They were living it.

The cavern walls flickered in dim light, as Rune's massive body crumpled against the stone. His breathing was shallow, his golden eyes resigned.

I showed them everything—the weight of his body pressing against mine as I knelt beside him. The sickening realization that there was no saving him.

Rune's voice echoed in their minds, as desperate and firm as it had been that night.

"You must kill me, Vale. Stab me right in the heart. And then you must stab Idris in his. Only through your power can we merge, and the curse be undone."

The silence from my mates was deafening. They felt the impossible choice sitting heavy in my gut as I begged Rune for another way.

"I can't, Rune. Rune, I can't do that."

Grief wrapped around them like iron chains. I let them feel the tears burning down my face, the helplessness strangling me as I lifted my glowing blade —as Rune gave himself to me, trusting me to end his life.

They felt the exact moment the sword pierced his heart.

The pain. His roar. The soul-deep agony as his magic shattered, flowing through me in a tidal wave so powerful it ripped me apart.

Then—Idris screaming.

His rage, his devastation, his breaking.

I let them feel what it was to die for him.

Then my memories shifted, turned. The air was thick—wrong. The cavern floor was ice beneath my cheek, my body empty, broken, unmoored. They felt my body breaking—they felt me die. The crushing silence, the weight of Rune's soul ripped from mine.

And then—Zamarra.

They saw the shadows curling around her, her unnatural beauty, her cruel smile. They felt the terror that had paralyzed me as her voice whispered through my mind.

"You freed him, little queen. But you freed me, too."

They felt my powerless struggle, my desperation as the shadows swallowed me whole, as her claws dug into my soul.

Then—Lirael's light. The warmth that dragged me back from death. They saw the goddess, the figure woven from pure light, the one who had touched my cheek and whispered the truth.

"The book, my daughter. You must go back to the book."

And then I woke up, but I wasn't the same. I was never the same.

They felt the sharp, bitter pain of rejection as I walked into the war room, as Idris barely even looked at me. The way the bond between us strained, the distance between us wider than it had ever been. And then, his words.

"You unleashed her, Vale. You broke the curse, and now the realm is at risk. So tell me—how do we fix this?"

The moment of pure devastation. The way my stomach had dropped, the way my fingers curled into fists, fighting back tears because I knew he blamed me. Because he wasn't wrong. They felt the betrayal coil in my chest when he spoke of Nyrah, when he dismissed my warning.

"I've already mourned you once. Do me a favor and don't make me do it twice."

I let them experience the agony of that moment, the way my heart shattered at his dismissal—let them feel everything. My abandonment, my confusion, my anguish. Even now, it hurt so bad I wanted to scream from the pain of it.

Gasping through my tears, I ripped myself free from the link, my chest heaving. Magic still crackled in my veins, raw and searing, but I didn't care. They'd finally seen it from my eyes.

The agony. The impossible choices. The unbearable weight of Rune's death and my own. The cruelty of Zamarra, the truth of the Dreaming, the moment Idris had looked me in the eyes and dismissed me like I was nothing.

My legs trembled, barely holding me up as I stared at the floor. Silence crushed the room, thick and suffocating. If they didn't believe me after that, there would be no repairing what was broken between us.

Kian's sharp inhale cut through the stillness like a knife. His hand dragged down his face, his shoulders stiff, his amber eyes wide and glassy. Through the bond, his emotions bombarded me—the horror, the ache, the sheer disbelief of what I had just forced them to relive. A broken sound escaped his throat, something raw and aching.

His fingers balled into fists at his sides. "Gods, Vale."

The weight of my name on his lips nearly shattered me. He didn't yell. He didn't rage. But his voice shook, and that—that hurt more than if he had screamed.

"You did all that alone."

Xavier let out a slow, shaking breath, his fingers twitching—then suddenly, he was moving. One second, I was standing there, still drowning in the magic of the bond, and the next, Xavier's arms were around me. He pulled me tight against him, his grip so firm, so grounding, it nearly knocked the breath from my lungs.

"Vale." My name came out in a whisper, hoarse and unsteady.

His chest rose and fell in uneven gasps, and when I tilted my head up, his blue eyes were burning, rimmed red, filled with something broken. He pressed his forehead to my hair, his grip tightening as if he let go, I might disappear again.

"You were breaking apart," he whispered, his voice shattered. "I should have known. I should have felt it."

I squeezed my eyes shut, fighting the sudden urge to sob. "You weren't supposed to," I murmured, my voice barely audible. "I didn't want any of you to. Sharing it felt cruel at the time."

Kian let out a slow, shuddering breath, dragging a trembling hand over his mouth. He took a small step closer, his eyes locked on mine.

"Why didn't you tell us?" His voice was softer now, grief-stricken rather than angry. "Gods, Vale. We would have found another way."

Would we? Would there have been another way? The answer didn't matter. Because I hadn't given them the chance to try.

My stomach twisted, my pulse pounding. "I couldn't," I admitted. "If I told you, you would have tried to stop me, and there wasn't time. We were under attack and Rune wouldn't let me wait. He was fading too fast. If I didn't do it then, the curse would have stayed unbroken."

Kian inhaled sharply, his throat bobbing as he swallowed. He extended a shaky hand like he wanted to reach for me, but he hesitated.

Xavier wasn't hesitating. He still held me tight, his face buried in my hair, his grip unyielding. His body was warm, steady, but I could feel the slight tremor in his hands.

Kian wasn't usually quiet. But he was now. Because this—this pain—was not something he knew how to fix.

And Idris—

The moment Idris broke, I felt it in my soul. His knees hit the obsidian floor with a brutal, echoing *thud*. I had never seen him like this—not when we fought. Not when we bled. His hands fisted in his hair, his jaw locking, his head bowing so low his forehead nearly touched the stone.

The King of Credour, the Beast, the man I'd feared all my life, the mate who had once sworn he would never kneel to anyone—was on his knees for me.

His broad chest rose and fell in uneven gasps, his

fingers digging into his thighs like he needed to hold himself together or he'd fall apart completely. Golden eyes—usually sharp and unreadable—were shattered. Ravaged. Ruined.

"I should have known." His voice was hoarse, wrecked, raw with agony. "Gods, Vale—I should have fucking known."

I had seen Idris furious. I had seen him cold, ruthless, terrifying. But I had never seen him broken. Not until right then.

His lips parted on a silent, ragged exhale, his whole body trembling as if my memories had burned through his soul and left him hollow—left him ruined.

My chest ached, and my throat burned. I should have hated him. If I were smart, I would hate him until the day I died. But when I looked into his eyes —into the sheer, unbearable guilt in them—I knew that he had hated himself a hell of a lot more than I ever could.

He lifted his eyes to mine, and the pain in them shattered me. Ravaged. Wrecked. Desperate. Tears lined his lashes, his golden irises flickering like molten light, like a star dying out.

Xavier's fingers tightened on my waist. Kian let

out a slow, shuddering breath. Idris' lips parted, but he didn't speak.

He reached for me and then stopped—like he didn't deserve to touch me. Like he had just realized how much he had broken us. I was his mate, carried his mark—all their marks. His gaze traced the swirling light tattoos embedded into my skin.

His lips parted, his jaw working, his breath coming too fast. But he didn't speak, didn't move—just knelt before me, waiting for judgment. Waiting for me to tell him he'd failed—that he'd lost me.

He thought he had ruined everything, and maybe he had. But gods help me—I still loved him. I still loved all of them. They were pieces of my soul. As much as I wanted to make him suffer, a part of me just couldn't twist the knife, couldn't make him bleed any more than I already had.

Reaching for him first, I allowed my fingers to graze across his cheek. The bond—that ancient magic that tied us so firmly together—snapped tight as his breath shuddered out of him.

My touch drifted lower, tracing the strong lines of his jaw, feeling the faintest tremble in his skin. His head tipped into my touch, his eyes squeezing shut like he couldn't bear to look at me. Like the weight of his guilt was too much to hold.

"I don't deserve your forgiveness," he whispered, his voice breaking.

The words twisted in my chest, a wound that still bled, still ached. I should have told him he was right. I should have told him he'd broken me. Instead, I clutched his shirt, pulling him closer.

I swallowed past the lump in my throat. "No, you don't."

His eyes snapped open, pain and desperation warring in their depths. His body tensed, waiting for the killing blow.

I exhaled, my throat burning. "But I still love you. I never stopped. Even when you left me standing in that war room, even when I carried all of this alone. Even when you hurt me."

His breath shuddered out of him, his body nearly collapsing forward as if those words had undone him completely. I slid my hands up, framing his face, forcing him to look at me.

"But I love them, too. I love all of you. And I am done trying to prove it. It's your turn. I need you to fight for this."

Something shattered in his gaze, something raw and aching, and then he crushed me against him. His arms wrapped around me, his grip desperate, his lips crashing against mine like he was trying to breathe me in. Like he would never let me go.

Every barrier between us fell away as he claimed my mouth, his emotions—raw and ragged—flooded my senses. I fell into the kiss—letting it leech all the poison from my veins as Idris bared his soul to me.

Kian and Xavier pressed in close, their heat surrounding me, steady, grounding, as their barriers lifted as well. Relief and desire warred in my chest as Xavier's lips brushed my temple, a breath of warmth before he pulled my lips from Idris and replaced them with his own.

It was slow at first. Soft, aching. A promise, a plea, a vow.

Kian trailed feather-soft touches down my spine, his breath warm against my neck, his fangs grazing the sensitive skin. "We won't fail you again, little witch," he murmured, his voice quiet but fierce.

Breaking from Xavier, I found Kian's mouth, his warmth, his taste. He groaned, his fingers tangling in my hair, pulling me deeper as he staked his own claim.

Everything that had been broken between us— the pain, the separation, the wounds too deep to name—began to heal in their touch. I gasped as

Idris' teeth grazed my neck, his lips tracing fire down my skin.

Xavier fisted my shirt, tugging me back into his kiss. Kian's arms wrapped around me from behind, his heat pressing against every inch of me, anchoring me.

I felt Idris' breath, his hands trembling as he slid them over my waist, up my ribs, as if memorizing me all over again. He let out a shaky exhale against my throat.

"I love you." The words were whispered against my skin over and over, remaking me in a way I hadn't realized I craved. I arched into them, my head tilting back as heat flooded my veins, the magic flaring bright between us. The bond crackled, pulling tight, snapping into place like a bone being reset.

It healed something inside of me—something I hadn't quite realized was broken. Their need, their desire filled my mind, my heart.

I had fought alone. I had suffered alone. But here, now, I was theirs again.

Idris gently pulled his tunic from my skin, his gaze reverent as he knelt at my feet. Kian hooked his fingers in the waistband of my underwear, dragging the flimsy garment down my legs as he, too, fell to his knees. Xavier pressed a hungry kiss to my neck, his strong arms holding me up.

The air was thick, pulled taut like a string ready to snap. The bond flared, crackling with power, with heat, with the slow, steady unraveling of everything that had kept us apart.

A fist slammed against the safehouse door, the force rattling the very walls.

The bond snapped tight. The magic between us recoiled, fracturing, as tension surged through me like a knife.

Xavier's curse was sharp, bitten off at the edges. Kian stiffened, his muscles locking, his head snapping toward the door. Idris was already on his feet, golden eyes burning, magic crackling through the air like a live wire.

No one was supposed to know we were here.

And yet—someone had found us.

The air grew thick and charged. Shadows pressed in around the edges of the room, whispering warnings in a language older than time.

I met Idris' gaze, my pulse hammering as I yanked my leathers up, fastening them with shaking fingers. His jaw tightened, and his golden eyes darted toward the door, then back to me.

Another *bang* rattled through the space, louder this time. Relentless.

A slow, cold dread slithered through my gut as I dragged Idris' tunic over my head, pulse hammering.

They weren't knocking.

They were trying to break in.

CHAPTER 12

VALE

The pounding on the door rattled through my bones, steady, relentless. The magic shielding the safehouse flared with every strike, resisting the force behind it.

Xavier stepped in front of me, magic thrumming through the bond, a silent promise of protection. Kian was already moving, his shadows wisping toward the door, twisting like living tendrils. Idris hadn't moved—not yet—but I felt the shift in him. He was watching, waiting, his golden eyes flickering with barely restrained power.

Suddenly, the banging stopped, and silence crashed into the room like a thunderclap. The absence of sound was worse than the pounding. My pulse hammered against my ribs as I inhaled sharply, magic sparking at my fingertips.

Before I could turn, a rough voice edged with exhaustion drawled, "Took you long enough."

A flutter of air glided along my spine, and I spun, my magic surging, but the figure in our midst brought me up short.

Talek stood in the middle of the room, breathing heavily, his cloak torn at the edges and his normally immaculate clothing streaked with his shimmering blood. His left sleeve was ripped, revealing a deep gash that had stopped bleeding but still looked raw. Even his short, dark hair shifted unnaturally, the strands lifting in a breeze that only he could feel. Honestly, he seemed half a breath away from collapsing.

I'd only met Talek once before—at the council chamber, on the day Idris presented me as his bride. He had been poised, unreadable, charming in a way that had felt more like a performance than sincerity. The second time I saw him, at my wedding, he'd been distant, calculating. But now?

He was rattled.

Xavier's blade was already at the Elemental's throat. Kian's sword was at his still-bleeding belly.

Idris didn't so much as twitch, but his golden gaze burned. If Talek blinked wrong, he was dead.

Kian's amber gaze burned with wrath. "You have a bad habit of showing up when you're least wanted."

Talek exhaled, brushing a speck of dirt off his tattered sleeve like he was sitting down for tea instead of bleeding onto the floor. "Nice to see you, too," he rasped, his voice raw with exhaustion, but still laced with his usual arrogance. His gaze swung to me. "You're welcome, by the way. I had to shake a few less-than-friendly parties off my tail to get here."

Idris wasn't buying it. He folded his arms, power thrumming around him like a barely leashed storm. "You're a survivor, Talek. I doubt you did anything out of the kindness of your heart."

I forced my magic down, exhaling sharply. "How did you get in?"

Talek's expression didn't shift, but something flickered in his eyes, the color shifting from pale to dark to pale again. "I found another way."

Xavier pressed his blade in just enough to bite. "Try again."

Talek sighed, rolling his eyes. "Your wards are strong, but nothing's impenetrable. And before you start throwing me through the nearest wall, you might want to ask yourselves how many other people could do the same."

A muscle in Idris' jaw twitched. His anger lashed through the bond, hot and crackling. He didn't like that answer.

Neither did I. I fought to keep my breathing even. The wards on this safehouse weren't just strong, if how we'd entered was any indication, they were damn near impenetrable. And Talek had found a way through.

My magic twitched beneath my skin, whispering warnings I didn't have time to listen to.

Kian's grip on his sword tightened. "I say we kill him now. Saves us the trouble later."

Talek let out a low, rough chuckle, but his usual arrogance was thinner than before. "Charming as ever, Kian." His gaze flicked to me, and his smirk faded.

"Tell us why you're here," Idris growled, the low rumble of his voice vibrating through the room.

Talek exhaled slowly, his usual bravado slipping just enough to show the exhaustion beneath. His body swayed slightly, and for the first time, I noticed the blood soaking through his cloak.

Not all of it was his, the red clashing with his iridescent blood.

"Nyrah," he said hoarsely. "She doesn't have much time."

I stilled at the mention of Nyrah's name, my pulse hammering so hard it felt like it would break through my ribcage. The bond flared, Kian and Xavier's emotions crackling through the connection, but Idris—

Idris was a storm barely contained. His rage burned through the space between us, a silent, seething presence.

Talek must have felt it, too, because, for the first time, his smirk vanished completely.

I took a step forward, pushing past Xavier's protective stance. "How the fuck do you know about my sister?"

Talek's gaze darted to mine, assessing. "Because I've been watching. Listening."

The room went still. All our magic flared.

"You've been what?" Idris' voice was lethal, his golden eyes flickering like molten fire. The air vibrated with his barely restrained power.

Talek sighed, running a bloodied hand through his hair. "Not like that, Your Majesty," he drawled, but there was no humor in it. He shifted his weight, wincing as his injuries caught up with him. "I had to keep tabs on the right people, and it turns out, your little sister happens to be one of them."

The words sent ice sliding down my spine.

Kian's fingers twitched at his sides, his voice dark with suspicion. "And who exactly are these 'right' people?"

Talek's jaw tensed. "The ones Zamarra is hunting."

My stomach plummeted.

The Dreaming throbbed at the edges of my mind, a whisper of shadows slithering too close.

"You said she doesn't have much time," I managed, my throat tight, and dry as the desert sand. "What does that mean?"

Talek hesitated. And that was enough.

"You don't get to be vague now," I snapped, my magic crackling in warning. "You found a way in here, past a fortress of protections, through a door that shouldn't open, with information you shouldn't have. Either you start explaining, or I'll—"

"The Dreaming is bleeding into the Waking." He interrupted, his voice sharp and urgent. "You think you have time, but you don't. Zamarra has her claws in Nyrah. If you wait, she won't be your sister anymore. She'll be hers."

A sharp inhale ripped from my throat.

No.

No, that wasn't possible.

Xavier's hand found my waist, grounding me as my body swayed slightly. Kian was at my other side, steady, warm, protective.

"Explain," Idris demanded, his voice so low and dangerous it could have cut steel.

Talek met his gaze, storm-gray eyes unreadable. "Zamarra doesn't just want Vale anymore. She needs a second vessel—one that can sustain her in both realms. Nyrah is the closest match to Vale's bloodline, and she's already tainted by the Dreaming's influence."

My lungs shrank to nothing, refusing to let air in.

My sister's face bloomed in my mind—laughing, teasing. We'd never been free—not really, but it was a hell of a lot better than the nightmare version Talek had just painted.

A slow, burning heat built in my chest—something ancient, something raging. I hadn't fought this long, suffered this much, just to lose her now. The bond hummed at my back—Kian steady, Xavier grounding, Idris still a storm on the horizon—but none of it stopped the weight crushing my chest.

I lifted my chin. "Where is she?"

Talek exhaled, his shoulders dropping slightly, as if he'd been waiting for that question.

"There's a place," he said carefully. "A sanctuary where she's being kept. I can get you in."

The words settled over the room like a challenge, a promise, a trap.

I stared at Talek, my pulse hammering like war drums against my ribs. My mind raced, not just through what he was saying—but through what he wasn't.

The last time we'd listened to Talek, we'd walked straight into a nightmare and almost didn't walk out.

Xavier tensed behind me, his fingers twitching against my waist. "The last time we followed your lead, we ended up in the middle of an ambush. Selene set a fucking kraken on us, and a mage nearly killed me. Now you just so happen to show up on our doorstep, bloody and out of breath, claiming you're here to help?" He took a slow step forward, his voice low. "Try again."

Talek sighed, his shoulders slumping. "I knew that kraken incident would come back to bite me in the ass."

Kian bared his teeth. "That's all you have to say?"

Talek met his glare with calm neutrality, but there was something behind his eyes, something shattered. "Selene was compromised. You know that now."

"You could have told us what we were walking into," Xavier pressed.

"I didn't know."

"Bullshit," Kian snapped. "You knew something."

Talek's jaw clenched for a moment, his nostrils flaring before he let out a slow breath. "Not enough to give you a heads-up. I knew Selene could be playing both sides," he admitted. "But I didn't know Malvor had his claws in her."

Xavier huffed, shaking his head. "And you conveniently forgot to mention that little detail?"

Talek's lips pressed into a thin line. "You wouldn't have listened—not then. Not only was I new on the council, but my predecessor was part of a coup to kill your bride. I had some information but not all of it, and if I came to you with a maybe and I was wrong, you—or she—would have had my head."

"And why should we listen to you now? " Idris growled, power whipping through the air like an oncoming storm.

His expression turned serious. "Because this time, the stakes are a fuck of a lot higher." Talek's gaze met mine directly. "Zamarra isn't waiting anymore. She's going after Nyrah. Soon."

My chest tightened.

"You're not getting a second chance at this." Talek exhaled sharply. *"If you wait, you won't find Nyrah—you'll find something wearing her skin."*

The room went still. Magic thrummed through my veins, rising like a tide. I forced a breath past my lips, tried to steady myself, but the words wouldn't stop echoing in my head.

Nyrah. My sister. The reason I'd started this fight in the first place.

The reason I'd run.

Talek dragged a hand through his bloodied hair, the dried cut across his temple standing stark against his skin. "I care more than you think," he said finally, before casting his gaze away, a thread of something like guilt crossing his expression before he shut it down. "I wouldn't be here if I didn't."

The air shifted, weight pressing down on my chest. Because despite everything—despite my distrust, despite the damage done—there was something in his eyes. Something unreadable.

Something that felt dangerously close to the truth.

"If you're lying to us—if this is another trap—you won't have to worry about Zamarra or the Guild," I whispered, my magic curling like smoke between my fingers. "Because I'll kill you myself."

Talek didn't flinch.

He just gave me a long, unreadable look before finally nodding. "Understood."

The weight of Talek's words still lingered in the air like a curse.

I barely felt Kian's hand at my back, barely heard the way Xavier exhaled slowly, trying to keep his own emotions in check. My body had gone numb, but my magic was screaming—pushing against my skin, clawing at my chest.

I clenched my fists, inhaling through my nose, grounding myself in the bond, in the feel of my mates pressing against me. But it wasn't enough to keep the storm inside me from rising. Nyrah was running out of time.

I wanted to go now. I needed to go now.

But then I looked at Talek—truly looked at him.

The cut at his middle was still bleeding sluggishly. His breaths came too fast, too shallow. His magic, normally a constant, unwavering thing, barely stirred in the air.

And if Talek—the one leading us in—was this close to collapse, we weren't getting far.

"We leave now," I said, forcing my voice to stay firm. "As soon as—"

Idris interrupted, stepping forward, golden eyes flashing. "No. We need to wait—at least until nightfall."

Silence rang throughout the room, sharp and unyielding.

I stiffened, trying my best not to scream. "We don't have time to wait."

His expression didn't change. "We don't have time to make mistakes, either." His golden gaze flashed to Talek. "And if you've led us into another trap, I will personally rip your lungs from your chest."

Idris wasn't wrong, but it still pissed me off.

Kian exhaled sharply, rolling his shoulders. "We're all running on fumes, Vale. Especially you."

Gritting my teeth, I tried to deny him. "I'll be fine."

Xavier huffed a bitter laugh. "You said that before you nearly died. Twice."

My hands fisted at my sides, any semblance of

calm long gone. "And Nyrah doesn't have time for us to rest."

Idris' fingers twitched, but his voice was steady. "And if we go now, charging in half-dead, we lose. We give Zamarra exactly what she wants. Trust me, you do not want to go in half-cocked. It will get us all killed."

The words struck low and deep, cutting through my stubbornness like a blade. Because they weren't wrong. If we went now, desperate and reckless, we'd lose.

I exhaled slowly, pressing my fingertips into my temples. "Fine," I muttered, the word tasting bitter as I swallowed. "We leave at nightfall."

A muscle in Idris' jaw twitched. "Good."

Talek didn't argue when I shoved him toward the nearest chair. He might have had a sharp tongue, but his body knew its limits, even if his pride didn't.

I worked quickly, tending to the gash along his arm while Xavier and Kian started gathering supplies. Idris leaned over the map on the table, tracing potential routes, his jaw tight with restraint.

The tension in the room was palpable. None of us liked waiting, but we needed to be smart, and that meant taking a moment to rest. The fire burned low as the sky deepened into twilight. The weight of what was coming pressed against my chest, threatening to crush me.

We were ready. The weapons were sharpened, the bags packed. Talek was as healed as he was going to get. Still, I couldn't rest. I stood by the window, watching the stars through the warped glass. My mind raced, my heart thundering too loud in my ears.

Xavier pressed a warm hand against my lower back. He didn't say anything—just stood there, solid, steady. His heat seeped into my skin, soothing the ache I hadn't realized was burrowing into my ribs.

Kian leaned against the opposite side of the window, watching me through the low firelight. "You thinking about backing out?"

I let out a short laugh, shaking my head. "Absolutely not."

His smile softened. "Didn't think so."

Xavier's fingers skimmed my waist before he turned me, pulling me flush against his chest. "You're carrying too much of this alone."

I swallowed hard. "I have to."

"No," Xavier murmured, tilting my chin up. "You don't."

Kian's arms wrapped around me from behind,

his breath warm against my temple. "You're ours, Vale. We protect what's ours."

The bond between us hummed, a living thing, wrapping around us like a pulse of heat.

Idris finally stepped forward, the golden fire in his gaze dimmed with something softer, something raw.

He didn't touch me—not yet. But his presence curled around me like something tangible.

"I failed you once," he said quietly. "I won't do it again."

The words caught me off guard, knocking the breath from my lungs. I turned, brushing his wrist. The contact sent a sharp, electric current through the bond, snapping something back into place.

He inhaled sharply, his golden eyes flickering— and then he gave in. His hand cupped the side of my face, his thumb brushing the edge of my jaw. He didn't kiss me. Didn't move closer. Just stayed there, his touch a promise.

The night pressed in, thick and waiting. The fire in the hearth had burned to embers, the only light coming from the sliver of moon spilling through the warped glass. It cast sharp shadows, twisting the edges of the room into something unfamiliar. Like the world was already shifting beneath us.

Breaking away, I adjusted the weight of my blades, fastening the last strap tight against my hip. My hands felt steady, but inside, I wasn't.

Xavier caught my wrist before I could move too far away, his grip firm, grounding. "We'll find her, Vale." His voice was steady, but the intensity in his gaze told me what he wasn't saying. Then his voice rang loud and clear in my mind.

"I won't let you lose her."

Kian leaned against the window, his amber gaze molten. "We're bringing her home."

Idris was quiet for a long moment, watching me carefully. Then, finally, he reached out, tracing along my wrist before his hand settled against the center of my chest.

The bond snapped into place like a breath of fire.

It wasn't just warmth—it was pressure, something sharp and sudden. My breath stuttered, the connection slamming open between us, unfurling with the weight of everything unsaid.

"I'm keeping my promise, Vale."

His voice—his thoughts—tore through me, sinking into my marrow. A rush of heat curled through the bond, familiar and devastating, like a home I hadn't realized I'd been locked out of.

I hadn't felt him like this in days. Not since I died. Not since he let me go.

The intensity of it made my knees weak. I gripped his wrist before I could stop myself, fingers digging into his flesh. And yet, he didn't pull away.

"You will get her back, no matter what it takes."

The certainty in his voice shattered something inside me. Relief burned through my every vein, fierce and raw. My chest tightened, my throat thick with words I couldn't say.

He was here. Truly here.

Tears welled in my eyes, and I blinked fast to keep them from falling. But I felt him catch the emotion anyway, his touch pressing against my skin in silent reassurance.

Xavier's arms tightened around me. Kian pressed his lips to my temple.

We weren't whole yet, but we were getting there. And gods help anyone who tried to break us again.

The night was deep when Idris finally pulled away, his voice low and certain. "It's time."

Talek shifted near the door, arms crossed, his usual smirk nowhere in sight. "If we're going, we need to move. The longer we wait—"

"—the closer she is to slipping away," I croaked, finishing the thought for him, my stomach knotting.

The weight of it pressed down on my chest. Nyrah was out there. My sister. My blood. And for everything I'd done, everything I'd sacrificed, if I couldn't get to her in time—

No. No more what-ifs. No more waiting.

I turned to my mates, inhaling deep, grounding myself in their presence.

"Let's bring her home."

And together, we stepped into the night.

CHAPTER 13

IDRIS

The cold bit deep, but it wasn't what chilled me.

We moved through the trees, our footfalls muffled by the thick hush of night, but every step felt heavier. The silence here wasn't natural. It pressed in, writhing beneath my skin, slithering through the cracks in my armor, like hands reaching for something buried.

I tightened my grip on my sword, flexing my fingers around the hilt, as though that alone could steady the sinking weight in my chest. But it wouldn't. Nothing would.

Not when I'd already made a promise I wasn't sure I could keep.

Vale walked just ahead, her golden magic

pulsing faintly beneath her skin, a beacon against the dark. She looked steady, composed, but I knew better. Knew the tightness in her jaw, the way her shoulders set too stiff, the way her power curled inward, as though she was trying to hold herself together by sheer force of will.

I'd failed her before. I would not fail her again.

Clenching my teeth, I forced the thought down before it could take root. But it was there—festering, lurking. I'd nearly lost her more than once, and if I let that happen again...

No. I wouldn't let it.

Ahead, Talek led the way, his movements strained but determined. He hadn't fully recovered, but there was no stopping now. Xavier and Kian flanked Vale on either side, close enough that their magic brushed against her own. She wasn't alone. None of us were.

Then why did I feel like I was?

I exhaled slowly, forcing my focus forward. The sanctuary was built into the cliffs of the northern mountains, an abandoned temple carved into the stone. The air was thinner here, the weight of old magic pressing down on my skin, slithering through the cracks in my armor. But the closer we got, the worse the air felt. Heavy. Rotten.

Vale slowed, her steps faltering. Hesitation rippled through the bond. Not mine—*hers*.

I rolled my shoulders, trying to shake the weight pressing against my chest. My magic felt sluggish—distant, almost. Like something was pulling at it from the edges, gnawing at the frayed parts of me that hadn't healed.

Maybe it was just exhaustion.

Maybe it was something worse.

I swallowed hard and refocused on the path ahead. We were getting close.

"Something's here." Her voice was barely a whisper in my mind, but it struck like a hammer against my ribcage.

I met her gaze, nodding once. We all felt it—that quiet, lingering wrongness in the air. And I should have listened to it sooner.

The first arrow came too fast.

I barely had time to shove Vale down before it slammed into the tree where she'd been standing, the splitting bark echoing through the quiet.

"*Move.*" Xavier snapped, already drawing his sword as figures erupted from the trees.

I spun, blade meeting metal, knocking back the first attacker before he could land a strike. They moved fast—too fast—but there was something wrong with them. Their movements were erratic and uncoordinated.

Kian's magic flared beside me, warping the air, making the world twist, tangling around the nearest enemy, wrenching him back. Xavier took the opening, driving his sword through the attacker's chest.

The man didn't scream. Didn't react.

He simply turned his head, looking directly at me with empty, vacant eyes. Something cold slithered down my spine. Vale's magic flared, and for the first time, I saw the faces of our attackers.

Not soldiers. Not trained fighters.

"*No.*" The word scraped from my throat, raw and disbelieving.

The man in front of me wore a butcher's apron, the leather tattered and smeared with old stains. His eyes—glazed, unfocused—locked onto mine, but there was no recognition in them. The woman Vale had thrown back clutched a broken pair of shears, her knuckles bone-white. A seamstress. Not a warrior.

Not an enemy.

But they kept coming.

Kian's illusions snapped, bending reality around them, but it didn't slow them down. Xavier cut one down clean through the chest, but the man barely staggered before righting himself again.

Their bodies twisted, bones cracking, wounds sealing with unnatural precision.

Talek let out a sharp curse as his opponent stood back up, his arm hanging at an impossible angle.

"They're not alive," Vale breathed, horror seeping into her voice.

And I knew she was right. I'd seen this before. Zamarra didn't need soldiers. She needed bodies.

They whispered as they moved, their lips forming soundless words—prayers, pleas, half-formed screams. And then, the cold came. Not the wind. Not the night.

Her.

A sick, clawing pressure snaked through my mind, slipping through the cracks of my defenses like poison through a wound. I staggered back, gasping, pressing a trembling hand to my temple. No. *No.*

This feeling—I hadn't felt it in centuries. Not since the day she cursed me.

A scream built in my throat, but I swallowed it down, slamming a barrier between us, forcing her out with every shred of strength I had left. My magic lashed back, raw, seething, fighting to keep her from pulling me under.

"She's here," I rasped, my voice barely my own.

Zamarra wasn't just sending her puppets.

She was watching.

Vale's magic crackled, brighter now, her fear bleeding through the bond. Xavier wrenched her back, shielding her as Kian threw his hands outward, his illusions expanding in a twisting veil of falsehoods.

I shoved her from my mind with a snarl, slamming a mental barrier between us, my magic crackling in protest.

"We can't win this." Vale's voice was sharp, her magic surging brighter.

Xavier's grip on her arm tightened. "We need to move. Now."

Talek stumbled toward us, one arm wrapped around his middle , blood trailing down his side. He looked ashen. "We have to *go*."

The sanctuary loomed ahead—a massive, jagged doorway carved into the cliffside—gaping like a hungry maw. I gritted my teeth. We had no other choice.

I forced my body to move. "Inside! Now!"

Vale hesitated, but Xavier was already dragging

her forward. Kian sent another wave of warped magic behind us, obscuring the battlefield, buying us seconds. Not much, but enough. We reached the entrance just as the first of them stepped through Kian's illusions, their glassy eyes locking onto us.

But they didn't charge. They didn't chase. They were waiting. And I didn't have time to figure out why.

As soon as the last of us stumbled into the sanctuary, a pulse of magic rippled through the stone, sealing the entrance. I exhaled hard, shoving my sword back into its sheath. My body ached, my magic still raw from forcing Zamarra out.

Silence crashed around us, thick and suffocating.

Vale turned to me, breathless. "You felt it, didn't you?"

I met her gaze, something raw clawing up my throat. I forced it down and nodded. "She was watching."

Kian ran a hand through his hair, his whole body wound tight. "She didn't send an army."

Xavier's jaw clenched. "She didn't need to."

This wasn't war. This was Zamarra sending a message. And we had just walked straight into her hands.

The moment we stepped inside, I knew we'd made a mistake.

The air pressed down, thick and wrong, clinging to my skin like unseen hands. It wasn't just the stink of blood—though that was bad enough. The stone beneath my boots felt slick, wet. The sigils carved into the floor weren't just dried marks—they were deep wounds in the rock, filled with flaking, blackened gore.

Some were familiar—wards, protection sigils, things meant to keep something in. But others? Others looked twisted, like whatever magic once lived in this place had been reshaped by something far older. Far worse.

This wasn't just an abandoned sanctuary.

It was a graveyard.

Something shifted in the walls. Not stone. Something deeper. Something alive.

I sucked in a slow breath, trying to steady my hands. They were shaking. I clenched them tight, but it didn't help.

I had already failed Vale once.

If I let her lose her sister, she'd never forgive me. I'd never forgive myself.

Kian let out a sharp breath beside me, his amber gaze flicking over the walls. "Yeah, great fucking idea coming in here." His voice was sharp, but underneath it, there was a sense of unease. He didn't trust this place. None of us did.

Xavier still gripped his sword, his knuckles white around the hilt. "I hate this," he muttered. He tilted his head slightly, listening to something none of us could hear. "Feels like the air is humming."

He was right. The walls bulged and contracted, like something deep in the stone was inhaling, exhaling, a slow, rhythmic throb, almost as if the stone itself had a heartbeat.

The sigils flickered erratically, reacting to our presence—not welcoming us. Marking us.

I felt watched.

No—worse.

I felt expected.

Vale exhaled through her nose, her magic curling around her fingers in golden wisps. "This is the Dreaming," she said quietly, her voice tight. "It's spilling through."

I felt it, too—the stretch of unreality, the feeling that I could blink, and the world would be different. The weight of it sat at the base of my skull, whispering of things that didn't belong here.

Talek was silent, his gaze skimming the sigils on

the floor, his storm-gray eyes unreadable. He was still—too still.

He stood just ahead of me, his head tilted slightly, as if he were listening. His eyes were sharp, but there was something wrong with his expression. Like he wasn't entirely here.

Vale noticed, too. She took a slow step forward, her magic flickering at her fingertips. "Talek?"

His fingers twitched. Then he inhaled—deep and sharp—like he was drinking in the air. "They're louder here," he murmured.

A chill swept down my spine. "Who?"

His gaze shifted to me, but for a second, I wasn't sure he saw me.

"The Luxa." His voice was hoarse. "They won't stop."

Silence.

Xavier and Kian both stiffened. They hadn't heard this before.

Talek exhaled through his nose, rubbing his temples as if trying to clear his head. "I tried to tell you," he muttered, his voice quieter now. "At the wedding. But how the fuck was I supposed to say it? 'Oh, by the way, the wind won't shut up, and the voices of the damned are keeping me awake at night'? Yeah, I'm sure that would've gone over well."

Xavier muttered a curse under his breath. "You should've said something."

Talek huffed a humorless laugh. "And what would you have done?"

No one had an answer for that.

He shook his head, his gaze sweeping the bloodied floor, the sigils carved deep into the stone. "It started as a whisper," he said, almost absently. "Just... fragments. Words I couldn't place. Names I didn't recognize." His hands curled into fists. "Then it got worse. They started screaming."

Vale's jaw tightened. "What did they say?"

Talek's lips pressed together. Then, slowly, he turned his head—toward the empty space at the far side of the room. His eyes narrowed slightly, his brows furrowing, like he was watching something move.

"They told me to find you. Help you."

Vale inhaled sharply, magic sparking between her fingers.

Talek's voice dropped lower, the words slower now, like they were pulling themselves out of him. "They told me you were running out of time."

Goose bumps rose along my skin, making me shudder.

Xavier's stance widened slightly, his free hand

twitching at his side. "And now?" he asked. "What are they saying now?"

Talek exhaled. His shoulders tightened, his jaw working. His gaze darted toward the far wall. The one where the sigils had shifted. The one where we had all felt something watching.

His voice was barely a breath when he said, "They're saying we're not alone."

The air shifted—a slow, sucking pulse, like the room itself had just taken a breath. The bloodied sigils on the floor shuddered, and the walls seemed to bend inward, the space feeling too small, too tight, too wrong. The metallic scent of blood thickened, turning the air damp and suffocating.

A low, distant hum rippled through the stone beneath our feet, as if something buried deep inside the sanctuary had just woken up.

Kian took a step forward, boots squelching against the blood-slicked ground. "Okay, tell me I'm not the only one who just felt that."

"You're not," Xavier muttered, his sword still gripped tight. "The air is...humming."

Talek exhaled sharply, his shoulders going rigid. "The voices—" He winced, his hand flying to his head. "Too many. Too loud."

Then something moved. A flicker in the shadows, a shifting of light, the suggestion of a shape that shouldn't be there. I stilled, fingers tightening around my sword hilt. My magic itched, whispering warnings I couldn't hear.

Vale froze, her golden light pulsing faintly against the gloom. Her breath hitched.

And then we saw her. A girl stood at the far end of the room. Unmoving. Unblinking.

I didn't recognize the girl standing in front of us, but Vale did.

She gasped, magic flickering wildly at her fingertips. "Nyrah?"

The name struck like a blade to the chest.

Nyrah.

Vale's little sister. The reason we were here. The reason she had started this fight in the first place.

A tremor ran through Vale's frame, but she took a hesitant step forward. "Nyrah—it's me. It's Vale."

The sigils on the walls throbbed, their glow flickering faintly like dying embers. The blood on the floor seeped deeper, as if something beneath the rock was drinking it in.

The weight of the wrongness pressed against my skin. I didn't know her—had never seen her outside of Vale's dreams weeks ago—but her body was too rigid, her hands clenched tight, her shoulders stiff. She wasn't breathing like she should.

Nyrah didn't move. Didn't blink.

Then, slowly, too slowly, her head tilted—like she was listening to something none of us could hear. And her eyes—they couldn't be hers. They weren't the pale blue Vale described when she spoke of her sister—nothing like the girl Vale had spent her life protecting.

They were glowing, but not with Luxa light. The color shifted, flickering between blood red and endless black.

And when she spoke, the sound curdled my blood.

"Vale. Good of you to show up."

But it wasn't just Nyrah's voice, something else was layered beneath it. A second voice, deeper, colder—older. Vale sucked in a sharp breath, her fingers twitching toward her blades.

Nyrah's lips curled into a smile—but it was wrong. Not hers—couldn't be. No, I knew that smile.

Nyrah didn't hesitate. She lunged, straight for Vale—not Xavier, not Kian, not even me.

Her movements weren't wild or desperate. She was focused. Precise. The kind of single-minded aggression that made my stomach churn. This wasn't the frantic strike of a trapped girl. This was a killing blow of a trained fighter.

I barely had time to shove Vale back before Nyrah's fingers curved like claws, aimed at her throat.

Xavier was already moving. His blade came up fast, a clean block between them—but Nyrah didn't even flinch. She twisted around him like he wasn't even there, so fast it left a blur in my vision. Kian threw up an illusion, warping the space around her, shifting the world into something impossible.

She cut straight through it.

Kian's jaw clenched. "She sees through illusions."

Vale scrambled back, breath sharp, magic flickering at her fingertips. "Nyrah, stop—"

She didn't. She didn't even react. Didn't blink. Didn't even flinch at the sound of her own name. Her glowing eyes locked onto Vale like she was the only person in the room.

Xavier caught her next strike, barely managing to wrench her wrist aside before she could claw at Vale's face. Her strength was impossible. He was twice her size, trained, experienced—and she still forced him back.

Xavier gritted his teeth, straining. "She's too fast —Vale, *move*."

Talek moved in to help, but Nyrah twisted, her foot slamming into his ribs and sending him staggering. Not the wild kicks of an untrained fighter. A precision strike. A deliberate, brutal move to clear the space between her and Vale.

She wasn't fighting like a child. She was fighting like an assassin.

Something ugly and sharp coiled in my chest.

Vale gasped, stumbling back again. Kian's illusions were useless. Xavier was defending, not attacking. Talek was already injured. None of them would strike her down.

And neither would I—I couldn't.

I lifted my hand, golden light sparking between my fingers, raw and instinctual. I hadn't used my magic much in this fight—not since Zamarra wormed her way into my head. But this wasn't the time to hesitate. I forced the light outward, a shield of golden fire bursting between Nyrah and Vale.

Nyrah hit the barrier and didn't stop, even when it singed her filthy tunic. Despite the flames, she ripped through it.

The gold sputtered, twisting, flickering—dying.

The moment she touched it, something sank into my skull. A familiar, terrible pull.

Zamarra.

My breath hitched, my head snapping back.

No—no, not again.

I wrenched away, ripping my magic back before she could sink her claws into me. But the damage was already done. My knees hit the ground, a gasp tearing from my throat.

Zamarra's laugh echoed through my head. Vale was running out of time.

Kian yanked Vale out of the way just before Nyrah's strike would have crushed her ribs. Xavier caught Nyrah's arms from behind, trying to restrain her—but she kept moving, kept twisting, kept fighting.

Vale gasped in pain, scrambling backward, eyes darting to me. But I couldn't help. I was still drowning in Zamarra's magic. And then I saw it— the truth of Zamarra's plan.

Torture, pure and simple. She needed Xavier, or Kian, or Talek—or me—to make a choice. A choice with no way to win. If we saved Vale from Nyrah, our mate would hate us until the end of time. If we let Nyrah go, we'd lose our mate forever.

A choked breath left me. "She's forcing our hands."

Vale's face twisted. She saw it, too.

Xavier's grip slipped, and Nyrah wrenched free.

And then Vale stopped running. Her shoulders squared, her chest heaving. She took a single, steady breath—then stepped forward.

Her voice cut through the air, sharp and breaking. "Nyrah."

Something flickered in Nyrah's expression. Just for a second. Her glowing eyes shuddered. Her lips parted.

I saw it. I fucking saw it.

Nyrah was still in there.

And then her body jerked, muscles tightening, like a puppet caught in its strings. She lunged one last time, and Vale let her. She let Nyrah close the space—let her strike.

Vale didn't dodge, but she *moved*. Her arm shot out at the last second, brutal and decisive, her fist cracking against Nyrah's temple. The impact sent a pulse of golden magic rippling outward—Vale's, not Zamarra's.

For the briefest moment, the entire room flashed with golden light. Nyrah's body shuddered. Her glowing eyes widened—just for a second, and then she collapsed.

The moment she hit the floor, the sigils on the walls stopped glowing. The pulse in the air faded—like something had been holding its breath. Zamarra's presence vanished, lifting from my mind as if Vale had driven her out.

Vale stood over Nyrah's unconscious form, breathing hard, hands shaking, the only sound her breaths wheezing in and out of her lungs.

Xavier knelt beside Nyrah, pressing his fingers to her throat. "Her pulse is faint," he said hoarsely. "But steady."

Kian exhaled sharply, dragging a hand through his hair. "Well... that was fucked."

Talek didn't speak. He just stared at the darkened sigils, his jaw jumping.

My own hands were trembling. Whether from exhaustion or fear, I didn't know.

Vale brushed a strand of blonde hair from her sister's forehead. "We got her."

Xavier nodded, tightening his grip around Nyrah's unconscious body. "Now let's get the hell out of here."

But when we turned, the door was gone. The sigils shifted again—slow, creeping, unnatural. The walls stretched, the air warped, and the world itself felt like it was breathing.

Kian swore under his breath. "The entrance was right there."

He moved toward where the doorway had been, reaching out, and then his hand passed through it. Like it wasn't real anymore. Like it never was.

Silence crashed over us.

The blood on the floor was dry, but the air was still thick with it. The feeling of being watched didn't fade. The air in the room felt heavier now, like the walls were pressing in, waiting.

Watching.

Vale's gaze flitted from me to Talek to the dark space just behind us.

She exhaled, slow and deliberate, as if the war raging in her thoughts wasn't echoing through all of us.

"So… anyone want to tell me how the fuck we get out of here?"

CHAPTER 14

VALE

The magic here twisted, warping the air itself into something that crawled beneath my skin. It wasn't just the scent of blood, though that was thick enough to coat my tongue. Not just the shifting walls, the flickering sigils, or the cold press of something unseen watching.

It was the Dreaming itself.

It slithered around us, curling through the cracks in reality, warping the stone beneath our feet, the space between breaths. It was alive. And it had no intention of letting us go.

I tightened my grip on my blades, my pulse hammering in my ears.

Xavier still held Nyrah, his stance firm, his grip

too tight. His fingers wrapped around her as if bracing for something to rip her away. His jaw was locked, tension rolling off him like a storm about to break.

Then Idris stepped forward, his golden magic flickering beneath his skin, faint but present, curling at his fingertips like it wanted her. Wanted to shield her. To keep her safe.

"Let me take her." His voice wasn't a demand. No sharpness, no edge. Just quiet certainty. A promise bound in four simple words.

Xavier didn't move at first, his grip on Nyrah tightening, his gaze shifting to me. He was waiting for my answer. I swallowed, ignoring the burn at the back of my throat, and nodded.

Xavier exhaled sharply and adjusted his grip, shifting Nyrah's weight. "Don't drop her," he muttered, but there was no real bite to it. Just the last vestige of reluctance before he finally let go.

Idris took her carefully, his arms solid and steady as he pulled her against his chest. And for the first time, I really saw it—how small she was.

Nyrah had always been tiny, had always needed me to protect her. And now she seemed more fragile than ever.

A sliver of gold flickered around Idris' hands,

unbidden, curling over Nyrah like a warding spell. His lips parted slightly, like even he hadn't expected it.

I felt the bond pulse. A quiet, unnamable thread pulled tight between us.

Idris swallowed hard and met my gaze. "I'll keep her asleep. I'll keep her safe."

Something inside me eased. Not completely. Not yet. But enough. I exhaled slowly and gave him a single nod.

I had spent my whole life protecting my sister. But right then—for the first time in ten years—I wasn't doing it alone.

Her body was limp in Idris' arms, her chest rising and falling in slow, steady breaths. She needed to stay unconscious. I wasn't ready to face the reality of what might happen if she woke up.

Escaping was my only focus.

The Dreaming disagreed.

The world lurched as a hallway stretched open ahead of us, impossibly long, impossibly dark. Torches lining the walls flickered sickly green, their flames casting shadows that moved when they shouldn't. A slow, rhythmic pulse crawled through the air, like something vast and ancient was breathing just beneath the surface.

I sucked in a sharp breath, steadying myself, but Kian cursed beside me, his illusions flickering wildly around his fingers.

"Don't trust it," he gritted out. "None of this is real."

He was right, but that didn't make it any less dangerous.

Xavier was next to me in a heartbeat, his grip firm on my wrist as the walls shivered like something beneath the stone was alive. "We move fast. We don't stop. We don't listen."

Talek exhaled sharply, his storm-gray eyes distant, his head tilted slightly, like he was hearing something we couldn't.

And then the Dreaming showed its teeth.

It gave us what we wanted to see.

For a second—a single, shattering second—I saw home.

Not the rough hovel of a cave I'd left behind, but the home I'd dreamed of when I let myself hope. Nyrah's laughter echoed down the hall. I heard her running ahead, her voice bright, happy—

What I'd always wanted for her.

My gut twisted. No. No, I knew better.

Idris had told me the rules of the Dreaming: "Believe nothing. Trust nothing."

Kian snarled. "It's playing with us—"

Then the illusion snapped.

The hallway melted away, and the ground underneath me vanished. I barely had time to react before Xavier yanked me back. My heart slammed against my ribcage. There was nothing beneath my feet—a sheer drop, black and endless. If Xavier hadn't grabbed me, I would have fallen straight into the void.

I whipped around, swallowing the bile in my throat. "Move. Now."

They didn't argue. I barely made it five steps before a whisper skittered along my skin.

"Vale?"

I froze at Nyrah's voice before turning sharply, heart in my throat, eyes locking on Idris.

Nyrah shifted in his hold. Her fingers twitched. Her face scrunched like she was about to wake up. Panic clawed through me.

Not yet. Not yet.

Idris' grip on her tightened. His jaw clenched. "No," he breathed, his voice raw, laced with magic. "Sleep."

A soft pulse of golden energy settled over Nyrah, pressing her deeper into unconsciousness. Her breathing evened out, and her body went still again.

I met his gaze. He was pale, his arms tight around her, his magic thrumming with something like desperation. I felt it. The sincerity. The promise. He would keep her safe.

I swallowed hard, nodding once. "Let's go," I muttered, turning away before the lump in my throat could strangle me.

Kian exhaled sharply. "Before she wakes up again, preferably."

Talek flinching was the first sign something was wrong. His head snapped to the side, his whole body going rigid.

Then Xavier stiffened, his sword already drawn.

A whisper crawled through the dark. Low. Amused. Familiar.

"What a tragic little group you are."

My breath froze in my lungs as the scars on my back ached. The shadows ahead thickened. Twisted. And then he was there.

Arden.

My hands clenched tighter around my blades. He looked... comfortable. Unbothered. Like he was expecting us. Like he had been waiting.

"Come now," he drawled, stepping forward as if he had all the time in the world. "No words for your rightful king?"

Talek's lips curled into a silent snarl. Xavier's grip on his sword was tight enough to break bone. But Idris hadn't moved.

His rage swelled through the bond, a dangerous, quiet thing.

I exhaled sharply, forcing my heartbeat to steady. Arden wasn't real. At least, that's what I wanted to believe.

The Dreaming shuddered. The world shattered. Walls twisted. The ground ripped away. I reached for Xavier—but my fingers passed through empty air. Kian's illusions flickered wildly, trying to fight the chaos.

Talek snapped his head up, eyes wide. "He's twisting it—he's twisting reality—"

A sharp tug yanked at my stomach, and I stumbled.

Then I fell—not into darkness. Not into nothing. Into something else.

With a gasp, I hit solid ground. Pain lanced through my knees and ribs. I forced my head up. And I saw them.

Idris. Arden.

They stood feet apart. Arden smirked, comfortably, like he had been waiting. Like this was exactly what he wanted. Idris was rigid, golden magic pulsing at his fingertips. But he wasn't holding his sword.

He was holding Nyrah.

She was still unconscious, limp against him, golden light curling over her like a protective ward.

My pulse hammered against my chest.

Shadows slithered around us, spiraling at the edges of my vision. The walls of the sanctuary stretched and twisted, shifting between solid stone and something else. Something living. The sigils carved into the floor flared, warping, their original meanings lost under layers of malicious intent.

I could barely hear my own breath over the weight of the magic pressing in, over the pulse of something massive, watching.

Arden sneered, his hands resting at his sides, casual as ever, but the air around him hummed with dark magic. Not just his own. Zamarra's, too.

"Come now, brother. We both know why you're here. You've been waiting centuries for this moment"—His fingers curled, and the walls of the Dreaming shivered—"So take it."

The Dreaming quivered, a subtle shift. A pull. It was baiting Idris—baiting him with vengeance.

Golden fire flared at his fingertips. The air around him crackled with restrained magic, a wildfire barely contained.

And for a split second, I thought he would do it. That he would choose vengeance over us.

Over Nyrah.

Over me.

I felt Idris tense through the bond, his fury sharp, burning. His entire life had led to this moment. His vengeance. His justice.

And then Nyrah stirred.

A tiny exhale, barely a whisper against his chest. Her fingers twitched. Not awake. Not yet. But close.

The moment Idris noticed, a war flickered across his face.

Arden saw it, too. His laugh echoed through the sanctuary, nearly splitting my skull.

"Oh," he said, mockingly soft, "what's the matter? Not willing to risk your precious mate and her little pet?"

The moment Arden spoke, the Dreaming pulsed, rippling through the air like a living thing—slinking, curling, twisting through the cracks of reality.

And then—it showed us.

It wasn't like an illusion. Not like Kian's magic. Not like anything I had ever seen before.

It was real—or it would be.

A soft, golden glow flickered over Idris' hands, curling over Nyrah's still form as he clutched her to his chest. His blade, poised midair, trembled slightly.

And then time fractured.

The walls around us melted, stone dissolving into shadow, light bleeding from the air until all that remained was the vision.

I saw it. I felt it.

Idris stepped forward. One foot. One second. His golden magic surged, swelling like wildfire, blazing through the suffocating dark. His sword—a gleaming arc of light—sliced through Arden's throat.

A clean cut. A swift execution. A king's justice.

Arden didn't scream. He stumbled, his smirk twisting—not in pain. Not in fear. In triumph. Then his body collapsed. And before his knees could even hit the ground, Nyrah gasped—a sharp, ragged inhale.

Her spine arched. Her fingers curled into claws. The light around her shattered.

Her lips parted—her breath became a scream— her body convulsed against Idris' chest.

And then... Silence. A cold, dead quiet that sank into my ribs like a blade.

Idris' arms tightened around her, his hands shaking.

"No," he whispered, hoarse and raw. "No, no, no—"

He shook her. Desperate, frantic—his golden magic spilling from his hands, trying to reach her, touch her, heal her. But there was nothing left to save.

Nyrah's body fell limp in his arms. Her skin ashen, her breath stopped. Her light, her soul, gone. Idris staggered back. His chest heaved, his golden magic flickering wildly as if it refused to accept what had just happened.

His golden eyes went wide as he broke.

I had never seen him like this—never seen anything touch him the way this did.

Not in battle. Not in rage. Not in grief.

But this? This destroyed him.

And the Dreaming wanted him to see it. It showed him every detail of what it would cost. The sound of Nyrah's final breath. The way her fingers went slack. The way I dropped my blades, scrambling forward to grab her—to hold her.

Because in the Dreaming's vision, Idris collapsed to his knees.

His hands—his hands, once strong, steady, unshakable—cradled her lifeless face. "No, please—Nyrah—"

The Dreaming was cruel. It let him hold her. It let him break. It let him feel what it would be like to lose her. And then, just before the vision ended, it showed me, it showed him.

My own body, collapsed at Nyrah's side. My light gone, too.

Idris didn't just lose her.

He lost me.

Because I would have burned this world to the ground before I let my sister die alone.

The Dreaming let me feel that choice settle in my bones. It let me hear Idris' scream. It let me watch the moment his magic turned to ruin. It let me see the exact second he lost everything.

And then the vision shattered. Reality lurched back into place. The walls of the sanctuary were whole again. The shadows reeled back into the corners. The Dreaming was silent.

And Idris stood there, shaking. I could still feel his magic pulsing through the bond—raging, fracturing. He stared at Arden, golden fire burning in his hands, and for a moment, I thought he would do it, anyway.

I thought he would kill him.

I thought he would burn the whole damn world down to take his vengeance.

Arden's smirk deepened. He knew.

"So what will it be, brother?" he whispered. "Me?" He spread his arms. "Or her?"

The air thinned.

Magic crackled around Idris like a dying star. His breath shuddered, fingers tightening around the hilt of his sword, his golden magic flaring bright, furious. The bond between us thrummed, screaming at me, at him—

Choose.

His knuckles went white. His jaw clenched so hard I thought his teeth might crack. Arden stood before him, so easy to kill. But Nyrah stirred in his arms. Just a tiny movement. A whisper of a breath.

Not awake. But alive.

And Idris... chose.

His sword lowered. His vengeance burned away like embers in the wind. And he let Arden go.

The moment the choice was made, the Dreaming reacted. The world lurched. The walls shrieked, collapsing inward, as if they had been waiting, watching, wanting him to fail. But he hadn't.

Arden's smirk twisted, his confidence wavering, just for a second, then he vanished.

Not dead. Not yet. But losing.

The shadows snapped back, and suddenly, Idris was there. He stumbled forward, golden magic flickering wildly, clutching Nyrah tight against him.

Xavier caught his arm, dragging him the last few feet.

The Dreaming howled, resisting.

But then Talek moved.

His head snapped up, his storm-gray eyes locking onto something none of us could see. His breath hitched.

"There," he said hoarsely. "There's a way out."

I couldn't see it—neither could Xavier or Kian—but Idris didn't hesitate. He turned straight toward Talek's voice, and then we ran.

I could still feel the Dreaming's hunger, its anger.

I knew Arden would be back.

I knew this wasn't over.

But when I looked at Idris—when I saw him clutching Nyrah so tightly, so carefully, his golden magic curling protectively around her, his jaw tight, his choice still echoing through him—I knew something else.

He had let go of his vengeance.

For me.

For her.

And when we escaped that cursed sanctuary, stumbling into the frigid night air, I didn't look back.

The cold cut like a knife, sharp and biting against my sweat-dampened skin.

I barely felt it. All I could see was Nyrah.

She was right *there*.

Her body was limp in Idris' arms but warm, her shallow breaths barely shifting the strands of golden hair stuck to her forehead. I stared, unblinking, waiting for the Dreaming to rip her away, for the nightmare to twist reality again. But nothing changed.

Nyrah was real. Here. Alive.

My hands shook as I reached for her. She looked small—too small.

Something inside me cracked wide open. I

reached before I could think, my fingers shaking, my throat raw. "Give her to me."

Idris didn't hesitate. His arms tightened around her for only a moment—a barely-there instinct—before he shifted, lowering her carefully into my waiting grasp.

The moment her weight settled against me, my knees hit the dirt. Hard. The pain barely registered, drowned beneath the crashing weight of *finally*. The tightness in my ribs threatened to snap. I clutched her to my chest, pressing my face into her hair, breathing her in, grounding myself in the rise and fall of her breaths.

Alive. Alive. Alive.

"Nyrah," I whispered, my voice cracking.

She didn't stir. Didn't move. But she was warm. She was here.

My body trembled, the last fraying strands of control unraveling as I curled tighter around her. I had spent weeks worrying she was lost to me, weeks clawing my way through hell to get to her. Had spent ten years keeping her safe. And now, finally, she was in my arms.

Kian knelt beside me, his hand a solid, warm weight against my back. "She's okay, Vale."

I couldn't answer. My throat was too tight.

Xavier's voice was a low rumble above us, sharp with tension. "We need to move."

I didn't want to let go—couldn't.

My arms locked around Nyrah, my body coiling around hers like I could shield her from everything —from Zamarra, from the Dreaming, from whatever else waited in the dark.

But we couldn't stay here.

A shadow moved beside me. Idris knelt, his golden eyes unreadable, the glow of his magic still flickering at his fingertips.

"I'll carry her."

I stiffened. Every instinct in me screamed "No." I had just gotten her back. Just pulled her from the nightmare I hadn't been sure she would survive. I couldn't hand her over again.

But Idris didn't push. He didn't reach for her. He just looked at me.

Through the bond, I felt the steady pulse of his sincerity, his certainty, his promise.

"You're exhausted," he murmured. "You need to stay in the saddle."

My hands refused to let go. A breath. A second. The kind of hesitation that could get someone killed in battle—but this wasn't battle. This was worse.

I had her. *I had her.* And now I had to let her go.

The bond pulsed—steady, warm, certain. I forced myself to exhale, to unclench my fingers, to trust.

Slowly, I exhaled and pressed one last kiss to Nyrah's hair before forcing my arms to loosen. Every movement felt wrong, like peeling away layers of armor I couldn't afford to lose. But when I finally, finally, handed her back, Idris held her like she was the most important thing in the world. Like he wouldn't let anything touch her.

I swallowed hard and nodded. "Let's go."

Talek was already moving, scanning the dark as he led the way. His voice was low, distant. "The path back isn't clear."

He hesitated, then exhaled sharply. "But there's something else. Something... watching."

No one questioned it. No one asked what. We'd already seen too much tonight. When we reached the clearing where we had left the horses, the air was too still. The animals were skittish, their ears pinned back, their bodies shifting uneasily beneath Xavier's calming touch.

Kian lifted a hand, murmuring a spell beneath his breath. A thin shimmer of magic wound through the trees, cloaking us in illusion. "This will help," he muttered. "But we need to move."

No argument. No wasted time.

I mounted quickly, my body heavy with exhaustion, but my eyes never left Idris as he swung onto his horse, Nyrah cradled against his chest.

I guided my horse forward, keeping close, watching.

Watching Nyrah. Watching Idris.

Watching the way he wouldn't loosen his grip.

The night stretched around us, thick and endless. The only sounds were the steady clatter of hooves against damp earth, the rustling of wind through the trees. I rode close, my hands tense against the reins, my eyes darting to Nyrah every few minutes.

Still warm. Still here. Still breathing.

Every few steps, I reached out—brushed my fingers through her tangled hair, touched the back of her hand.

She didn't stir—not once—and I feared she should have. Idris' magic wasn't keeping her asleep anymore, so why wasn't she waking up? The weight of unease bore down on me, but I kept my silence.

Instead, I shifted my focus to Idris.

He hadn't spoken since we left the sanctuary. He hadn't loosened his grip. Hadn't let her go. Sparks of golden magic still undulated around his fingertips, pulsing faintly, protectively, but I felt the tension in him through the bond.

His shoulders were rigid, his jaw tight. His guilt was deafening.

Silence stretched between us until I finally broke it. "You haven't even exhaled, have you?"

His jaw flexed. He didn't look at me. "I told you I'd keep her safe."

"You did."

I studied him carefully, taking in the way his grip grew tighter around Nyrah every time the horses shifted beneath us. The way his magic wouldn't settle. The way he hadn't let himself breathe since making his choice.

I reached out. Not for Nyrah. For him.

My fingers brushed against his arm—warm, steady, real.

"You chose us," I murmured.

He let out an uneven breath. It sounded shattered, broken.

His arm twitched beneath my touch—just the faintest, involuntary reaction, barely there before his grip shifted. And then—finally—Idris moved his hand, tightened it around mine, and held on.

As we rode, the night stretched around us, vast and unrelenting. The wind whispered through the trees, too quiet, too knowing. The hoofbeats of our horses muffled against damp earth, the weight of silence pressing against my skin.

I rode close to Idris, my gaze alternating between Nyrah's still face and the rigid line of his shoulders. She hadn't stirred. Not once. I told myself it was exhaustion. That she needed rest, that her body was just reclaiming its strength. But the thought curdled in my gut.

Kian skimmed my wrist. A light touch, barely there, like he wasn't sure if he needed to comfort me or just remind himself I was still there. Xavier rode a little ahead, but his head turned slightly, catching my gaze. Not speaking—just checking.

Always watching.

Always ready.

A low exhale from Kian drew my attention. His posture was deceptively relaxed in the saddle, but his fingers flexed around the reins, his knuckles pale. "You'd think after all that, we'd at least get a dramatic sky split or something," he muttered. "You know, a little divine intervention, a whisper of Fate saying, 'Congrats, you survived. Have a cookie.'"

I huffed a breath that might have been amusement if we weren't running for our lives. "Hate to break it to you, but Fate doesn't give out riches and gold for surviving. In my experience, that only gets more shit shoveled your way."

Kian clicked his tongue. "Yeah, well, Fate can kiss—"

"Focus," Xavier cut in. His voice was low and controlled, but I caught the sharpness in it. He didn't like this silence any more than I did. His gaze swept the darkness around us, his grip firm on his sword's hilt, even as he rode. "Something still isn't right."

Talek made a quiet sound. He was a little ahead of us, his head tilted like he was listening to something we couldn't hear. "We aren't alone," he murmured. "I don't know if it's watching or waiting, but it hasn't left."

A sense of unease slithered up my spine. "Can you tell what it is?"

Talek's jaw worked, but he shook his head. "Not yet, and the spirits or whatever the fuck they are aren't being very forthcoming."

That wasn't comforting.

Xavier grunted, his fingers twitching like he was resisting the urge to pull his sword free. "Then we ride faster."

No one argued.

The horses shifted restlessly as we picked up speed, their hooves pounding harder against the damp earth. I pressed my knees against the saddle, adjusting my grip on the reins, keeping my eyes on Nyrah—on the way her body barely moved with each breath.

She was still too pale. Too still.

Idris' magic curled faintly around her, not enough to force her into sleep anymore, just... there. Guarding. Watching. As if his body hadn't fully registered the battle was over.

I swallowed hard. "Idris."

He didn't react right away. His gaze stayed locked forward, but I saw the tension in his features, the flicker of something unreadable in his expression.

"I'm not putting her down," he said quietly. "I told you I'd protect her and I—"

"I know." I exhaled, shifting closer, just enough that my knee brushed against his. "But you can breathe now."

His hand flexed against Nyrah's side, but he didn't answer.

The ride through the dark was silent, save for the clatter of hooves, the muffled rustle of wind through the trees.

I rode close, my knee brushing Idris', my fingers skimming Nyrah's arm. Still warm. Still breathing. But her body was too still, her breaths too shallow.

Something wasn't right.

A sigh from Kian cut through the quiet. "So. I know of an inn somewhere around here."

Xavier shot him a look. "Is it still standing?"

"Probably."

"Is it defensible?"

Kian hesitated. "It has walls and a strong 'Don't ask, don't tell' vibe. Not the best clientele, but it's better than staying in the damn forest for the night. I don't know about you, but frostbite is a worry of mine."

Xavier exhaled sharply, already shaking his head. "Is this the same inn where all your clothes were stolen from the bathhouse, and you had to fly home in shame? Please tell me how that's better than the forest?"

"Not good enough." Idris' voice was flat, cold.

"We need more than walls and the illusion of safety."

I barely recognized his tone—his voice was all steel and finality.

"Where, then?" Talek murmured, glancing back. "We can't keep moving forever."

Silence. Then Idris spoke again, quiet but absolute. "There's an estate. My grandfather's—well, mine now. We can go there."

As the trees thinned and the estate's towering wrought-iron gates loomed ahead, a faint shimmer of protective runes pulsed through the air.

Something skittered through the trees beyond the edges of Kian's illusions.

Just the wind. Just a trick of the light. Just—

I swallowed hard, keeping my gaze forward. *Don't look back. Don't let it see you.*

The gates groaned open under Idris' silent command, and the estate swallowed us whole. The silence here was different—not empty but listening. Magic crackled against my skin as we passed into the land proper. Ancient. Waiting.

The shift was instant.

The air settled. The weight of pursuit, of the Dreaming, of the Sanctuary—it all dulled beneath the layered wards of the estate.

But we weren't alone.

A figure stood at the base of the massive front doors, hands clasped neatly in front of her, her sharp gaze sweeping over us like a blade.

Small. So small. She barely reached my chest, her white hair twisted into a neat bun, her crisp brown and gold gown unruffled despite the late hour. Her aged face was pinched with disapproval as she took in our ragged, bloodstained state.

And then, she sighed. "I was expecting you hours ago."

Kian let out a low, exhausted chuckle. "Damn, Briar. Good to see you, too."

The Brownie lifted a single, unimpressed brow. "I would say the same, but you smell like wet dog and bad decisions."

Kian clutched his chest. "Right for the heart, huh?"

"I would have to aim much lower to hit something functional."

Xavier grunted in approval. "Gods, I missed her."

Idris, who had yet to let go of Nyrah, exhaled slowly. "Briar."

Her sharp eyes snapped to him, scanning him from head to toe. She took in the tight set of his jaw, the lingering flickers of golden magic rippling around Nyrah, the way exhaustion lined every inch of his frame.

And just like that, the disapproval cracked. Her expression softened just a fraction, and she let out a low, muttered curse. "You foolish boy."

Idris' jaw twitched. He didn't argue.

Briar huffed. "Inside. All of you. Baths have been drawn, the rooms are warm, and the food is waiting. You look half-dead, and frankly, you're bleeding on my doorstep."

I blinked. "You knew we were coming?"

Briar's lips twitched like she was fighting a smirk. "I didn't need to know. I just needed to prepare. And don't worry. My son is taking care of the castle in my absence."

My throat tightened. Gods, I had missed her.

Kian slung an arm over Talek's shoulder, grinning despite the filth on his face. "See? This is why I love her. She just knows."

Briar sniffed. "If you really loved me, you wouldn't track filth through my halls. Take off those bloody boots before I find a switch."

I breathed out a laugh.

Then, finally, I swung my leg over the saddle—only to find Xavier already there, one steadying hand at my waist as I landed. Kian was just behind him, his fingers brushing my arm like he wasn't sure if I needed support or if he just needed to touch me.

"You good?" Xavier's voice was low, quiet enough that only I could hear.

I nodded, even though my legs wobbled. Kian didn't seem convinced. His eyes flicked between me and Nyrah, his magic winding faintly at his fingertips.

"I'm fine," I murmured, pressing a quick, reassuring squeeze to his wrist before stepping toward Idris.

Briar's gaze shifted to Nyrah once more, and she exhaled sharply. "Your sister's still unconscious?"

"She hasn't woken up," I murmured. "Not since the Sanctuary."

Something unreadable flashed across Briar's face. Not surprise. Not exactly. But something deeper. Briar pursed her lips, moving closer. The sharp glint in her gaze softened—just slightly—as she reached for Nyrah's wrist, pressing two fingers against her pulse. Something flickered across her face—something that made my stomach twist. But she didn't say it. Not yet.

"Then let's get her inside."

She stepped aside, the massive double doors swinging open at the wave of her fingers. The relief hit like a flood, unraveling the tightness in my chest. The scent of lavender and polished wood wrapped around me, rich and grounding. It was more than warmth—it was safety, woven into every candlelit corridor and shimmering rune along the walls.

Safe.

I exhaled.

We were safe.

At least, for now.

CHAPTER 16

VALE

The warmth hit all at once, sinking into my frozen skin, weaving around the aching, frayed edges of my magic. I'd been running for days, and now it was as if I'd skidded to a stop.

For a heartbeat, I could only stand there—blinking against the golden glow of candlelight, the scent of polished wood, old books, and something richer beneath it. Something woven into the very bones of the estate.

Magic. Old. Familiar. Expectant.

A shiver rolled up my spine. It knew Idris.

It knew he'd come home.

Idris stood just ahead, Nyrah still tucked against his chest. His golden eyes flicked upward, scanning the vast, open space of the entrance hall. A massive chandelier of sculpted crystal hung from the vaulted ceiling, its enchanted light shimmering off the carved stone walls. Pillars of dark marble, streaked with veins of gold, lined the room, leading toward the twin staircases winding to the upper floors.

It was a place built for a king. And yet, for all its grandeur, it wasn't cold.

Not like the just-out-of-reach Guild chambers. Not like the throne room. This was a home.

Briar sniffed, already moving past us with the sharp, no-nonsense precision of someone who had ruled these halls longer than their owner. "Don't worry, your horses will be taken care of." She shifted her gaze to Idris. "Your chambers are as you left them."

Kian exhaled lowly beside me. "You mean when he was a child?"

Briar shot him a withering glare. "You mean when his father's people still thought to lock him and his brother away in the east wing? *No.* His proper chambers. The ones his grandfather prepared for him." Briskly, she pivoted on her heel, already leading us deeper into the halls. "But first—this way."

She didn't need to say it. Nyrah came first.

I barely noticed my feet moving as we passed through towering arched doorways, down a hall lined with tapestries of dragons and gold-threaded sigils. Everything here was heavily warded—I could feel the enchantments thrumming softly beneath the surface, layered over generations. Protection. Preservation.

Xavier's gaze flicked over the doors we passed, eyes narrowed, body still tense despite the security of the estate. His fingers tightened and released, like he was resisting the urge to keep his sword drawn. He didn't trust this place yet.

Neither did I.

Not until Nyrah was safe.

Briar led us through an ornate doorway, pushing through heavy double doors into a chamber bathed in blazing firelight.

The moment I saw the canopied bed, the thick, fur-lined blankets, the carefully stoked hearth, my legs almost buckled.

The room had already been prepared.

Soft linens. Fresh water sat on the nightstand. A basin, still steaming. Everything was ready for us.

She knew. She always knew.

Idris hesitated for just a breath, then carefully

lowered Nyrah onto the bed. He didn't let go immediately.

I stepped forward before I could stop myself, reaching, until Briar smacked my hand away. I startled, blinking at her. "What—"

"You stink," Briar said flatly. "Vetra is a fine horse, but you smell too much like her for a queen."

Kian choked on a laugh. "I take it back. I missed you so much."

Briar ignored him, already pressing two fingers to Nyrah's wrist. Her sharp gaze scanned my sister's too-pale face, her chest barely rising and falling.

The pause was just a breath too long.

"What is it?" I demanded.

Briar exhaled through her nose. She didn't look at me right away, her thumb brushing once, twice over Nyrah's pulse point.

"She's steady." A pause. "For now."

For now.

A sharp knot twisted in my chest, but before I could demand more, Briar tilted her head toward the door. "Now—out. All of you."

I blinked. "What?"

Briar's lips twitched like she was fighting a smirk. "You're tracking filth through my halls. You think I'd let you put those bloodstained boots on my rugs? I'd sooner let a wyvern roost in the dining hall."

Xavier crossed his arms, unimpressed. "You have a dining hall?"

Briar didn't even look at him. "You won't be seeing it until you scrub the battle off your skin."

Kian elbowed him. "You heard the woman. Scrub first, feast later."

I hesitated. My fingers curled at my sides, my pulse thrumming too fast. Every instinct screamed at me to stay, to keep watch, to protect her. I had spent weeks clawing through hell to get to her. And now, I was supposed to just walk away?

Briar must have seen it, because she sighed. "I'll stay with her," she said simply. "You know I would sooner chew glass than let anything harm that girl. I'll get her cleaned up and see what I can do to ease her."

That... helped.

A little.

"Talek?" she continued, eyeing the Elemental like she could see every wound and every brittle, weary part of his body through his clothes. "Your room is two doors down and to the left. Do use the healing balm beside the tub. I'd rather not scrape your withered corpse off my clean linens."

Briar turned to Idris, waving him toward the door with a flick of her wrist. "You know the way. Now *shoo*."

Idris didn't move. The bond pulsed between us, thick with lingering magic and the quiet war raging in him. His golden gaze shifted back to Nyrah, his hands still hovering as if he wasn't convinced he was allowed to step away. Like letting go was breaking a silent promise.

Without thought, I grabbed Idris' hand, twining my fingers with his. *"You can stand down,"* I murmured through the bond. *"You did everything you promised. It's time to breathe, my love."*

Then, finally, he exhaled as he turned toward me, then toward the door, leading us out into the candlelit hall.

I followed, his grip tight as he led the way.

The silence inside the estate was heavy. Not the unnatural hush of a battlefield after the last body fell. Not the eerie quiet of the Dreaming, waiting to show its teeth. This was something else. A place steeped in magic, in memory, in expectation.

And it was listening.

I felt it in the way the sconces flickered the moment Idris stepped deeper into the halls, in the thrum of something vast beneath my skin—the weight of the wards pressing into my ribs. Like the estate recognized him.

Recognized that its king had finally come home.

But I barely processed it.

The warmth hit all at once, the contrast so sharp it nearly stole my breath. The scent of polished wood and lavender drifted in the air, but beneath it —the faintest trace of salt, of steel, of something alive.

I followed Idris through a gilded archway, my steps slow, my body too heavy, too spent. I should have been relieved. Should have let go of the tension coiling through my ribs, the fight locked tight in my spine.

But I couldn't.

Not yet.

Not until I saw Nyrah wake up. Not until I felt the heat of my mates pressed against me, solid and real.

The room was massive, carved from warm stone and dark-veined marble, the high vaulted ceiling arching above us like a cathedral. A dozen lanterns flickered along the walls, their golden light reflecting off the polished surface of the water.

The bathing pool itself stretched nearly the entire length of the chamber, its edges sculpted with intricate sigils and dragon motifs, their golden inlays glowing softly beneath the steam. It wasn't just a bath—it was a sanctuary. A place meant for kings and queens, for the bloodline of rulers long past.

A massive hearth crackled to the left, its firelight casting long shadows against the stone. A low, ornate table sat nearby, stocked with lush towels, delicate crystal vials of oils and scented balms.

The water glowed faintly, the heat rippling in waves, enchanted to remain perfectly warm. At its deepest point, it would reach my waist, but there were shallower ledges carved along the edges, places to recline, to soak. To rest.

A smaller pool sat off to the side, cooler, meant for rinsing, its surface edged in delicate silver runes. Another reminder that this was a royal bathing chamber—a place for kings and queens, not warriors smelling of blood and exhaustion.

And yet, despite its grandeur, its sheer size, the space felt intimate. The lanterns burned low, the hearth cast everything in soft gold and amber, and the walls wrapped around us like something safe. Something belonging to us alone.

Standing in the vast bathing chamber, I should have been relieved. I should have felt the tension drain from my bones, should have let the steaming water pull me under.

But my body refused to unwind.

I stood at the edge of the pool, the marble beneath my bare feet warm from the water's lingering heat. Steam curled into the air, thick and fragrant—lavender, bergamot, something grounding and rich.

I barely registered it.

Because Idris stood just beside me, silent, his golden eyes locked onto me like he could see every war still raging inside me.

Because Kian and Xavier were already in the water, their bodies slick with steam, their sharp gazes pinned on me, waiting.

Waiting for me to let go.

Waiting for me to breathe.

Xavier's long white hair was damp, curling slightly as he pushed it back from his face, his broad shoulders tense, waiting. He was always watching me, always reading me, but now, that sharp, assessing gaze was gentle.

Kian's amber eyes flickered as he shifted in the water, the scar along his jaw catching the candlelight. His bronze skin gleamed, no longer streaked with the remnants of battle and blood and exhaustion.

They should have looked worn down. Instead, they looked hungry—not for sex, not yet.

For me.

For the space between us to disappear.

For the last threads of battle to finally unravel.

Idris' fingers ghosted along my spine, slow, careful, measured.

"You're shaking," he murmured.

I hadn't noticed. The fight, the blood, the weight of everything we'd just survived—it was still locked in my bones. I turned, slowly, and Idris was already unfastening my dragon scale corset before I could reach for it myself. He wasn't hurried. Not rushed. Just steady, deliberate.

Piece by piece, he stripped all my armor away, and not once did Kian or Xavier take their eyes off me.

The moment my tunic hit the ground, Kian reached for me. Of course he did. His fingers skimmed my wrist, his usual smirk nowhere to be found.

"You coming in, Vale?" he murmured, voice low, rougher than usual.

I hesitated, the fight still coiling in my ribs, in my stubborn, aching refusal to surrender. The need to keep moving. The need to hold everything together.

They felt it, too.

Kian flexed his fingers, and his amber eyes scanned my face, reading every hesitation, every fractured piece of me still refusing to let go.

"Tell me you don't want this," he whispered. "Tell me you don't want us."

Xavier hummed low, the sound sliding over my skin like silk. "She won't say it."

"Because she does. She always does," Idris finished.

The bond flared between us, sharp and bright, tangled with so much need it made my knees weak. But still, I stood there.

Kian exhaled sharply, shaking his head. "So be it, little witch."

Then his arms wrapped around me.

Solid. Unyielding.

Before I could step in on my own, before I could think, before I could find another excuse to fight, Kian scooped me up.

My breath left me in a startled gasp, my body instinctively curling against his as he waded deeper into the water, pulling me with him.

I let myself sink.

Let myself fall.

At last.

CHAPTER 17

VALE

Warmth.

It sank into my frozen skin, wrapped around my aching muscles like silk.

I sagged without meaning to.

Idris followed, his golden eyes dark as he lowered himself onto a shallow ledge, watching as Kian and Xavier positioned me between them.

I didn't fight when Kian tipped up my chin, his fingers warm against my jaw.

"Let us take care of you."

He wasn't asking.

Kian moved behind me, positioning me so I leaned against his chest. His strong, wet arms braced around my waist, locking me against him.

Xavier knelt in front of me, his hands gliding over my arms, soothing me in a way I didn't know I needed. His calloused fingers skimmed over fresh bruises and cuts I hadn't noticed, and one by one, he healed them, pressing his power into me.

I could feel Idris' gaze on me as he watched from his seat. I wanted him nearer, and as if he read my mind, he moved closer, kneeling at my side.

Xavier plucked a small glass vial of oil from the side of the bath, pouring shimmering drops into the bathing pool. The scent of amber and myrrh unfurled in the steam as Kian scooped warm water over my shoulders, his hands skimming my arms, my ribs, my thighs.

Then Xavier took a washing cloth from the pile and ran it over every inch of my flesh, massaging my palms, my wrists, anywhere and everywhere. I squirmed and bucked as he washed me, but I didn't want him to stop. I never wanted him to stop.

Then, Idris plucked me from Kian's hold, turning me so my back was to his front. Then his impossibly strong fingers were at my scalp. They worked through my tangled hair, washing the strands of days of fear and despair.

Every single one of their touches were slow. Intentional. Reverent.

Kian hummed against my ear, pressing a lingering kiss just beneath my jaw.

"Relax, little queen."

I tried. Gods, I tried.

But the longer they touched me, bathed me, worshipped me, the more my pulse thundered.

Xavier's fingers brushed lower, trailing down my stomach, teasing, but not quite touching where I needed.

Idris' voice was soft at my ear, his lips grazing my temple.

"Let us do this for you."

The warmth of their hands, the scent of the oils, the ache of being held and touched but not quite taken—it all built inside me, a slow, exquisite torture.

My hips shifted involuntarily, seeking more.

Idris' lips ghosted across the column of my throat. "We're just getting started."

Golden threads of magic coiled around my wrists, my thighs, my waist, a question rather than a command. His voice was soft at my ear, but there was nothing soft about the promise beneath it.

"You are safe," he murmured, with a slow brush of his lips against my temple. "You are ours."

I swallowed hard, my body shuddering as my

resistance cracked—just enough for Idris to see it. His magic tightened. Not trapping, not forcing, but reminding. I inhaled sharply, my body bowing against his hold, an internal struggle still warring within me.

But then Xavier's fingers drifted lower—just a tease, just a whisper over my skin.

Kian's lips dipped to my collarbone, his fangs scraping the sensitive flesh, sending heat surging through me.

Xavier kissed me then, slow and devastating, swallowing the last fragments of my control.

"Let us take care of you," Idris whispered against the shell of my ear, his teeth grazing my skin. "You don't have to think, my love. Just feel."

I shuddered. And then—then I let go.

"Yes," I moaned.

The moment the word left my lips, Idris' magic surged. Not just around me, but through me—golden threads of restraint and pleasure sinking into my skin, into my bones, into the bond between us. Kian's fingers ghosted over my stomach, lower, lower, teasing, not giving me what I needed—not yet.

Xavier kissed me again, rougher this time, claiming my mouth, dragging me deeper into them.

Then the bond exploded—breaking wide, tearing away every barrier, every wall.

Waves of their pleasure crashed over me all at once—Kian's raw hunger, Xavier's agonizing restraint, Idris' need to unravel me completely.

I felt them. All of them.

Idris groaned, his magic tightening—thick, whisper-thin ropes holding me exactly where he wanted me.

Xavier's touch moved lower, brushing over my aching, desperate clit. Just a tease. Just enough to make my hips jerk against the magic holding me still.

Kian's lips found my breast, his tongue flicking over the peak before his fangs scraped down. My back arched, but I couldn't move.

I was caught—held, trapped, owned.

And I loved it.

"You're ours." Idris' magic tightened around my wrists, my thighs, a whisper of silk and steel. "Say it."

I swallowed hard, the heat in my belly twisting, tightening. My breath left me in a shaky exhale.

Kian's teeth scraped my skin, his voice wicked at my ear. "She can't. Not yet. She's still fighting us."

Xavier's breath ghosted against my throat, his

fingers just barely pressing against my clit. "Then let's make her beg," he rumbled, with a slow, deliberate stroke and an aching press of his fingers. "We're going to break you apart, Vale. Over and over again."

My entire body shuddered.

Idris' breath skated over the nape of my neck, moving slowly, his lips grazing my pulse, his magic coiling tighter. "Say yes, my brave one." His fangs raked over my throat, making me tremble. "Let us worship you."

My head fell back against his shoulder, my lips parting on a gasp, a plea, a surrender, and I gave in. *"Yes, please. I'll do anything. Please—"*

Xavier rewarded me instantly, his fingers filling me just right, enough to make my hips jerk against Idris' hold.

Kian groaned. "Fuck, you are so perfect when you beg."

Idris' hand slid up, cupping my jaw, forcing my gaze to meet his. His golden eyes burned.

"Free me," I begged, not knowing if I spoke it aloud or inside their heads. *"I want to touch you. I want to feel you."*

Then the bonds dissolved, releasing me from their hold, and I reached. Not just with my hands, but with my magic. The second it hit them, they groaned in unison—their pleasure slamming into me through the bond, so potent it stole my breath.

Idris had once spun me into mindlessness with his magic. Now, it was my turn.

Hot flesh bloomed underneath my hands as I turned on Idris' lap, straddling him with a single-minded focus of blind need. My aching center rubbed against his thick cock, and I wanted it inside me. Needed it. Idris fisted my hair and captured my mouth with his. I was free, but he still controlled every movement, every kiss, every touch.

Yes, I was at their mercy, but they were also at mine.

My power raced over their flesh, touching them everywhere, feeling everything. Kian and Xavier's heat blossomed over my back as they crowded in, caging me in the very best of ways. Kian pulled my mouth to his, stealing my lips as my hips rolled, giving me the best pressure against my aching clit.

Kian's grip loosened when Xavier stole my kiss, but his fingers found my ass, pressing against the puckered ring of muscle as I rubbed against Idris' cock. The dual sensations had me panting into Xavier's mouth, my desire so acute, my skin felt too tight.

And then Idris stood, yanking me with him before planting my ass on the edge of the bathing pool.

"Gods, you make me fucking crazed. I can't wait anymore. I have to taste you." Hooking his hands behind my thighs, Idris spread my knees wide before he dropped his mouth to my center.

A guttural growl left his throat, the vibration of it making me gasp. His hot tongue lashed my clit, as his claws pricked the tender flesh of my thighs. My back bowed as he devoured me, my hands scrabbling for something—anything—to hold onto.

Kian and Xavier didn't let me down. One moment, I was untethered, and the next, Kian's lips were on mine as Xavier left biting kisses to the tops of my thighs, my belly, my breasts.

And all the while, Idris didn't once temper his onslaught. He filled me with his fingers, ramping me higher and higher as I mentally begged for release.

"Fuck, little witch. You taste so fucking good," Idris groaned into me, driving my need higher as the tendrils of his magic raced over my flesh.

My only answer was a moan as my hands found Xavier's hair, and I dragged him to my mouth, needing his heat. Kian moved lower, his biting kisses driving me to madness as he gripped my thigh, holding my legs wide for Idris' feast. And feast, he did.

My orgasm raced for me, threatening to pull me under, and gods, I wanted to drown. All the worry, all the fear, everything shriveled to the back of my mind until there was only their touch, only their mouths on me, only their hands.

"Come for us, *oroum di vita*," Kian growled into my flesh, his fangs grazing my hip. "Let us feel it."

But Idris wouldn't allow it. Not yet. The golden bonds wrapped around my hips, pulsing with heat as they kept me still, teetering on the edge, unable to fall. I whimpered, pleading, twisting in his hold.

Xavier smirked, pinching my nipple, giving me the seductive bite I craved. "You can take more."

I didn't think I could—not until they made me. Idris devoured me, licking, sucking, filling me so full, I thought I would die from the pleasure. Kian nipped at my skin as Xavier kissed me mindless, and it wasn't until I started begging did Idris finally, finally, set me free.

"Come, my love," Idris growled, his voice vibrating through my mind like the most blissful command.

As if my body was waiting for the order, my release pounced, yanking me under as my back bowed on the tile. My scream was silent, my breath caught in my lungs as wave after wave crashed into me. Idris' tongue never left, continuing his lashes against my clit until each one felt like lightning zipping through my body.

And then his tongue left me, only for the heat of his cock to rest against my slit. My core ached even though I'd just come, mindless need building in my body until I felt like I would break.

"Please," I gasped, every part of my body trembling. I needed them inside me, filling me, making me whole again. *"Please."*

At my plea, Idris filled me with one long stroke, his talons digging into my hips with the most delicious pain.

I didn't care if I bled, if the world fell apart around us. Idris filled me to the brim, stretching my walls until there was nothing but him. My eyes rolled into the back of my head as pleasure raced across my flesh.

And still, I wanted more.

My greedy hands reached for Kian and Xavier. I wanted them to feel what I did, wanted them just as mindless, just as needy. My fingers closed around Xavier's cock, his oil-slicked skin sliding through my hold as he groaned into my mouth.

Xavier's kiss turned punishing as Kian's strong grip flexed against my throat, not squeezing—just anchoring. Claiming. My pulse thrummed against his hold, the steady drumbeat of surrender. I gasped, and Xavier swallowed the sound, his kiss turning from coaxing to devouring, his teeth nipping just hard enough to remind me who was kissing me.

Then his mouth was gone, and I tugged on his cock, slightly begging him to fill my mouth. Kian guided my lips to his best friend's cock, setting the pace as Xavier thrust down my throat.

"*Fuck*," Idris growled against my breast, his lips brushing my nipple. "Push her harder, fuck her face. Gods, she clenches so fucking tight when you make her."

Xavier obeyed his King, his fist tightening in my hair as he fucked my mouth. My sex tightened, as a wave of heat threatened to drown me again.

"Oh no you don't," Kian rumbled, lifting me off Xavier. "You don't get to come again until I've had a taste."

A second later, Kian filled my mouth while Xavier guided my hand to his slick length. I flexed my fingers around him as he thrust into my grip, and I couldn't help my moan as his rough fingers found my clit while Idris continued his punishing thrusts.

I loved the way they demanded their pleasure and mine. Loved how affectionately rough they were with me, like they knew I wouldn't break.

The pressure built higher and higher until I stood on the precipice, waiting to fall. And fall, I did. And as much as I'd wanted it, this release still caught me by surprise, and I screamed around Kian's cock as spurts of his hot seed lashed my throat when he fell with me.

Then Idris yanked his cock from me, leaving me empty, and I whimpered at the loss. In a single moment, I was up off the tile and in his arms, my back hitting soft sheets seconds later. Then it was Xavier between my thighs, his large, hulking frame spreading my legs wide as he notched the head of his cock at my opening.

"Look at you," Xavier murmured, brushing his thumbs over my slick folds. "Fucking ruined for us. And we haven't even given you everything yet." He dragged himself against my entrance, teasing, not giving, just making me feel the weight of him.

"You want it, don't you, little queen? Want to be so full of us you can't think anymore?"

I whimpered, arching my back, reaching for him.

But Xavier didn't move. Not yet. He just watched me squirm under his gaze.

"You take us so beautifully." With a slow, torturous roll of his hips, he filled me. "Let me give you what you need."

Then he was covering me, consuming me, filling me so full, I forgot what being empty felt like. A moment later he flipped us, settling me on his lap as he drilled into me, his wide palm grasping my throat.

"Keep your eyes on me when I take you, Vale." Xavier's voice dipped, dark and promising. "I want to see you fall apart."

Those brilliant blue depths called to me, and I couldn't look away—not until Kian's heat covered my back. Slick oil dripped between my cheeks, and Kian's already-hard cock brushed the tight ring of muscle.

"Gods, look at you, Vale." Kian's voice was thick with hunger as his slick fingers pressed deeper, stretching me, working me open. "Taking Xavier so perfectly, and you're still greedy for more."

He leaned in, biting my shoulder, sinking his fangs so deep I nearly came. "I bet you don't even realize how fucking beautiful you look like this"—Another slow, torturous press of his fingers made me whimper—"spreading yourself open for us. For all of us."

I gasped, my hips rocking between them, chasing *more, more, more.*

"Patience, little queen," Kian groaned. "We're going to ruin you first."

Then his fingers were gone, and the hard press of his cock breached my ass, filling me until I couldn't breathe. And when I did, the sound that came from me was nothing short of crazed.

"That's it, my brave one." Idris' voice was velvet over steel, his fingers tilting my chin, forcing my eyes to meet his. "Look at me while he takes you. Let me see how much you love this."

I whimpered, my body shuddering between them as Kian's thick length stretched me open, as Xavier filled me so full.

"You were made for this, weren't you?" Idris' golden gaze burned as he brushed his thumb over my kiss-swollen lips. "For us. To take us. To let us ruin you."

Then, he pressed his cock against my mouth, teasing the seam of my lips. "Open, little queen. I want to feel your moans around my cock while they fuck you senseless."

I couldn't deny him—I needed it too badly. And

when he drove his cock into my mouth, the bond between us all seemed to erupt, spilling from me, anchoring me to them—to their hearts, to their minds. I was filled so completely, so completely theirs. My body was at their mercy, and they knew it, craved it.

They were in every facet of my thoughts, every cell, every single piece of me. I lost all sense of time, place, there was only them, only this, only the pleasure they wrung from me. I felt like I was falling, breaking apart at the seams. Their bodies—their warmth—pressed against mine.

It was all too much and not enough, never enough.

Kian's grip on the back of my neck tightened, his voice a low snarl in my ear. "Take it, little queen. Take it all."

Xavier groaned, his breaths just as ragged as mine when his hands slid to my throat, squeezing as he forced me to feel every single inch of him surging inside me.

"You're so fucking perfect like this, Vale. So full of us. So wrecked."

My body trembled, my magic spilling from my skin, bathing us in golden light. Then Idris cupped my jaw, his golden eyes burning into my soul.

"Let go, my love." Idris' voice was the last tether holding me together. "No more holding back. Let us feel you fall."

My body obeyed before my mind could catch up. Pleasure slammed into me, breaking me apart in a thousand bright pieces, leaving me gasping, shaking, lost in them.

The bond tore wide open, pouring light and sensation through every part of me. I felt Xavier's sharp pleasure, Kian's raw hunger, Idris' deep satisfaction as they pulled me under. They didn't let me go—they followed, drowning with me, until I was nothing but one with them.

Bliss took over every part of my body, tearing the bond, reshaping it, making it something new.

And through this bond, I felt everything. Not just the raw heat, the pleasure—their emotions. Kian's quiet awe, a deep, unspoken reverence as he traced his fingers over my spine.

Xavier's fierce devotion, the way his arms tightened around me, anchoring me even now. Idris' possessive adoration, so vast and absolute, it left no room for doubt.

This wasn't just magic. This wasn't just claiming.

This was a connection we couldn't break.

This was forever.

Xavier's sharp pleasure flooded my senses as my sex clenched around him, and his release dragged me into another as he lost his control and let go. Kian's low growl surrounded me as he followed, claiming me completely as I fell again. Then Idris lost his ironclad control, filling my mouth with his release, and I felt every second of it. They dragged me down into the abyss with them, their releases crashing over me like fire and gold—until I was boneless, trembling, and completely theirs.

The world blurred at the edges, the bond between us still thrumming, golden threads of magic twining around our limbs like silk. I tried to catch my breath, but my body felt too heavy, too spent.

Only the sound of my own breaths, ragged and uneven, filled the room as the unsteady pound of my heart beat against my ribs.

A warm hand skimmed down my spine.

"Breathe, little queen." Kian's voice was soft now, no longer teasing, no longer demanding. Just full of something deeper.

Xavier let out a low groan, pressing a slow, lingering kiss to the damp skin of my shoulder. "Are you with us?"

The best I could manage was a hum, my voice too wrecked for words.

Idris chuckled, his voice like honeyed embers. "We may have broken her."

My thighs shook as Kian slowly withdrew, pressing a kiss to her spine, murmuring something I couldn't quite hear, but felt all the same. A second later the steady fall of the shower began.

Xavier slipped from me next, moving slower, more reverent, like he was reluctant to leave my body.

Idris trailed a soft touch, brushing my lips in praise.

"You were perfect," he murmured, his golden eyes burning into me. It was bigger than adoration, bigger than love.

Before I could move, I was being lifted—strong arms cradling me, pressing me against warm, solid chests.

"Shh," Xavier whispered, "we've got you."

Soon, water sluiced over my skin, washing away the remnants of pleasure, of sweat, of the battle we had barely survived.

Xavier held me up, arms firm but gentle, supporting my weight as Kian smoothed soap over my shoulders.

Idris' hands were in my hair, his fingers massaging my scalp, his voice a low murmur at my ear. "That's it. You're safe now."

I swallowed hard, my chest still heaving. My body was spent, but my mind was still spinning, still caught in the gravity of what had just happened.

Kian pressed a kiss to my temple, his lips lingering. "Still with us, little queen?"

I hummed, too exhausted to speak. They cleaned me like I was something precious—and that, more than anything, made my throat tighten. I had fought so hard, endured so much, but here, in their hands, I didn't have to fight at all.

I just had to be.

Before long I was clean, and the soft sheets graced my skin again as my mates curled around me. Idris' hand in my hair, Kian's lips at my temple, Xavier's arm around my waist—it was all too much, and yet, exactly enough.

I exhaled, my body sinking into the warmth of them—of home.

For the first time in too long, I let myself be held.

Warmth coiled around me, deeper than skin, deeper than magic.

And for the first time in my life, I let myself believe it.

CHAPTER 18
VALE

Heat. Deep, bone-deep heat.

It wrapped around me, cocooning me in the scent of embers and something spiced, something rich. My mates.

Idris lay beneath me, his chest rising and falling in a slow, steady rhythm, his heartbeat thrumming against my ear. My legs tangled with his, my body draped over him like I never wanted to leave. Maybe I didn't.

Xavier's hand rested low on my hip, his breath slow and even at my back. Even in sleep, he anchored me, his fingers curled over my skin in that quiet, steady way of his. Kian was at my other side, his arm flung loosely over my waist, his fingertips tracing idle patterns along my spine.

Held by them, wrapped in their warmth, I should have felt safe. I should have been dead to the world.

But something was wrong.

Beneath me, Idris went still. Not just still—rigid. Every muscle in his body locked, breath turning shallow. A slow, quiet inhale through his nose. A controlled exhale through his mouth.

The kind of measured breath someone took when they were trying not to move.

A warning.

Sleep bled away in an instant. My pulse kicked up as I stiffened against him. "What is it?" My voice was barely more than a whisper.

He didn't answer right away. His golden eyes flickered in the dim light, his grip tightening on my waist.

Kian hummed low, half-asleep, and drowsy, his lips brushing my shoulder. "What's got you all wound up?"

Then Idris exhaled. The bond between us pulsed. "She moved."

I blinked, sleep draining from my limbs. "Who?"

His jaw clenched. "Nyrah." Idris paused for a beat. "She moved."

Then he shook his head like he was trying to clear it. "I spelled her to sleep. It... connected me to the Dreaming inside her." His golden eyes burned, unfocused. "I just felt her move, but she didn't wake up."

The bond between us all thrummed with something restless, something cold. I went still. My breath caught, my fingers clenching against Idris' chest.

Nyrah.

I scrambled upright, but Idris was already moving, shifting me effortlessly as he sat up.

Awake in an instant, Xavier's hand wrapped around my hip to steady me. The bond surged, thick with golden fire and something sharper—something like dread.

And then a pulse rippled through the air.

I didn't think. Didn't hesitate.

My hands flew out, grabbing for the first thing I could reach. A tunic—soft, oversized, Idris' scent still clinging to it. I yanked it over my head, not bothering with laces, just enough to be covered. Underwear, boots, blades.

Behind me, the bed shifted violently as Idris

stood, golden magic flickering over his skin. He dragged his leathers up his legs in one fluid motion, practiced and precise.

Kian was already moving, his usual mirth replaced with sharp, lethal focus. He grabbed his pants first, but his weapons second, the blackened scales of his dragon flitting over his skin.

Xavier barely took the time to shove on his trousers, snatching up his blades before he moved.

The house trembled again.

I didn't wait. I ran, bursting from the room into the corridor.

The hallway stretched. Just for a second, just for a breath. Then the walls shuddered, pulsed, the wood bending inwards, curving toward me. A whisper—too low to understand, too high to ignore—brushed over my ears.

Then everything snapped back.

The door to Nyrah's room was ahead—Briar's voice sharp on the other side.

I didn't slow. I threw the door open. And everything stopped.

Nyrah was there, still unconscious, still asleep. But something else was, too.

The air twisted. The air warped, the space around Nyrah bending like ripples over glass. Magic thickened, twisting, shifting—like a veil between realms had just torn open.

Briar covered Nyrah with her small body, doing her best to protect her.

I barely had a chance to take one breath.

The Dreaming didn't pull. It ripped.

One breath, I was standing in Nyrah's room, the scent of old magic thick in the air. The next, I was wrenched downward, yanked from reality with an unnatural force.

Cold.

Not the crisp bite of winter, not the creeping chill of a shadowed room—this was deep cold. Ancient. A void that had never known light. It wrapped around me in an instant, numbing my skin, clawing at my bones.

I reached—for the bond, for my mates, for anything solid. But there was nothing.

The world around me warped. Up and down bled together, gravity shifting sideways, backward —wrong.

A heartbeat pounded in my ears, but it wasn't mine.

I gasped, trying to orient myself, but the floor wasn't there. There was no floor. No sky. Just an endless stretch of swirling, fractured light.

And then I hit the ground.

Hard.

The impact cracked through me, stealing my breath, sending pain lancing up my spine. My palms scraped against stone—smooth, shimmering like molten silver. The air vibrated, thick, humming, alive. Like it had been waiting.

I sucked in a sharp breath and pushed up onto my hands and knees, blinking fast, my body aching from the landing.

And that's when I saw him.

Rune.

He stood at the center of it all, his massive scarlet form coiled around something—*someone*. His wings were flared, talons digging into the ground, his golden eyes burning through the shadows.

Defiant. Furious. But fading.

The edges of his scales flickered, unstable, as though he was barely holding himself together. And between his massive claws, Nyrah lay motionless.

My stomach lurched. "Rune," I breathed, scrambling to my feet.

His head snapped toward me, golden eyes locking onto mine, and for the first time in my life, a dragon looked afraid.

And then the shadows moved.

Terror flooded my chest, but it wasn't mine. It poured through the air, thick and suffocating, snaking through my bones like smoke. Heavy. Old. And laced with something sharp, something ragged and raw.

This wasn't my fear.

It was Rune's.

My stomach knotted, the bond flaring white-hot inside me, surging past Idris—past all of them—and into the heart of the dragon who stood before me.

Rune's massive chest heaved, his form shimmering at the edges, struggling to hold its shape. His talons flexed against the iridescent stone beneath him, his scaled lips peeling back in a warning snarl, his golden eyes full of fire and death.

A growl rumbled through the void, low and lethal.

"You are not welcome here."

I flinched. His voice wasn't like Idris' anymore. It was deeper, older, a living storm ready to break.

But he was wrong.

"I am," I said, lifting my chin. "And you know it. You *know* me."

Rune's wings flared, his massive form blocking out everything else, but I wasn't afraid of him. Not when I could feel the truth beneath his fury—the pain. The fear. The looming death sinking its claws into him.

He was dying.

And if he died—really died—so could Idris.

Rune bared his fangs, golden light cracking along the seams of his body. His voice came as a snarl of pure agony. "I will not let you take her."

My gaze traveled to where she lay curled beneath his massive form. Unmoving. Pale. Barely breathing. Her pale hair and small form a dead giveaway.

Nyrah.

He was protecting my sister. Guarding her from Zamarra's influence, from the Dreaming that wanted to swallow her whole.

The shadows around them twisted. Reached.

Zamarra.

I didn't think. I lifted my hands, and power surged outward. It wasn't the flickering flame of my magic before—it was more. Bigger. Brighter.

The moment it hit the air, the Dreaming screamed. The shadows reeled back, hissing, writhing like steam meeting fire.

Rune flinched. His massive body recoiled, his wings rustling, his golden eyes going wide.

He didn't just see me. He felt me.

His breath hitched. *"You—"*

The bond flared, and for a second, Rune shivered—trembling as I spoke into his mind.

"It's me, Rune. It's Vale."

I stepped forward, my magic burning through the dark, illuminating the twisted world around us.

"You're not alone." My voice was quiet, but steady. *"I'm here, Rune. And I will not let you fall."*

A scream tore through the Dreaming. Not a voice—the realm itself.

The moment my power lashed out, the void around me twisted, shrieking, as if I had burned it. And then it fought back. The darkness lunged forward. I gasped, staggering as it slammed into me, sinking its claws deep into my chest.

Cold. Bone-deep, soul-deep cold.

It wrapped around my limbs, my throat, slithering like something alive. A breath. A whisper.

"You do not belong here."

I choked, my body jerking, but the shadows coiled tighter. My magic flared too slow. I couldn't move, couldn't break free.

"Vale!" Rune's voice was a snarl of fury, of pain.

I twisted in the dark, barely able to see him through the shifting void. He fought the shadows, tearing at them with his talons, but he was losing.

The edges of his form wavered, his massive scarlet body phasing in and out like he was barely clinging to existence. His claws dug into the stone, his tail lashing wildly as he tried to shield Nyrah, to hold onto what little strength he had left.

But the Dreaming wanted him gone. It wanted him devoured. Shattered. Erased. And if I couldn't stop it—if I couldn't free him—it would succeed.

My pulse thundered. I reached, straining for my magic, shoving it outward with everything I had, but the shadows crushed down, drowning me.

No. I was so close to fixing everything. Nyrah, Rune—everything I'd ruined.

A sudden roar shook the realm, deep and shattering, and then...

Idris was there—they all were.

Magic exploded through the Dreaming, a shockwave of raw, furious power. The shadows reeled back, hissing, retreating into the void as golden flames ripped through the darkness.

A blast of wind slammed into my chest as Kian's illusions unraveled the Dreaming's hold on me. Xavier was already moving, his blade slicing through the air, his magic snapping like a whip as he severed the threads trying to pull me deeper.

And at the center of it all—Idris burned.

His golden eyes locked onto Rune, onto me, onto the void trying to steal us away. His voice was steel, fire, an unshakable command that shook the Dreaming to its core. "*Enough*."

The realm shuddered. Rune staggered, his massive body barely holding together, his golden eyes blazing with desperation, with defiance, with fear.

And then the final battle for his soul began.

The Dreaming raged—it lashed, howled, tore at the edges of reality, trying to consume everything. But my mates stood like unbreakable pillars, golden fire, and raw power slashing through the dark.

Rune trembled. His body shuddered, flickering, his massive form struggling to stay whole. The void clawed at his wings, his talons, trying to rip him deeper into the Dreaming's grasp. And Rune—for the first time in centuries—was losing.

"I won't let it take you." The words burst from me, fierce and unwavering.

Rune's golden eyes locked onto mine, burning through the shadows. For just a second, uncertainty cracked through his fury. He was terrified.

Not of me. Not of the Dreaming. Of what would come next.

"If I do this." Rune's voice cracked—raw, old, haunted. *"If I merge with him... do I disappear?"*

The Dreaming lurched. The void screamed. Rune's massive form fractured at the edges, gold light spilling from every crack.

This wasn't just pain—this was annihilation.

I grabbed onto him. Not just his body—his soul. Rune had saved me over and over again. I wouldn't let him fall—not ever.

"No." I breathed it, willed it, carved it into the bond between us.

My magic surged, flooding the space between us, burning through the cold, through the dark, through every inch of him. I felt him.

Not just his power.

Not just his fire.

Him.

Rune—the dragon who had once been Idris' other half, the guardian who had fought for me, who had always fought for me.

"You don't disappear," I whispered. *"You become whole."*

His eyes widened, moving a single step forward as the darkness threatened to pull him back.

And Idris met him halfway.

The Dreaming shuddered as he moved between us, his golden eyes locking onto Rune's.

"I am not whole without you." Idris' voice was low, raw, absolute, echoing through the bond that was so much stronger now. *"I never have been."*

Rune's form flickered, his massive chest heaving, his claws gouging into the stone beneath him.

The void tightened.

Rune flinched, but Idris did not. The golden fire around him surged.

"I will not be ruled by the years we lost," he said, stepping closer. *"Not the mistakes, not the failures. Not anymore."*

A muscle in Rune's jaw ticked. His great wings shuddered, his tail flicking in hesitation.

"I'm afraid," Rune admitted. The words were so soft, I barely heard them over the roar of the Dreaming.

Idris lifted a hand—not demanding, not forcing, but offering. *"Then let's do this together."*

Rune stared at him.

Then, slowly, painfully, he reached forward, skin meeting scales, and the Dreaming exploded.

Light surged outward—blinding, burning, golden fire consuming everything. Rune's massive form shattered like breaking starlight, his body collapsing into Idris, golden magic wrapping around him, sinking into his King.

And Idris' back arched, his body bowing, golden fire consuming him.

For the first time in two hundred years, the missing piece of himself returned.

The shadows screamed. The Dreaming fractured. Magic crashed through me, through them, through everything.

A deafening silence followed like the whole realm had exhaled. I staggered forward, blinded, breathless, heart pounding.

And when the world finally settled, Idris stood before me.

Whole.

Alive.

Changed.

His golden eyes burned, brighter than they ever had before. And when he finally spoke, his voice was steady, unshaken, absolute.

"My Queen."

I felt relief for one shining second before the Dreaming twisted around us. The void lurched, the fractured light of this realm pulsing like a dying heartbeat. Then the walls of the Dreaming tore open.

A shockwave of golden fire erupted from Idris, forcing reality back into place. The void shuddered, howling, but it didn't collapse.

It bled.

Like darkness seeping into twilight, the edges of the Dreaming leaked into the waking world, a creeping, hungry rot slithering through the seams of existence.

My breath caught. "No."

Nyrah.

She was still there—still trapped beneath where Rune had shielded her. The Dreaming buckled. Shadows snapped at my ankles, a new wave of darkness cascading toward her.

I lunged for my sister.

Idris' magic snapped out, gripping my wrist before I could touch her, before I could dive into the dark and take her with me.

"Vale—" His voice was sharp, commanding, but edged with something raw. Desperate.

She was right there. I couldn't leave her.

The Dreaming screeched, a sound that rattled through my ribs. The ground beneath her cracked, split.

"Let me go!" I yanked against him, fighting, reaching, clawing, but Nyrah wasn't there anymore.

The shadows surged, swallowing her whole.

"No!" I reached with my magic, my power screaming outward, but Idris' magic collided with mine, wrapping around me, yanking me back.

"We have to go!"

The Dreaming collapsed inward.

Xavier and Kian were already moving, their magic shredding a path toward the waking world, tearing open an exit.

My breath hitched, my body shaking, my magic still straining for her—for my sister.

Then the world snapped, and the Dreaming spat us out. I hit the ground hard, gasping, the waking world crashing back into me. The scent of embers. The solid floor. The glow of golden magic still flickering over Idris' skin.

And the sharp, terrifying absence where Nyrah should have been.

I didn't even feel the tears spill down my face before Idris was there, before Xavier caught my shoulders, before Kian's voice murmured something —anything—to bring me back.

But all I could do was stare at the empty bed.

Empty.

Nyrah was gone.

And the Dreaming was coming for us next.

Vale's scream didn't just shatter the world, it tried to unmake it.

Magic detonated, not just inside her, but through the bond, through us, through everything. It was a rupture. A snapping, violent unraveling, a force so raw it ripped into my chest, my mind, my soul.

I choked on it, staggered under the weight.

Because it wasn't just grief.

It was loss sharpened into a blade. It was rage wrapped in lightning. It was power with nowhere to go—surging, splitting, breaking.

And it would kill her.

Her magic flared too bright, too unstable.

My breath caught in my lungs, the memory of

losing her wrapping around my heart and squeezing. Vale couldn't use this much power and not—

A surge of magic flashed from her, and the whole room warped. The walls didn't just bend inward—they cracked, black veins splintering through the stone, through the wards, through reality itself. The floor shuddered, the wood twisting as if it were alive, fighting to pull itself apart. The air thickened, turning into something crushing, suffocating, as reality seemed to coil in on us.

And still—Vale didn't stop. Didn't breathe. Didn't fight.

She was breaking. And worse, I felt why.

Nyrah was gone.

My chest tightened, clenched, ruptured because I'd promised. I'd been the one to spell her to sleep. I'd been the one to shield her, protect her. I was the one who told Vale she would be safe, that she could relax, that she should rest.

And I'd failed.

I'd saved Vale instead of letting her fall with her sister. I'd pulled her free when I could have let them go together.

But I wouldn't have. Not then. Not now. Not ever.

I would choose her a hundred times over, a

thousand, a million. Even knowing the cost. Even knowing what it would do to her. Even knowing she might never forgive me.

Because Vale was mine. My mate. My Queen. And I had already watched her die once.

I would burn the world down before I let it happen again.

I forced myself to breathe. Forced myself to move.

Vale stood in the wreckage of her own power, her magic slamming into me, into all of us. She wasn't just breaking—she was coming apart. She'd risked everything to bring Nyrah back, and now she'd lost her again.

And it was my fault. I had to face her. I had to face the storm I'd unleashed.

The bond twisted, pulled, suffocated, driving me into the heart of her ruin, forcing me to feel every fracture, every unraveling thread.

Rune's voice rose in my mind, fire and judgment, and a fury so blistering it burned through my whole body. *"You let her fall."*

I flinched. Not from Vale. Not from Kian. Not from Xavier.

From him. From the dragon now rooted inside me, bound to me, part of me.

"You promised. Did you think I was guarding her for my health? After all she sacrificed for me—for us."

"I know," I croaked as I watched my mate crumbling before me.

"And you failed."

My jaw locked as guilt threatened to pull me under. Because I had, and now Vale was unraveling before my eyes.

She swayed, barely breathing, barely standing, but the Dreaming hadn't taken her. It had taken Nyrah instead. Why?

Realization washed over me.

Because it *couldn't* take Vale. Not yet. Not while she was still standing, still fighting, still too powerful to be claimed.

The bond between us pulsed, not just between me and Vale, but deeper—through Kian, through Xavier, through Rune, through the Dreaming itself.

And I felt it—a whisper of something watching. Waiting.

This wasn't an attack. It was a test.

Zamarra's magic coiled at the edges of the room, but it didn't lunge. Didn't try to drag Vale back into the Dreaming. Because it didn't need to.

Vale was breaking herself. If she shattered

completely, if she lost control, if she let herself fall, Zamarra wouldn't have to steal her.

Vale would hand herself over.

A sharp burning sensation flared in my skull as Rune's voice seethed through me, through the bond. *"She's waiting. Watching. You feel it, too."*

I clenched my teeth. "Why take Nyrah instead?"

A growl rumbled inside me, low, full of bitter understanding. *"Because Nyrah is young and weak. Because she is poisoned. Because Vale is still whole."*

I swallowed hard.

Vale wasn't corrupted. She wasn't tainted. But she was breaking. And if she didn't pull herself back together, she wouldn't need to be taken.

She would go willingly.

Xavier moved first. Fast. Ruthless. Unrelenting.

He caught Vale's face between his hands, tilting her chin up, forcing her to see him. "Vale. Look at me."

She didn't blink. Didn't breathe. Blood dripped from her nose as her magic rippled, vibrating through the air, a living, feral thing with claws. It wasn't just power anymore—it was instinct, raw and unchecked. And it was hunting for something to destroy.

"Please, Vale," Xavier whispered. "Don't do this."

Kian pressed against her back, his hands gripped the fabric of her tunic, her shoulders, his heat flaring as he tried to anchor her. His illusions pushed against the Dreaming, against Vale's power, but they weren't a match for it. They crumbled to dust as soon as they touched her light.

"Breathe, little queen," he pleaded, his voice like broken glass.

She inhaled, but it was shallow, jagged, barely enough.

Then, her magic detonated, lashing outward—wild, uncontrollable, devastating.

The force slammed into Xavier's chest, knocking him back a step. It snapped against Kian's skin like a live wire, burning, cutting, threatening to break. But neither of them let go.

A snarl ripped from my throat, pure instinct, primal and protective. I surged forward, catching Vale's arm, grounding her. I wouldn't lose her again—couldn't.

She didn't fight. Not because she was listening. Because she was *gone*.

Her eyes were vacant, the green burning too bright, too untethered. She was slipping, the pull of the Dreaming stretching toward her like a black tide.

I tightened my grip, digging my claws into her

skin—not to hurt, but to remind. "You think this is what she would want?"

Her breath hitched. Magic snarled, coiling at the edges of the room like a storm waiting to break.

"You think Nyrah would want you to die for her? Think she'd want you to let Zamarra win?"

"She's gone. I lost her. I was supposed to keep her safe. I promised."

A sob heaved in her chest, ricocheting through my heart, my lungs. It burned like acid, and worse, when she let out the sob she'd been holding inside, I worried it would break her in half.

"She was mine. My responsibility, my sister, my charge. My light. I would have withered away a thousand times if I didn't have her and now—"

The walls pulsed with power as she broke, but we wouldn't let her do this alone.

"Come back to us, Vale. You can't help your sister if you break now." Kian's voice cut through the chaos, steady, firm—iron forged in fire.

Vale shook, like she was physically straining against the truth of those words. Her power faltered. And then her eyes cleared, the warped reality bending back to rights.

"Then we get her back," she growled, her voice firm, her shoulders straight.

"That's my brave one," I murmured through the bond, and those gorgeous green eyes found me. In them wasn't blame or hatred, only determination.

Suddenly, magic swirled in the room, knocking the doors wide open.

Not from the Dreaming. No, this was new magic.

Not Vale's. Not mine. Something else.

Talek staggered inside, his odd, color-shifting eyes burning, his entire body vibrating with strain. Magic clung to him, raw and jagged, crackling through the air like lightning with nowhere to go.

But he wasn't looking at Vale.

His gaze locked onto me, sharp, cutting—like he knew something I didn't.

A cold weight twisted inside my gut.

Then he spoke, his voice sounded hoarse, wrecked. "They took her."

Vale stilled, her body snapping rigid. Her lips parted, and her breath hitched. "Nyrah?"

Talek nodded, and this time—his voice was sharper. "Briar, too."

A sound ripped from Vale's throat. Not a cry. Not a scream. A sound of something waking up.

Talek swiped a hand through his hair, his usually composed expression fractured with something close to grief. His magic still hummed, still churned, but he wasn't letting it loose.

"She wouldn't leave Nyrah," he said, his voice raw. "When the Dreaming came for her"—He swallowed hard, jaw tightening like a vise—"she fought it."

Vale swayed, and all three of us strengthened our grip on her so she wouldn't go down. Talek's fingers twitched at his side, like he wanted to do the same—but he stayed where he was.

"I tried to pull them back," he continued, his voice dark, chilling. "But Briar wouldn't let go. She held onto Nyrah. And then—" He exhaled sharply. "They were gone."

Silence slammed into the room.

Vale's chest heaved, and her hands shook uncontrollably.

I felt it through the bond—the moment she shattered all over again.

Her power rippled, not just reacting, but pulling, latching onto the edges of the Dreaming, yanking at the veil like she could rip it open and step through.

Talek took a sharp step forward, his gaze locking on her hands. "Vale."

She didn't answer. Her magic wasn't stopping. It wasn't contained anymore. It pulsed again, and

Xavier, Kian, and I were knocked back, away, her power ripping us from our mate.

Talek swore, stepping toward her fast. "Fuck, this is going to hurt."

His fingers latched onto her wrist and magic exploded. Pain whipped through the bond. Vale gasped, wrenching back, but Talek held her firm. His magic surged, ripping through her, through the room, sending fractures through reality itself. Light bent. Shadows lengthened. The walls shuddered, the air thickening.

Then the veil split open. Not just a crack, but a doorway, and they stepped through.

Not just flickering echoes. Not just whispers caught between realms. The Luxa.

More solid than I had ever seen them. Their presence pressed against the air, like a law of nature that had always existed but had never been fully realized.

The one in front—tall, regal, terrifying in her grace—lifted her chin, eyes gleaming with silver light as they locked onto Vale.

Recognition flashed in her expression. Not surprise. Understanding.

Talek exhaled sharply, his grip loosening. He stumbled back, sweat beading along his brow.

"Vale." Xavier moved, reaching for her, but she didn't budge. She was locked in place.

Because the Luxa leader bowed, with a slight tilt of her head. A flicker of deference.

Something ancient recognizing something older still.

Vale flinched. "What—"

And then—the Luxa spoke. Not just words. A prophecy.

"The Blood of the First will show the way."

The air vibrated, rippling with power.

"Seek the one lost to the Dreaming."

Xavier tensed, Kian reached for Vale's shoulders, and my pulse hammered.

I'd seen that first line before, carved into the walls of the temple, but I had never heard the rest.

Vale's golden eyes narrowed, sharp with confusion. "What?"

"The blood awakens. The Dreaming calls."

The words were woven with power, a thread through reality itself.

Vale swallowed hard, glancing at me, at Kian, at Xavier. None of us had heard this before. None of us had known. Except Vale.

Her lips parted, her pulse pounding through the bond. "You—you've said this before."

A trace of something knowing passed across the Luxa leader's face. "Yes."

Vale's breath hitched. "Then tell me"—Her hands clenched into fists—"what the hell does it mean? Who is the first? What do you want from me?"

The Luxa leader took a single step forward, her head tilting to the side with a ghost of a smile flitting across her lips, the first crack in her unreadable expression. "Your burden is great for someone so young, but you will bear it. It can only be you because Lirael is your mother."

The world stopped.

I felt it through the bond, the way the revelation pierced Vale's very being.

Her breath left her in a harsh exhale, her pulse hammering through the mate bond, a staccato rhythm of shock and denial.

"I—" She shook her head. "That's not true —"

The Luxa leader's silver eyes softened. "Your parents came to the goddess of the Dreaming for help to stop what we all knew was coming."

A whisper of something old drifted through the air, something almost tender, as if the Dreaming itself was listening.

"And the goddess answered."

The Luxa stepped closer, her gaze unwavering.

"She conjured you from the Dreaming itself. You are not just Luxa, Vale. You are of the Dreaming. Born from it. Bound to it. It's why your power is different. Why Zamarra wants you. Why she will stop at nothing to possess you."

The room trembled.

Vale's hands curled into fists, shaking. "No."

Not a scream. Not a roar of defiance. Just one small word, breaking at the edges.

The Luxa leader canted her head. "You have always felt different... always known you were not like the rest. Because you are more."

Vale flinched.

I moved closer, every instinct screaming at me to do something, to protect her from this, but there was nothing to fight.

Because deep in my heart I knew it was true. It was the only explanation—why the Dreaming always reached for her, why she could pull objects from it, why it called to her more than any Luxa I'd ever met.

The bond pulsed.

The walls shuddered.

The Dreaming watched.

Then the Luxa leader's voice shifted, turning

sharp as glass. "You cannot defeat Zamarra without us. As strong as you are, you will still need our help."

Vale's blazing green eyes snapped to hers. Her breath was still unsteady, but her spine straightened.

The Luxa stepped forward, the silver glow in her gaze burning brighter. "We are the lost."

My pulse hammered.

Vale's fingers flexed at her sides. "What?"

"We have been trapped between realms for centuries. Waiting. Watching." The Luxa's gaze sharpened. "You are the key."

A ripple of power pressed into my chest, into all of us, as the words filled the space.

"Find us. Free us. And we will bring down the sleeping one before she fully wakes."

Vale's magic coiled in the air, no longer snapping wild—but focused. Controlled.

And when she finally spoke, her voice rang clear, steady, commanding.

Unbreakable.

"Tell me where to find you."

The Luxa leader lifted her head, silver-lit eyes burning with something deep, old, knowing. "Follow the fractures."

A pulse of power rippled through the air—not an attack, not a retreat. A parting gift.

She raised a hand—just barely. It wasn't a spell. It wasn't an attack. It was... a call.

The air shifted. A whisper of wind that wasn't wind. A pulse of something felt in the bones. A small satchel on the end table twitched. It was dirty and tattered like it had been through war. *Nyrah's.*

Vale's breath caught as the air in my lungs froze.

Crumpled papers rose into the air. Three, maybe four, edges torn and wrinkled. They didn't fall. They floated, spinning gently, glowing faintly.

The book. The Luxa history book Vale plucked from the Dreaming. It had pages torn from it. Nyrah had them all along.

The Luxa leader's eyes shifted to Vale. Not a command. Not a question. A choice.

Vale reached out, and the pages didn't hesitate. They snapped to her palm, pulsing with energy.

"She sought the answers before you," she whispered, the edges of her body fading. "Now, they are yours."

The room warped around them, the unnatural shadows twisting, curling. The air shimmered, like the space between worlds was fraying at the edges.

And then, they began to fade. Not vanishing.

Unraveling. Like a tapestry being unwoven, thread by thread.

The Dreaming recoiled, retreating, like a beast slinking back into the dark. The room settled. Solidified. But Vale's hands were still trembling around the pages Nyrah had stolen from the book.

Vale inhaled slowly. Deeply.

"Follow the fractures," she whispered as she gently wrapped her fingers around the ripped pages. Then she turned, her green eyes shining like emeralds.

"Get the book."

The room was too quiet in the aftermath of the Luxa's disappearance.

But inside me? There was nothing but chaos.

I shoved my fury, my rage, my despair into a little box inside my head, trying to slam the lid shut before it could consume me. Because if I let it out—if I let myself break again—there would be no coming back from it.

I'd set out to save my sister, and that was exactly what I was going to do.

My gaze flitted to the torn pages in my hands, the weight of them pressing down on my bones. It wasn't just that Nyrah had stolen them. The weight was because they meant something.

She'd hidden them, having the answers before I even thought to look for them.

And now, she was gone.

I clenched my fingers around the fragile papers, my heart pounding, mind racing. The Luxa's words echoed in my skull.

I stared at the torn pages, my breath sharp and uneven. Nyrah's handwriting still marked the edges, hurried notes scrawled in a script I knew better than my own. My throat tightened, a painful, sharp ache pressing into my very soul.

She had found the answer first. And I hadn't even known.

What if this wasn't enough? What if I failed her again?

I wrapped my fingers around the parchment. *No. No more waiting. No more second-guessing.*

"Follow the fractures."

Her voice echoed in my mind, looping over and over again like a chant. A command. An order that was already shoving me forward.

The book. I needed the book.

I turned sharply, locking eyes with Idris, my breath still ragged. "The book. It's in our room."

Xavier shifted immediately, muscles coiling

tight, energy crackling off him like a live wire. "Then why the fuck are we still standing here?"

I didn't answer. I just ran.

The halls blurred around me, my boots pounding against stone—mine first, then theirs. My mates were close on my heels, but I barely noticed.

The castle felt different, like the walls were holding their breath. Like the Dreaming had sunk into the bones of this place and refused to leave. It made my skin crawl, made the magic under my skin itch, and burn like something was trying to get out.

By the time I reached the doors to our room, my pulse was hammering in my ears, louder than the sound of my own breath. I threw the doors open, the hinges groaning under the force. The room was still —too still—a stark contrast to the wildfire burning in my chest.

The book was there, where I'd left it in my pack, but it didn't feel like a book anymore.

It felt like a living thing.

Like it was waiting. Watching. Aware.

I moved without thought, without breath. I dropped to my knees, pressing the torn pages against their place in the binding. The moment the edges met, the ink throbbed. Like a heartbeat. Like recognition.

The book hummed. Not a sound, but a low, insistent vibration that rattled through the floorboards, slithering up my spine. The air thinned, the temperature dropping enough that frost spider-webbed across the nearest window.

The ink on the pages didn't shift or rewrite itself. It had always been waiting to be whole again. It bled outward, stretching, mending the gaps where the pages had been torn.

The book drank in the magic, absorbing it like it had been starved for completion. And then the words surfaced, dark as night, sharp as carved stone.

Ancient. Older than Luxa history. Older than any magic I'd ever seen. A pulse of power shot through me, through my bones, through my blood. Through the room. Through my mates.

Deep. Black. Ancient.

Magic poured off the page, heat rising in waves, too old, too powerful to belong to anything but the Dreaming.

Xavier staggered, a hand flying to his temple. "Fuck—"

Kian flinched, his jaw clenching. "I fucking hate when books do shit like this."

Idris didn't move, but his golden gaze was locked on the book—watching, waiting, calculating—like the book itself had just become a threat.

I understood why. Because the words had weight to them. Like they weren't just meant to be read. They were meant to be *spoken*.

And they were meant for me.

Kian's illusions rippled to life around him, flickering like shadowed afterimages—four of him, shifting between real and unreal, instincts pulling him into defense. His jaw clenched. "I don't fucking like this."

Xavier ran a hand down his face, muttering a string of filthy curses under his breath before snapping, "Tell me we're not walking into another one of Zamarra's fucking traps."

Idris didn't move. But his chest rose slowly, controlled, measured—too measured. His golden eyes had gone fully molten, his pupils sharp slits.

Rune was watching.

The spell whispered through me, spiraling into my bones.

Blood of the First. Light of the Dreaming. Show me the way.

Blood.

The truth settled in my ribs like a weight, like something final, undeniable. For the first time since

Nyrah had been ripped from me, my mind was clear. There was only one way forward.

I barely noticed my own breath. Barely felt my own hands. My dagger was in my palm before I had even registered grabbing it.

Kian moved toward me, a hint of hesitation in his gaze. "Vale, wait—"

The sharp sting of metal cut across my palm.

A sharp, clean cut. No hesitation. Blood beaded, then spilled, sliding over my palm, dripping onto the pages. The scarlet lifeblood smeared across the parchment, soaking into the coal-black ink.

The book shuddered. And then the ink moved. It didn't just absorb the blood. It drank it. The ink twisted, curled, spread like cracks in shattered glass.

Fractures.

Then one line burned. A single point pulsed, glowing like a beacon, like a heartbeat. A location. A weak point in the Dreaming itself.

A path forward.

A door.

Kian exhaled sharply, rubbing at his temple like something had just scraped across his mind. Xavier's fingers twitched, as if he wanted to rip the book from my hands and throw it across the room.

"And what if this is a trap?" Xavier's voice was sharp, razor-edged.

Unflinching, I met his gaze. "Then we fucking spring it. I'm not letting her get her claws into my baby sister, and I'm not leaving Briar to that woman."

It didn't matter if it was a trap to me. I was tired of Zamarra's snares.

The air tightened—not like before. Not violent. Not dangerous. But watching.

The house groaned under an unseen weight, the very foundation seeming to exhale. Not collapsing. Not breaking, but bowing.

I froze. An unknown pressure settled against my skin, my lungs, and my bones. Not a hand. Not a force, but a presence. Like the Dreaming had stretched through the fractures in the map and found me.

And it knew me now.

The walls didn't just breathe—they bent. The air crackled against my skin, a phantom pressure brushing across my arms, my throat, my chest.

Vale.

The voice wasn't spoken. It wasn't whispered.

It was felt.

A hum curled in the marrow of my bones, a presence pressing between the worlds, watching. Waiting.

Idris shifted closer, his hand brushing my back. His voice was steady, low, and tense. "Vale—"

Kian swore under his breath, his illusions rippling, flickering like dying embers. "What the fuck is this? Why does it feel like—"

Xavier snarled and lunged forward, trying to grab my arm—but something stopped him. He swore, shoving against the invisible force, his blade flashing as if he could cut through air.

"Vale, you better tell me this isn't what it fucking looks like." His shoulders bunched, his body coiled to fight. "Of course the fucking book had to be haunted."

But it wasn't the book.

It was me.

Kian's illusions rippled again—but they weren't his anymore. The Dreaming twisted them, warping them into something else, something wrong. He swore, snapping his fingers, banishing them before they could shift into nightmares.

Idris didn't flinch. But Rune pushed forward, his presence a low, simmering heat against my skin, and gods, how I missed it.

This new presence didn't press—it cradled. A

whisper of silk sliding over my skin, enveloping my body like warmth on a wintry night. My heart-beat slowed, calmed, as I tilted my head into its touch.

The air smelled of something ancient, something impossible—moonlight and jasmine, the first breath of dawn.

A voice—soft but distant, familiar as my own in a way I couldn't explain—filled my mind. *"My daughter, my light... you have always been meant for this. You were woven from the Dreaming, Vale. You are stronger than you know. Trust what you are. Follow the path. It will lead you exactly where you are supposed to be."*

The words slid over my senses, threading through my veins, sinking into my bones. My breath hitched—not out of fear, but recognition.

Lirael.

She'd saved me once before. Had pulled me back from the void, had steadied me when I was lost. And now—I felt her. Not just in the voice threading through my senses, but in my very bones. Like I had always been meant to hear her.

She had never been absent.

I just hadn't known how to listen.

The Dreaming wasn't pulling me under, it was

coaxing me forward. It wanted me to find the fractures. It wanted me to follow them.

And then another voice filled my mind—one I worried I'd never hear again.

Rune.

"Listen to your mother, Vale."

His voice enveloped me: steady, warm, familiar. Like the heat of a fire against winter's bite. Like the first deep breath after a storm.

"She's never led you wrong before."

"Trust her."

My breath caught as my fingers curled into fists. I wasn't falling or losing myself. I was being shown the way. I swayed, but a pulse through the mate bond anchored me. Idris. His golden eyes locked on mine—he had felt something, but he didn't know what.

But I would take it on my own terms. With a pulse of magic, I pushed back—not a rejection, but a promise.

"I'm coming."

The weight eased. The house exhaled again, the walls creaking, the pressure fading. The Dreaming did not vanish, but it retreated.

And it left a path in its wake.

A heavy silence fell over the room. I could feel their eyes on me. Waiting. Watching. I turned to them—calm, unwavering. "We're leaving. Now."

Kian exchanged a quick glance with Xavier, both of them tense but resigned. Idris' gaze held mine, searching. He knew something had happened—something just for me. But he didn't ask.

Not yet.

Talek still watched me, his odd, color-shifting eyes burning with something unreadable. He shook his head once, more exhaling than laughing. "You don't stop, do you?"

I met his gaze, waiting for him to challenge me. "Not when it matters. Now are you going to fight with your King or bow out while you still have a chance?"

His gaze shifted to Idris, then back to me. "Him, I could take or leave." A smirk tugged at his lips. "But you? I'll gladly follow a goddess into battle, my Queen. Just say the word."

I turned, gripping the book tighter, the map now etched in blood and fractures.

A promise.

A destination.

A warning.

I met each of their gazes, one by one. Idris. Kian. Xavier. Talek.

"No more waiting. No more running. No more fucking games. We bring them back. One way or another. Understood?"

At their chorus of nods, I lifted my chin. "Then get your weapons."

CHAPTER 21

KIAN

The house was too quiet.

That wasn't right. Not after what just happened. Not after the Dreaming had looked at us. Not after Vale had stood there, hands covered in blood and fractured light, and told us exactly where we were going.

She should've been shaking. She should've been uncertain.

But she wasn't.

She was standing there, one hand on the book, her jaw tight, green eyes glowing in the dim candle-light, like she was *carved* out of something more than just flesh and bone.

Like she belonged to the Dreaming itself.

It made something inside my chest squeeze *too hard*.

"Vale," I said, my voice lower than I meant it to be. "You wanna explain to me why you're so fucking sure about all this?"

Vale gripped the book like it was the only thing keeping her tethered to the ground.

Her breathing was even, too even. The kind of calm that came before a storm, the kind I'd seen before a battlefield of slaughtered men who weren't prepared for it. My gut twisted. I didn't like this. I didn't like the look in her eyes, the surety in her stance —like she'd made peace with something we hadn't.

Then she exhaled. "I died."

The room stopped. No breath. No sound. Just that quiet, suffocating pause where the world wasn't sure whether to keep turning.

Xavier stiffened first, his entire body tensing like he'd just been punched. "Vale—"

"I died," she repeated, her voice quiet and steady. Too steady. "When I tried to merge Rune and Idris the first time—when I failed. My heart stopped before I could finish it."

Something ugly and sharp lodged in my chest.

I knew. Of course I knew. I was fucking there. I

saw her body go slack, saw the light in her eyes flicker out. I remembered how it felt—standing there, watching my mate die, and being unable to do a damn thing about it.

But hearing her say it now? Like a fact, like something already buried in the past?

Like she'd made peace with it, and we hadn't?

No. Fuck that.

Idris was the only one who didn't react—because he'd already known. Rune knew. Of course they had.

But Xavier—Xavier was staring at her like she'd just cracked the ground open beneath him.

Vale inhaled. "Lirael brought me back."

Xavier's throat bobbed as he swallowed hard.

I clenched my fists. My mouth opened to say something, but nothing would come out. I had no words. Nothing. I had a lot to say, but I just couldn't. Not yet.

"You were gone," Idris murmured. "We all felt you go."

She nodded. "She told me my time wasn't up." Her fingers curled around the book. "And now, she's telling me to trust what I am. Who I am." She lifted her gaze, and something deep and unwavering settled there. "And after everything, I have to believe her."

I exhaled sharply, shaking my head. Fuck. I turned, raking a hand through my hair, forcing down the sharp, visceral instinct to grab her and make her stay.

Because what the hell was I supposed to do with that? She had already died. And she still wanted to walk straight into the lion's den?

I clenched my jaw. "I don't fucking like it."

She huffed a quiet breath. "Noted."

Xavier let out a long, slow exhale, dragging a hand down his face. "I think what Kian means is that none of us like knowing we can't protect you from this. We weren't even the ones who brought you back."

Vale's gaze softened. "But I am back. And now, I'm going to save my sister because I know she's telling me the truth. I was made for this."

My pulse hammered, my mind already working through contingencies, exits, fallback points. I needed a plan. I needed a way to keep her alive—again.

I wouldn't lose her twice.

I moved forward, crossing the space between us in three strides, ignoring the weight of Idris' stare and Xavier's tension. I stopped just close enough to press a hand to her hip, my fingers curling into the fabric of her tunic as I fought off the urge to toss her over my shoulder and race off the continent so she would be safe.

"If you die again," I muttered, "I'm going to be fucking pissed."

Vale's lips twitched. "Good."

Idris had been standing beside her, silent, his golden eyes dark with something unreadable. But at that, something in him shifted—like something had just clicked into place. He reached out, his fingers brushing her wrist, grounding her.

She let out a slow breath. "We don't have time to waste," she continued. "If the fractures are visible here, if the Dreaming is already bleeding into this world—then it means Zamarra is closer to waking than we thought."

I exhaled through my nose. My grip on her tunic was too tight. I made myself loosen my fingers.

Fine. We were doing this.

There was something ritualistic about getting ready for a fight.

Shifters often undressed for a battle, refusing to lose gear or weapons to the changes in our bodies. Vale, meanwhile, did the opposite.

She tightened the buckles on the leathers covering her arms, adjusted the straps at her waist, prepared like she was walking onto a battlefield rather than mounting a dragon's back. Because in a way—she was.

Talek muttered something under his breath as he pulled his own armor into place. He rolled his shoulders like his body was still weighed down by the magic that still clung to him in faint wisps. Like he was unraveling from the inside.

He was drained. Even if he wouldn't admit it.

"You good?" I asked, because I wasn't that much of an asshole.

He shot me a dry look. "I'm always good. Even when I'm not."

Idris exhaled, cracking his knuckles. "You used a lot of magic earlier."

Talek didn't respond, but he didn't have to. He was exhausted—anyone with half a brain could see it.

There was a brief pause before Idris lifted his palm, his magic flaring to life. "Take some."

Talek's eyes snapped to his, sharp with immediate refusal. "No."

"You're running on fumes," Idris said flatly. "Take some."

Talek's jaw tightened. I wasn't sure if it was pride or sheer stubbornness, but he didn't move. Idris didn't, either. Just waited. It took a long moment before Talek finally let out a slow breath, stepped forward, and pressed his palm to Idris'.

Magic lashed between them—sharp, bright, like a blade dragging through the air. Sparks crackled across their skin, power arcing from Idris' palm to Talek's fingers, disappearing into him as if he were drinking in a storm.

Talek swayed, just slightly, then exhaled, rolling his shoulders like he'd just dropped a heavy-laden weight.

When it was done, he pulled back, flexing his fingers as if he were testing them. He huffed. "I'll pretend I don't owe you for that."

Idris smirked. "I was planning on pretending the same."

The house groaned behind us as we stepped into the night, the last remnants of its warmth shutting out like a door closing behind us. Cold air bit at my skin, but I barely felt it.

Because for the first time, I saw them. The fractures.

Jagged lines of glowing light stretched across the sky, sharp and unnatural, as though someone had taken a knife to the fabric of the world. They pulsed in time with something I couldn't name—something deeper, older, something watching. I swore under my breath. The map hadn't lied.

The fractures were real. And they were everywhere.

Vale stopped dead beside me, her green eyes locked on the sky. "Gods."

Xavier let out a slow, steady exhale. "Well. That's fucking ominous."

Idris said nothing, but his gaze tracked the fractures, sharp and assessing.

Even Talek—who never shut up—was quiet, his expression unreadable as the light of the fractures reflected in his strange, shifting eyes.

I lifted my arms above my head, stretching, forcing the tension down. We didn't have time to stand around staring at the sky. I turned back to my brothers. "Shift."

Xavier was already unstrapping his weapons, pulling them free and stuffing them into the leather satchel that would hang around his neck once he shifted. Idris did the same, moving with his usual efficiency, his expression tight, controlled. I shoved my own weapons into my satchel and pulled my shirt over my head.

Vale, meanwhile, was strapping the book to her chest beneath her armor.

I caught her wrist before she could pull away. "You stay on Idris. Talek's with me."

She frowned. "I could—"

"I'm not fucking arguing with you." My voice was sharper than I meant it, but I didn't care. "You're safer with him."

Vale's mouth pressed into a thin line, but after a moment, she nodded.

The shift happened in quick succession.

Idris went first. The air around him warped, rippling outward in a blast of heat, and a moment later, the massive scarlet dragon, who had once been my King, stretched his wings wide. Xavier followed, the crackle of magic vibrating through the air as he changed, pale and sleek in the night.

Then I let go.

The shift slammed through me, wrenching muscle and bone, tearing me apart to remake me into something more. Power flooded every inch of my being as I stretched into my full form, wings snapping wide, talons sinking into the dirt beneath me.

Talek let out a low, impressed whistle. "You lot are ridiculous."

I paid him no mind, my gaze locked on my mate. My mate that was not moving. Not an inch.

She was standing rigid, still as stone, staring at Idris' massive form like it was the enemy, like it was something she had to conquer but wasn't sure she could. Her breath had turned shallow, too controlled, like she was forcing herself to be fine when she wasn't.

Fuck. I forgot.

Vale wasn't just *afraid* of heights. She was terrified of them. After being forced to watch people die from falling in the Guild, this wasn't just discomfort. It was a trauma response.

She tried to mask it, but I saw the way her fingers trembled against the straps of her pack. Saw the stiffness in her shoulders, the way her jaw locked tight.

And I hated that she was scared. Hated that, once again, circumstances were forcing her to do this. Hated that I couldn't stop the fear clawing at her chest the way I wanted to.

But there was no other way.

I barely flicked my tail before Idris moved. He turned his massive scarlet and gold head toward her, lowering it, slow and steady. He exhaled softly, his breath ruffling her hair, warm instead of scorching. He wasn't rushing her.

Neither did I.

She had already agreed to this. She had already decided she was going to do this. She just needed a second.

Idris made a low rumble in the back of his throat, something soft, something soothing.

Vale closed her eyes, just for a second. Then she let out a breath, grabbed the ridges of his scales, and hauled herself up.

I felt Xavier's pulse through the bond, steady and careful.

"You good, Vale?" Idris' voice was quiet, even in my mind.

Her grip tightened. *"No. But I won't let that stop me."*

I turned away before I did something stupid, like telling her we could find another way, and shook out my wings before lowering myself enough for Talek to climb on.

Talek exhaled sharply as he hauled himself onto my back. "You're all very casual about using me as an accessory."

I didn't answer because frankly? I couldn't feel him.

On my back, he weighed about as much as a feather. I didn't want to bruise his ego by saying as much, but luckily in this form I didn't have to bite my tongue. Unfortunately, that didn't stop Vale from hearing me, anyway.

My voice slid into her mind, dry as hell. *"Apologies, your highness. Should I make sure my scales are softer next time so your delicate ass is more comfortable?"*

Vale snorted. Loudly. Then she let out the most beautiful laugh—one I'd been dying to hear for days now.

Talek blinked. "What the fuck did he just say? I know he said something."

Vale coughed, struggling not to grin as she tightened her grip on Idris' spines. "Nothing."

Her heartbeat eased in my chest, her fear dimming. I huffed out a breath as I met Idris' gaze.

"Let's go."

The wind howled as we tore through the sky, our wings cutting through the night like blades. The world below shrank, swallowed by darkness, while ahead, the fractures bled light into the night.

Vale was too quiet.

She clung to Idris' back, her fingers locked around his spines in a white-knuckled grip. Her breathing was too controlled, her entire body coiled, as if she were forcing herself to be fine when she wasn't.

I felt it. Sharp. Visceral.

Xavier's voice crackled through the bond, low and careful. *"Vale, you're safe."*

She didn't answer. Didn't loosen her grip.

Then she did something that cracked my chest wide open.

She pressed her forehead against Idris' scales, but only for a second.

A breath of trust.

A moment of grounding.

Then she straightened, her shoulders set, and her fingers flexed slightly against his hide.

That was it. Just a moment. But I felt it settle in my very being.

Good girl.

I forced my attention back to the sky—back to the fractures.

At first, they were just glowing wounds in the world—crawling over mountains, winding through forests, cutting through rivers. Some were thin, barely visible. Others were deep, gaping fissures, splitting the land like a blade through flesh.

And then I realized something else.

They weren't static. They were moving. Shifting. Like something on the other side was trying to push through.

A low growl rumbled through my chest. Xavier let out a sharp snort from my left, and I felt him glance toward me. *"You see it, too?"*

"Yeah."

Ahead, Vale turned slightly, her hair whipping in the wind. *"The Dreaming is shifting. The fractures are getting worse."*

Great.

Then, a voice cut cleanly through the rushing wind, crisp and unnaturally clear.

Not a shout. Not a yell. A whisper carried on the air.

Talek. "We're being followed."

I didn't react outwardly, but I flicked a glance behind us. He wasn't wrong. In the distance, far below, shadows slithered through the fractures. Moving. Twisting. Watching.

Zamarra's creatures.

Talek's voice rose on the wind again, his magic carrying it straight to me. "They're not attacking yet." He paused for a beat. "They're watching."

I bared my teeth as heat coiled in my chest. *"Then let's move faster."*

We cut through the night like a blade, chasing the fractures as they bled across the land. The farther we went, the more real they became. They weren't just cracks anymore.

They were bleeding.

And up ahead, I saw it. A convergence. The fractures twisting together, merging into something denser. A focal point.

A door.

A low vibration throbbed through my bones. Not an attack. Not yet. Something was waiting.

And that's when the sky erupted.

They came from everywhere.

Shadows ripped free from the fractures below, exploding upward in a storm of black fire and claws, their skull-splitting screeches deafening.

A pulse of dark magic slammed into my chest, forcing me to snap my wings wide to counter the force. I snarled, whipping my head around as another blast shot toward Xavier.

He twisted sharply, his pale form cutting through the sky as he narrowly dodged.

The creatures were wrong. They flickered between solid and smoke, reforming mid-lunge. They moved too fast, like they were skipping through time. And when Idris crushed one in his jaws, it shattered into black glass.

But it didn't stay dead. No, the shards twisted and writhed, reforming before my eyes.

"Well, that's fucking great."

Talek cursed every god he knew of as we banked to avoid them. "Of fucking course. Because why would this ever be fucking easy?"

His voice carried effortlessly through the howling wind, his magic slicing through the storm like a razor.

I bared my teeth. *"Remember when all we had to worry about was Girovian mages with dragon bolts?"*

Xavier snorted through the bond as his talons shredded another shadow. *"Damn, I miss those days."*

Then one grabbed Vale.

It happened in a flash: a blur of shifting shadows, claws wrapping around her like a noose.

Before Xavier or I could get to her, Talek ripped the air apart. A blast of wind howled between us, peeling the creature back before it could wrench her from Idris' back.

I snapped my jaws shut, catching it midair. It shattered between my teeth, dissolving into smoke.

Vale's grip tightened, but her voice rang clear

through the link. *"Stop talking and start killing these fuckers."*

Xavier let out a sharp, rumbling laugh, already twisting midair, his wings beating hard as he spun to face the oncoming wave.

"Gladly."

I didn't hesitate. I let the heat in my chest build. Let it grow wild, feral, uncontrollable.

Then I opened my jaws and let hell rain down.

But my flames could only do so much.

Talek's voice cut through the chaos. "Something's coming. Bigger."

I didn't need to ask what. I didn't even want to know what. Too bad I most definitely would find out.

The fractures below pulsed violently. Something was pushing through. The creatures weren't attacking anymore—no, they were falling back.

Not retreating. *Waiting*.

Xavier banked toward the convergence. *"We need to move—now."*

Idris surged forward, Vale holding tight.

The convergence opened —a slashing tear in reality itself, pulling us forward.

I unleashed one last burst of dragon fire, carving

a burning path through the creatures still swarming below.

The moment we crossed the threshold, I felt it. A ripping sensation, like something had just grabbed hold of my ribs and yanked me forward.

The world fractured.

One of the creatures slipped through with us. With a final shadow-laced snarl, its twisted form flickered between solid and smoke. Mangled claws stretched for me—for Vale.

Then the world wrenched sideways.

The convergence tore open wider, the pull of it a force stronger than gravity, stronger than the wind. A rush of silver light, burning cold and endless.

The Dreaming swallowed us whole.

As a violent crack of reality split apart, everything fractured, ricocheting through my chest.

And then, we fell.

CHAPTER 22

VALE

We kept falling.

Silver light swallowed us whole, stretching out in every direction. There was no sky, no ground—just a weightless descent into nowhere.

I couldn't breathe. Not from pain, not from fear, but because the Dreaming itself was breathing around us. The air pulsed. A heartbeat, too deep, too vast, vibrating through my bones.

Then, everything snapped.

First, the ground wasn't there, and then it was.

I hit *hard*. The impact should have shattered me, it should have broken bones, but instead, it was soft. Like sand, like silk. Shifting, shifting—then suddenly, solid.

I gasped, the air was thick and wrong in my lungs.

Somewhere beside me, Talek swore. "Fucking —" He cut himself off, rolling onto his hands and knees, his usually wild magic crackling uneasily around him. His gaze flicked to the silver-lit sky. "This place feels... wrong."

Xavier growled, pushing himself up, his pale, iridescent scales blinking bright in the never-ending light. A heavy, dragging breath pulled from Idris' lungs as he stood, his massive body trembling for a breath before he found his balance. Then Kian let out a low, sharp growl.

The moment we landed, the Dreaming settled. The ground stopped shifting, the pulse in the air slowing. Everything stilled.

And then something *moved*.

Talek stiffened. His nostrils flared, his color-shifting gaze snapping to the shadows. "That's not—"

A snarl tore through the stillness—sharp and wrong.

I twisted toward the sound—just in time to see it rising.

The last of Zamarra's creatures.

I shoved to my knees, my breath sharp as the beast unfurled from the darkness, blotting out the light. It was different now. Bigger. More real. No longer flickering between shadow and smoke, no longer just something summoned from the fractures.

Now the Dreaming had twisted it into something worse. A creature of pure void, its body moved like black fire, but its limbs?

Those were solid—too solid.

Its claws, sharpened to razor points, gleamed, even in the strange silver glow of this place. And it was coming right for me.

Kian was already moving. He lunged first, his massive dragon form snapping toward the beast with brutal force—only for his jaws to clamp down on empty air. The shadow passed through him like mist, reforming on the other side.

"Oh, fuck this," Talek snarled, slamming his hands forward. The wind roared, a force meant to rip the creature apart—but it didn't even shift. Talek bared his teeth. "Are you shitting me?"

Xavier snarled, his pale-blue eyes narrowing. Magic curled around his claws, power building—then releasing in a blast of blue flame. It burned, searing hot, but the beast didn't scream. It didn't even slow. The fire licked over its body, slipping off like it wasn't even there.

"*Shit,*" Xavier hissed.

Idris braced his stance, golden eyes flashing. *"It's not corporeal. Our magic won't work."*

Kian twisted midair, banking hard to avoid another lunge. *"Well, that's fucking convenient."*

I knew.

I didn't know how I knew, but I did. This thing wasn't something my mates could fight. But I could.

I moved without thinking, and the Dreaming answered my plea before I even asked. Light flared in my hands, unbidden and alive. I didn't summon it. I didn't shape it. It shaped itself.

A dagger materialized, gleaming and wicked, formed from pure light. It wasn't the first I'd ever conjured, but this was something more. This wasn't just my light—this was pure magic pulled directly from the Dreaming.

The creature lunged for me as I leapt for it, far faster than I should have. It swung, claws streaking toward my throat.

I ducked, twisting beneath its reach, then drove the dagger into its chest.

The creature screamed—a bitter plaintive cry that threatened to shatter my skull. It wasn't like before—not like the others, no black mist, no dissolving into nothing.

It *shattered*.

A burst of darkness ripped apart, pieces of it distorting, writhing, and then the Dreaming devoured it.

I stood there, my chest heaving, hands clenched around the blade. The dagger pulsed once before it vanished into thin air.

Silence descended as I tried to grasp what I had just done.

Xavier exhaled sharply, his voice reeling through the bond. *"What the fuck was that?"*

Talek didn't hear him, but he didn't need to. His magic was still snapping at the edges, the Dreaming's pulse twisting through the air. He let out a slow breath, rubbing at his forearm like he was trying to shake off a static charge.

"That was *not* normal," Talek muttered, casting a wary glance at the shifting air around us. His voice was low but edged with something uneasy. "You didn't just kill that thing, Vale. You changed something."

Kian, still in dragon form, stepped forward, his molten amber eyes narrowing at me. *"Vale?"*

I lifted my chin, the power still thrumming

beneath my skin. *"Me. There might be something to this whole 'born of the Dreaming' nonsense."*

My words settled between us, heavier than the silence.

Then Idris shifted. His great dragon form melted away, his golden magic curling around him until he was standing in front of me once more, but he didn't say anything.

He just reached out, fingers brushing mine, feeling the power still crackling against my skin. The power of the Dreaming.

Of who I was.

I let out a slow, steady breath and met his gaze.

The Dreaming wasn't done with me yet.

It shifted as the silver light that stretched into eternity pulsated, deep and rhythmic, like the breath of something vast and ancient. The ground beneath my feet rippled, not like solid earth, but like something alive, something aware.

The air felt different now, charged with a quiet knowing. I exhaled slowly, trying to steady myself as the last echoes of the creature's existence faded into nothing. My body still hummed with power, the pulse of the Dreaming settling in my bones.

Then, the air moved.

No footsteps. No warning.

Just a whisper of light, forming shapes.

A dozen figures emerged from the glow. Not stepping forward, not appearing, but becoming. Their bodies flickered, shifting between solid and translucent, as if they weren't fully here, not completely separate from the Dreaming itself.

The Luxa.

I knew them instantly, not by their faces—most were unfamiliar, their features blurred at the edges —but by their presence. A shimmering thread of recognition tightened in my chest. The Dreaming was part of them. And now, they stood before me.

A woman in the front moved closer. Her hair was pale as starlight, her form draped in flowing silver that melted into the space around her. She didn't walk so much as drift, the air shifting lazily with her movements.

Her gaze found mine.

"You came," she murmured. Her voice wasn't a sound, not really. It was a feeling, a resonance that settled deep into my bones.

"It's not like you gave her much of a choice," Kian muttered beside me, his stance still braced like a fight might break out at any second.

The woman's unreadable gaze flicked toward him briefly, then back to me.

"You are as she said you would be," she said. "Just as Lirael promised."

At the name, my throat tightened. My... *mother*. The being who had created me from this place. I was still having trouble wrapping my mind around it.

"What is this?" Idris asked, his voice low and controlled, though I could feel the tension threading through our bond. "Why are you still here?"

The woman directed her full attention to him. "Because we had to be."

Her words hung between us, heavy with meaning.

Another figure stepped forward, a woman with sharp, angular features and a gaze like fractured light. "Two hundred years ago, we should have died. Our magic should have burned out when Zamarra took everything from us." Her voice was rougher, more human, more real.

"But we fled," she continued. "We clung to what little we had left and escaped into the Dreaming before we could be destroyed completely."

Xavier let out a pensive growl . *"And now?"*

The woman looked at me. Only at me. "Now, we give what remains to you."

Silence. It stretched on for what seemed like an eternity.

Meanwhile, her words dropped like a stone in my chest. I already knew what she meant before she said it, but hearing it aloud sent a chill through my veins.

They weren't just giving me power.

They planned on giving me themselves.

Kian tensed beside me, his wings ruffling as his entire body tensed. *"No."* His voice was low, sharp— an order wrapped in fear. *"She can't take any more power. You don't know what it does to her."*

"We do," the woman said softly, answering my mate, even though she shouldn't be able to hear him. "And so does she." Her gaze met mine, full of quiet knowing.

I swallowed hard, my throat tight. "If you do this... what happens to you?"

The Luxa didn't hesitate. "We move on."

The way she said it—gentle, unafraid—sent an ice-cold tremor racing up and down the length of my spine.

"No." Kian's voice turned dangerous. *"Fuck that. Find another way."*

Xavier's power crackled through the air, the bond between us throbbing with a storm of emotions. *"Vale."* His voice was taut, fraying at the edges. *"Tell me you're not actually considering this."*

I clenched my fists. "I don't want to do this." My voice was quiet, but it still cut like a knife. "I don't want to take this risk. I don't want to leave you."

The bond pulsed, grief and rage coiling around me.

Kian's expression twisted. *"Then don't."*

I let out a shaky breath. "I made a promise."

Xavier let out a sharp, ragged exhale, pacing like he needed to move, or he'd explode. *"To your parents before they died."*

"And to all of you." My throat burned, but I kept going. "I swore I would stop Zamarra. I swore we would win. And I can't do that like this. She's too powerful."

Xavier's tail snapped, his eyes wild. *"Then we'll find another way—"*

"We don't have time." My voice cracked. "Nyrah doesn't have time."

My words hit like a blow, and they all felt it.

Idris closed his eyes for the briefest second. Then his golden gaze locked onto mine, fierce and steady. "My brave one," he murmured. "Are you sure?"

No, I wasn't sure. I wasn't sure of anything. But I knew exactly what would happen if I did nothing.

I inhaled slowly, my voice barely above a whisper. "I don't want to die."

Kian let out a guttural snarl, his body shimmering with the telltale heat of magic. In a flash of golden fire, his dragon form melted away, leaving him standing there, bare-chested, fury burning in his molten gaze. He took a sharp step toward me, fists clenched. "Then *don't*."

"I don't plan to." I forced my shoulders back, trying to steady the tremor in my breath. "But I have to try. I have to keep my promise."

Kian swore, turning away like he couldn't look at me.

Xavier exhaled hard, his massive wings flaring wide before snapping tight to his sides. His head tilted back, a deep, rumbling growl vibrating through his chest—like he was pleading to the gods without words.

Idris was watching me with something unreadable in his molten gaze, his magic curling against mine like an unspoken plea.

They all hated this.

So did I.

But I still stepped forward.

Kian made a low, guttural sound of frustration— his fury, his fear—before he stormed closer and caught my chin in his fingers, forcing me to meet his gaze.

"If this starts killing you," he rasped, "we stop it. I don't give a fuck what happens after that. Do you understand me?"

I nodded, my throat too tight to speak.

He let out a slow, shaking breath and pressed his forehead against mine. "I hate this."

"I know."

Xavier's jaw clenched, his massive body vibrating with barely contained emotion. *"Vale—"*

I turned to him, moving closer, pressing a hand to the thick scales over his chest, feeling the deep, powerful thrum of his heart beneath my palm.

"I choose you," I whispered. "I choose all of you."

Xavier let out a ragged breath, his dragon form dissolving into shadows and light. When he stood before me again, his bare chest heaved as his hand covered mine, fingers tightening. "Then stay."

I let out a breath, something breaking inside me. "That's the plan."

It was a promise—one I intended to keep.

The woman lifted her hand, her fingers glowing with soft, burning light.

"This is not a burden," she whispered. "It is a gift."

My hands were trembling, but I reached out, anyway.

The moment my fingers brushed hers, light erupted—not a simple glow, not a shimmer, but an explosion that split the air like a crack of lightning. The Dreaming surged, the very fabric of it folding over my senses like an unstoppable tide.

I gasped, but there was no pain—only fire. Not the kind that burned, but the kind that remade. It sank into my skin, my veins, my bones, forging me into something else, something more. The air vibrated with the power—a pulse of energy so intense it felt like a second heartbeat slamming into my chest.

The Luxas' forms wavered, their outlines breaking apart—not gently, not peacefully, but like glass fracturing under pressure. The woman's lips curved into the faintest smile, but her body was already scattering, the pieces lifting into the air, like threads being unwoven from existence.

The Dreaming itself shuddered.

A ripple spread outward, warping the space around us, sending a deep, resonant hum through the ground, through my body, through my soul. My mates felt it, too—Kian snarled, his hands reaching for me, Xavier staggered as he clutched his chest, and Idris let out a ragged breath, golden eyes burning as if he could see what was happening inside me.

One by one, the Luxa faded, their remnants streaking through the air like falling stars. Their power wasn't just filling me. It was changing me.

The Dreaming itself exhaled—a final, breathless sigh.

Their voices, their magic, their very essence settled into my bones, into the very fabric of my existence. The last echoes of laughter, of sorrow, of love, filled my heart before the Dreaming took them home.

And then, the light collapsed inward.

For one breathless moment, everything compressed, squeezing so tight I thought I might shatter. My pulse skipped—once, twice—before it detonated outward, a final burst of raw, blinding force that shook the ground beneath me.

The power settled.

The Luxa were gone.

And for the first time, the Dreaming was quiet.

CHAPTER 23

VALE

I exhaled sharply, my body trembling, burning from the force of it. The light inside me coiled like something alive—too much, too vast, too deep. It wasn't settling—it was stretching, expanding beyond the limits of my skin, filling the space between my ribs until I thought I might break.

My legs buckled as the world tilted.

Strong hands caught me before I could collapse.

Idris. Kian. Xavier.

Their touch grounded me, anchoring me to reality, even as my body shuddered beneath the weight of the power now thrumming inside me.

Taking a step back, Talek hovered, his expression tense and wary. He didn't reach for me, but his sharp eyes scanned my face, tracking every tremor, every breath. He didn't know what was happening, but he knew enough to be on guard.

Idris' grip was firm, unwavering. His warmth bled into me, steady, solid, and unshakable—a tether pulling me back from the edge of something I didn't understand.

Xavier was there, too, his palm pressing against my back, fingers splayed, his breath warm against my temple. A silent promise, unspoken, but felt through the bond: "I've got you."

And Kian—Kian's presence coiled through the bond like a vice, sharp with worry. His fear wasn't loud, wasn't spoken, but I felt it in the way his magic ghosted against mine, like he was testing, searching, making sure I was still here.

But I wasn't.

Not completely.

The power in my chest vibrated. My vision blurred—

"Shit," Talek muttered under his breath.

I barely heard him before I was gone. Not watching. Not distant. I was *in* it.

I stood in a grand temple—no, what was left of it. The golden stone was already cracking, magic unraveling from the walls like dying veins. The Luxa were here, their bodies bent in agony as their power was ripped from them, as the temple groaned beneath the weight of an ending.

The sky above churned with silver and black, the Dreaming itself screaming in protest.

And at the center of it all—

Idris.

Not as he was now, but as he had been. A king in golden armor, blood streaked across his face, his power pulsing at his core—whole. Still whole.

I wanted to run to him. To stop this. To rip the magic apart with my bare hands. But I couldn't move. I could only watch.

Standing across from him was Zamarra.

She was beautiful. Terrible. A being of luminous grace, her pale hands stretched outward, fingers delicate as she pulled at the strands of power, weaving them tighter, binding them together with an expertise that made me sick.

Her expression wasn't cruel. It wasn't gloating. It was focused. She knew what she was doing. Knew what this would cost. Knew exactly what her magic was about to break.

This wasn't emotion. This wasn't rage.

This was science. This was her craft.

She didn't revel in it. She didn't cackle or sneer. She simply worked.

She was so focused, so intent, that it took me a moment to see him.

Arden.

He was standing beside her, his face alight with devotion. Not to his brother. Not to his blood.

To her.

His hands moved in tandem with hers, his own magic threading into the curse, reinforcing it. Strengthening it. Feeding it. He didn't hesitate, didn't falter, didn't even look at Idris writhing before him.

Zamarra whispered something I couldn't hear.

And Arden smiled, a slow, terrible thing, as if this betrayal were a gift.

My stomach twisted. My heartbeat pounded in my ears.

Zamarra lifted her chin. And for the first time, I saw it. The moment she realized. The moment she knew.

Idris had loved her. Not as an infatuation, not as a passing romance. But as something more. And she didn't hesitate for a moment.

Idris was fighting it. His body strained, his hands fisting at his sides, his power fighting back—

But the curse was stronger.

The moment it took hold, I felt it—the severing. The pulling. The undoing.

Idris let out a strangled gasp, his back arching—his

golden eyes going wide as the magic tore into him, burrowing deep, tearing something apart. Not something.

Someone.

A roar shattered the temple as Rune ripped free from his skin.

The dragon erupted from him, bursting into being in an explosion of fractured light. A great scarlet beast, claws scraping across the golden stone, his wings beating wildly—fighting what had been done.

But the bond was already gone.

Rune stumbled, massive golden eyes wide with confusion, with panic. His mouth opened, but there was no voice. No thoughts through the link.

He turned—instinct pulling him toward Idris, but Idris was collapsing. The scream that followed wasn't a scream at all. It was a death. It was a severing.

It was a soul being torn apart.

He hit the ground hard, panting, his hands clawing at his chest, as if trying to grasp something that was no longer there. His power had been ripped in half, and he had no way to reach what had been stolen.

And then the curse settled.

The power locked inside Rune, swelling and destabilizing. The air shuddered. The magic of Credour fractured. The world broke apart at the seams.

And still—Zamarra wove the spell.

Still—Arden watched with devotion.

Still—the Luxa fell.

My people, the dream-walkers, the light-bearers. Their bodies wavered between form and formlessness, their light dimming, draining. Their screams tore through the air, soundless in this place, but I still felt vibrations of agony in my bones.

One by one, their bodies crumpled, the last remnants of their power siphoned into the curse. The temple trembled, the stones cracking, their golden light dimming as their lives were extinguished. The last Luxa, the leader— the woman who had spoken to me—reached for something, her gaze lifting skyward.

The last thing I saw was Idris reaching for Rune— his fingers stretching toward the great beast that had been his.

And Rune turned away—not because he wanted to, but because he had no choice.

I gasped, my knees buckling, the world careening back into focus. The ground was solid again. My heart slammed against my ribs. My breath came too fast, too sharp, my lungs trying to catch up to a body that no longer felt like mine.

Hands caught me—strong, steady.

Idris.

Kian.

Xavier.

They were here. They were real.

And Idris' golden eyes burned as he looked at me. "Vale?" His voice was raw.

I swallowed hard, my entire body trembling with the weight of what I had just seen. "They didn't just curse you," I whispered.

His grip tightened as his gaze burned even brighter. Idris' pain, rage, and betrayal—it was palpable—I could feel it through the bond.

"They tore you apart."

And Arden had let her. No. Helped her.

I felt it now—the hatred bubbling beneath my skin, the fury clawing its way up my throat. Zamarra had been a monster. But Arden? He had been worse. He'd loved his brother, and he had betrayed him, anyway.

The curse had settled. The temple had fallen. The Luxa had been stripped bare, their bodies flickering like dying stars. Everything had been lost.

And yet, somewhere beyond the ruins, beyond the devastation, beyond the grave of what had been —hope still remained.

A whisper cut through the Dreaming. Soft. Steady. Not magic, not a spell—a prayer—and I was pulled into a vision as reality around me shifted.

The shattered temple, the broken bodies, the echoes of betrayal—they faded. Instead, I was standing in the Dreaming. But this time, it was whole. Vast. Infinite. The night sky swirled into a spiral of colors stretched in every direction, a place unbound by the rules of the mortal world.

And at the center of it—

Them.

I knew them. I had always known them. Their faces, their voices, the way their love had shaped every moment of my childhood, even in the direst of places.

My parents.

They were kneeling before a figure wreathed in light, a goddess standing in the heart of creation itself.

Lirael.

Her presence filled the Dreaming like a rising dawn, her hair shifting with the silver glow of the stars, her gaze vast and endless as the sky itself.

My father's voice broke on a whisper, a plea carved from his very soul.

"Please, my goddess."

My mother clutched at her robes, fingers trembling. She had lost everything. I had never heard her voice like this—raw, breaking. Not the steady strength I remem-

bered. Not the quiet warmth that had carried me through my childhood.

"We need your help. We can't do this on our own."

Lirael did not move. Did not speak.

She only watched them—watched the grief that had hollowed them out, watched the prayers that had been whispered into the void, the love and the desperation wrapped in every syllable.

"You ask for salvation," Lirael murmured.

My father swallowed hard. His hands were shaking. "We ask for hope."

Lirael lifted her hands to her chest before drawing it away with light gathered in her palms. The light curled, shifted, reformed, and all too soon, an infant was nestled against her chest.

A child. Small, fragile, but burning with something vast.

The breath wrenched from my lungs.

Lirael held the baby tighter, pressing a kiss to her forehead, a tear falling down her cheek as she offered the infant to them.

She did not say, "This is my daughter," or "This is your salvation." She didn't have to.

And my parents—my mother, my father, the people who had loved me, raised me—reached for the baby.

For me.

Tears blurred my vision. I wanted to scream, to cry out, to warn them. I wanted to tell them what this would mean, what would happen. But I was powerless to stop what had already been.

I watched, helpless, as they took me into their arms, held me close, whispered promises into my newborn skin.

"We will love her."

"We will protect her."

"We will keep her safe."

And Lirael, the goddess who had given me to them, only whispered one thing in return.

"Until it is time for you to let her go."

The Dreaming wavered. Shifted.

The vision of my parents blurred, their whispered promises fading like echoes on the wind. I reached for them—too late. The world around me bent, twisted, and then I was somewhere else.

Pain. It wasn't mine, but I felt it.

It dragged me under, sharp and unrelenting, sinking deep into my bones. The air around me grew thick, vibrating with magic—old, hungry, and devouring. Shadows curled along the edges of my vision, twisting, shifting, feeding.

And then I saw Nyrah.

She was on her knees, wrists bound, golden skin pallid, her breaths coming in weak, trembling gasps.

Her light was flickering—too dim. Draining. Being taken.

And Zamarra—

Zamarra stood over her like a goddess in the dark.

No, not a goddess. Something worse. Something that had been broken and reforged into something stronger, something terrible. She was almost whole now. The hollowness in her face was gone. The cracks in her form had sealed, her magic burning with cruel, unyielding life.

She met my gaze, smiled, and then the Dreaming shattered.

A hand closed over mine.

I gasped, my vision snapping back into focus, the weight of the Dreaming pressing against me. My heartbeat thundered in my ears, my skin still burning from the echoes of what I had seen.

Idris.

His golden eyes bore into mine, searching, anchoring me to the present. "Vale." His voice was rough, a command and a plea wrapped into one. "What did you see?"

I shuddered. The images burned behind my eyes —Nyrah's fading light, Zamarra's terrible smile, the magic still siphoning, still taking. But worse than that—Arden was nowhere to be seen.

And that made my blood run cold.

I lifted my gaze to meet his. "We don't have time." The words scraped from my throat. "She's almost whole. And she has Nyrah."

Xavier swore under his breath.

Talek went still. Not in the same way as my mates, whose emotions pressed through the bond— he had no link to me, no way to feel what they did. But I saw it in the way his jaw locked, the way his fingers flexed at his sides. This wasn't his fight. Not really.

And yet, he was still here.

But it was Kian who spoke first, his thoughts following mine before I ever said a word. His expression was dark as night. "And Arden?"

I exhaled sharply. "I didn't see him."

A heavy silence settled between us. Then Xavier stepped closer, his voice tight. "Which means he's not with her."

Kian's amber gaze flicked toward the distance, toward the fractures in the Dreaming still shimmering in the air. The pieces slotted into place.

Zamarra was still gathering her power, and Arden wasn't at her side. Which meant—

"He's waiting for us." Idris' voice was steel, final. "He knows we're coming."

A slow, creeping fury coiled in my chest. I had seen what he had done to Idris. I had felt his betrayal like a knife through my gut. And now he was standing between me and my sister?

Not just no. *Fuck* no.

I gritted my teeth, light searing beneath my skin, my resolve solidifying into something sharp, something unbreakable.

Kian exhaled sharply, rolling his shoulders. The anger was there—but so was the weight of everything I had just seen. I still felt it in my ribs, in my skull, the power pressing like an unhealed wound.

I clenched my fists—not just at the pain but at the fury. At everything Arden had done. At the fact that he was still breathing.

Kian's amber gaze met mine, and the bond between us throbbed.

"Then let's go ruin his fucking day."

Kian cracked his knuckles, his grin sharp, Xavier exhaled hard, rolling his shoulders, and Idris' golden eyes burned.

Talek didn't speak, but his fingers flexed, a small storm of energy flickering to life at his fingertips. He wasn't bonded to this war, wasn't bound to these choices the way the rest of us were.

But he still took a step forward.

Vale swayed.

Not much. Just enough that if I hadn't been looking straight at her, I might have missed it.

I inhaled slowly, feeling the charge in the air, the way the very fabric of this place seemed to pull toward Vale like she was its anchor now. She stood at the center of it all, her breaths shallow, her hands trembling at her sides. Power coiled beneath her skin, quiet but endless, rolling off her in steady waves.

But I didn't miss it. And neither did Idris.

His golden eyes burned as he reached for her, but she took a breath—a sharp inhale like she could force her body to hold, to stay upright.

It didn't work.

The next second, her knees buckled.

I lunged, catching her before she could hit the ground. Kian was half a second behind me, hands gripping her arms, steadying her between us.

"Vale," I rasped, my palm pressing against her back, feeling the unsteady rhythm of her breathing. "Breathe, sweetheart."

She exhaled shakily. "I'm fine."

I knew better. Magic like that didn't settle without a cost. Didn't take root without a price. I'd seen it before—power unraveling a body from the inside out. Too much, too fast, too soon.

Kian's growl rumbled through his chest. "You're about as fine as a fucking landslide."

Vale managed a sharp, humorless breath of a laugh. "That bad?"

Talek shifted somewhere behind me, his voice deadpan. "You look like someone pulled you inside out and then stitched you back together with raw magic."

I pressed my fingers to her pulse. Too fast. Not dangerously so, but high enough to have my instincts on edge. And she was too warm. The Dreaming had branded itself beneath her skin, and her body was struggling to hold it.

"That's basically what happened."

She stiffened slightly. "I don't have time to be weak."

"No one said you were weak." I tilted her face up with my fingers, meeting those too-bright eyes. "But if your body gives out on you mid-fight, we're fucked."

A slow, ragged breath shuddered through her. Her chin lifted slightly.

She hated this. Hated feeling fragile. Hated us seeing it.

But she didn't fight me when I ran my hands over her arms, checking for injuries. Kian pulled one of her hands into his, his thumb brushing over her palm, grounding her with his touch. Idris stayed close, his golden warmth weaving through the bond, steady, solid.

She exhaled slowly, pressing her hand to my chest, her fingers splayed against the bare skin there.

I choose you, she had said. *I choose all of you.*

I felt it now—the steady hum of the bond between us, even as it trembled under the weight of what she'd just done. What she was still becoming.

Vale inhaled through her nose, steadying herself.

"I can't just sit here and wait to feel better. We have to move."

A muscle ticked in Kian's jaw. "Not until we talk about where the fuck we're going."

Idris' golden eyes darted toward the fractures in the Dreaming still shimmering in the distance. "With Arden missing from the vision, it throws up too many red flags. We can't fight a war on two fronts. We need to kill Zamarra first. She's the one with the real power."

There was a tense beat of silence before Kian laughed. It was a sharp unamused bark that would have chilled me to the bone had he not been one of my oldest friends.

"No." His response wasn't a discussion. It was an execution. Brutal. Final. Unyielding.

I dragged a hand through my hair, letting out a slow breath. "Arden wasn't in the vision. We don't know where he is or what he's planning."

Kian's grip on Vale's arm tightened. "Then we need to find out."

Idris' magic reeled through the bond, molten and simmering. "If we go after Arden first, we risk giving Zamarra more time."

Talek exhaled, crossing his arms. "And if we go

after her first, we give Arden time to do whatever the fuck he's planning."

Vale's voice was quiet. "Nyrah doesn't have time to waste."

Kian's jaw flexed. "Neither does anyone else if Arden is out there scheming."

Then Idris stiffened—not in response to Kian—to something else. His golden eyes darkened to something unreadable as he took half a step back, almost like something had just hit him in the chest.

And I felt it.

The bond twisted—something breaking. Something wrong.

Then the Dreaming ripped apart.

The air cracked open, silver light slashing through reality like a wound forcing itself into existence. Magic seared through the space in front of us, curling, flickering—showing us exactly what we needed to see.

Tarrasca was burning.

The castle gates had been torn apart, the stone spattered red. The banners had been ripped down, bodies littered the steps, and through the smoke—

Arden.

His golden eyes gleamed when he cut through a soldier as if he were nothing. Magic burst from his fingertips, latching onto another, wrenching the life from their body.

And he was smiling.

A sharp clang of steel rang through the air as Freya's blade crashed against his.

She was holding her own. Even outnumbered, her movements were sharp, calculated—not desperate, just fucking furious. Every strike hit hard, meant to break, meant to kill.

And for the first time, Arden didn't look amused.

His smirk slipped, and his eyes sparked with rage.

She snarled something I couldn't hear—but I saw his lips pull back in a sneer.

He lashed out. A wave of magic slammed into her midsection, sending her crashing into a stone pillar. Then the vision collapsed.

The rift snapped shut so hard the ground shuddered beneath our feet.

Idris sucked in a breath. His chest heaved, power flowing from him in waves full of rage, raw and seething.

Talek was the first to speak, his voice grim. "Well. That's fucking settled, then."

Vale's hands balled into fists, and the light beneath her skin burned hot—too bright.

No one spoke. They didn't have to. They all knew exactly what needed to be done.

Vale inhaled, slow and steady. The glow beneath her skin burned hotter, her magic seething, stretching, demanding. The Dreaming quaked around her, an extension of herself, no longer just something she walked through—but something she could command.

She lifted her hand, and the air shivered.

"This place brought us here," she murmured, her voice steady despite the storm raging beneath her skin. "It can take us where we need to go."

Kian's brows pulled together. "Vale—"

But it was already happening.

The Dreaming answered her.

A crack split through reality, light slashing through the air, curling at the edges like a wound trying to heal but held open by her will alone. The world pulsed around them, the very fabric of this place bending beneath Vale's grip.

Wind roared through the fracture, pulling, shifting, and opening.

The world twisted. Folded.

For half a breath, everything was weightless. The Dreaming twisted around us, stretching reality into ribbons of silver and black—until it snapped.

We were falling.

No, not falling—being thrown.

The Dreaming spit us out like it was done with us, hurling us straight into the throne room. Hard stone met my knees, the force of our landing rattling my bones. Behind me, Kian let out a sharp curse as he steadied himself, and Idris slammed a palm into the marble to keep from falling.

But Vale—Vale didn't even stumble.

She landed like she belonged here.

Like the Dreaming had placed her exactly where it needed her to be.

The air was thick with blood and magic. Smoke billowed from collapsed pillars, the remnants of a battle still raging beyond the shattered doors. The metallic bite of iron clashed with the acrid sting of burning spells.

And at the center of it all—Freya and Arden.

Freya's blade met Arden's in a shower of sparks, her fangs bared, copper hair tangled with blood. She wasn't losing. She was pushing him back. But even as she struck again, faster, sharper, her magic crackling around her like a second skin, Arden smirked.

That slow, infuriating smile.

"Finally," he breathed, golden eyes flicking toward us.

Freya didn't hesitate. She drove forward, striking again—her sword a blur of steel and fury.

The bond throbbed. Idris and Kian were already moving, stepping into formation beside me. Talek's magic bent the air, shifting in a way that made my instincts prickle. My own power coiled, ready to be unleashed.

But Vale?

She hadn't moved. She just stood there. Her gaze locked on Arden.

And then there was a slow, crawling shift in the air, like the Dreaming itself was watching through her eyes. Magic curled off her in waves, but it wasn't just magic anymore. It was something else.

Something vast. Something ancient. Something that made even Arden's smirk falter. A flash of something passed through his golden eyes. Not fear —not yet. But uncertainty.

Because he'd expected us. But he hadn't expected her.

And the Dreaming?

The Dreaming was hungry.

The room shrank around Arden. Not physically. But in the way that a predator's gaze made the world tighten around its prey.

Freya's sword scraped against his, her breath

labored but steady. Blood slicked the marble beneath them, pooling in jagged streaks, and still, she stood. Still, she fought.

She didn't give him an inch, didn't give him room to breathe, let alone time for a monologue. But she did give him a smile.

"All these years, and you're still living in Idris' shadow," she taunted, her sword sliding against his, the clanging of steel on steel ringing in my ears. "No wonder you're so desperate to stand in his place. Too bad you'll never fill it."

Arden sneered. "The throne should've been mine. I just had to clear a few obstacles." His golden eyes flicked toward us. Toward Idris.

And that was his first mistake.

The temperature in the room dropped as ice crackled around me, rage on Idris' behalf calling my magic forth. The air stopped moving as the very castle seemed to hold its breath.

Oh, so slowly, Idris stepped forward.

He didn't unsheathe his sword. Didn't lift his hands. Didn't need to.

Instead, he said—quiet, controlled, and razor-sharp, "You betrayed your own blood. For what?"

Arden's smirk twitched. Just barely.

Idris didn't stop. He took another step, power

weaving in and around him in a slow, lethal burn. "A woman that never wanted you and a crown you'll never wear?" The words landed like a verdict. His golden eyes gleamed. "You ripped me in half and still you weren't strong enough to take it then. You sure as fuck aren't strong enough now."

The fucker's smirk vanished, and Arden's grip on his sword tightened.

And then he lashed out. "And yet, for two hundred years, you were nothing more than a broken toy," he spat, golden eyes burning. "You *still* are."

Idris didn't falter. "And for two hundred years, you were nothing more than a shovel, digging Zamarra out of the prison she made herself. How does it feel to be nothing more than a pawn, brother?"

Vale moved as the Dreaming vibrated around her.

The castle hummed. The very air shifted. The banners on the walls trembled, the torches flickered, and the room bent.

Arden felt it, and for the first time, he hesitated. "You're wrong. You're all wrong." He beat the hilt of his sword against his chest. "I am the rightful king.

Zamarra is my queen, and you are nothing. You're *nothing*."

When Freya saw the flicker of uncertainty, she struck. *Hard*.

Arden barely caught her blade in time. Metal shrieked against metal, their magic sparking in the space between them. But the balance had shifted.

And he knew it.

"Now you're just stalling," Kian muttered, rolling his shoulders, magic coursing between his fingers. "We doing this, or what?"

Freya lunged again, teeth bared. And the fight began.

Arden snarled, twisting as Freya pressed him harder, her blade a blur of steel and fury. He'd expected us to come, but he hadn't expected this.

Hadn't expected Vale. Hadn't expected Idris standing whole before him.

Magic *cracked* through the air as their swords met, the impact sending sharp echoes throughout the throne room. The golden banners were torn, the marble slick with blood. The battle beyond the shattered doors still raged, but this fight—this moment —was the only one that mattered.

Freya struck high, forcing Arden back, his stance shifting as irritation flashed across his face. He caught her blade, pushing her off, and finally looked up.

Looked at Idris.

The smirk returned. That same fucking smirk.

"You came all this way to die for me, brother?" Arden breathed, his eyes gleaming. "I'm touched."

Idris didn't smile. He walked forward, slow and deliberate, his power swelling around him like a gathering storm. "You should be afraid."

Arden scoffed, shaking out his wrist like this was just another match between them. Like he hadn't shattered the world with his betrayal. "You've always been dramatic. Still waiting for someone to save you?" His golden eyes darted to Vale. "Or do you actually think you can win this time?"

Vale exhaled, her magic humming at the edges of reality, twisting, watching. The Dreaming curled toward her, hungry and waiting.

"You should be more worried about yourself," she said in a soft but sharp voice. "Because this time, we're not playing your game."

Arden barely had time to frown before Idris was on him. Their blades met, sparks flying.

And then Vale moved as the Dreaming exploded.

The very air shuddered as she pulled the magic through her veins, twisting reality as if the castle itself wanted this fight over. The throne room tilted —no, not physically, but around Arden. The world was shifting, centering on him.

And he felt it. For the first time, he looked unsure.

Freya was still locked in combat, their blades flashing between bursts of golden magic, but the air was already shifting. Pulling. Rearranging.

And Arden felt it.

His foot slid back. His shoulders tightened. He swung for Freya's middle, but he was slower now.

The Dreaming had caught him.

Vale's eyes burned, the golden glow beneath her skin pulsing in time with the fractures around them. Reality itself was curving inward, the Dreaming reaching toward him like fingers through a veil.

Arden snarled, ripping his blade away, his golden eyes cutting toward her.

"This isn't your fight!" he spat, his voice sharp and desperate.

Vale tilted her head, watching. The Dreaming shuddered at her fingertips, waiting for her command. "You made it my fight when you killed my parents," she murmured. "When you starved me, cut me, branded me. When you tied me to a stake to burn. When you went after my sister. When you attacked my mates."

Vale's gaze never once wavered. "After all you've done, and you think I'll let you keep breathing? I didn't let your son live a single second after he put his hands on what was mine. Why would you think my judgment for your crimes would be any kinder?"

Her words settled, and Arden's hands clenched.

Then she moved.

Magic ripped through the room.

Not just magic. Not just power. The Dreaming itself.

It latched onto him.

A pull at first. An invisible thread tightening around his limbs, wrapping, binding—until it became something else. Something alive.

Arden staggered. His free hand went to his chest as his breath hitched, his body jerking as if something inside him had twisted wrong.

The glow beneath his skin—his stolen magic—flared.

Then dimmed.

"What—" He let out a sharp breath. "What did you do?"

Vale moved closer. She raised her hand—just one—and the air obeyed. Tendrils of the Dreaming tightened, sinking into his skin, latching onto something beneath his flesh.

His magic.

His soul.

He choked on his next breath. His sword slipped an inch in his grasp.

"You spent your whole life trying to take what wasn't yours," Vale said softly. "A throne. A kingdom. Power."

The Dreaming tightened. Arden's spine arched as it dug in, snaking through his veins, weaving into him like a second set of bones.

"And yet," Vale murmured, watching him unravel, "you never learned how to hold on to anything."

The floor cracked beneath him. He stumbled, but there was nowhere to go. Nowhere to run.

Vale had him trapped, and for the first time, he looked afraid.

His golden eyes snapped to his brother.

A plea—not with words, but in the way a dying man searched for mercy.

And Idris? He only watched.

For a long moment, no one spoke. The only sound was the war beyond the shattered doors, the distant clash of steel.

Then Vale turned and met Idris' gaze.

She didn't have to ask. He already knew—we all did. The bond throbbed with the silent question, but all I could think about were the scars on her back. The heretic brand burned into her skin. The stab wound in her middle that had taken nearly all of me to heal. Her parents.

Idris exhaled, power rising through the air like a final breath. "Do it."

Vale lifted her chin and let the Dreaming hum beneath her skin.

And for just a second—just one—I saw it. The hesitation. The part of Vale that still held space for mercy.

I knew that part of her. *Loved* that part of her.

But not now. Not for this.

Not for him.

Her fingers trembled, light blooming across her flesh, waiting. And for a breath, I thought—*fuck, she's actually considering it.*

And for that moment, Arden saw it.

His golden eyes latched onto hers, breath ragged, body rigid as the Dreaming held him tight. His hands twitched, the last dregs of stolen power curling at his fingertips like dying embers. He had no fight left, no last move, no way out.

Then her gaze flicked down—to Freya's blood on the marble.

To Idris, whole again, but still standing in the wreckage of what Arden had done.

To the bastard himself, struggling, trapped in the web of his own making.

And still—he tried. His lips parted, a snarl half-formed, maybe a plea, maybe one final insult, but Vale just tilted her head.

Not with pity. Not with regret. With something sharper, something colder.

Then, in a voice as steady as the storm inside her, she murmured, "Say hi to your son for me."

Arden barely had time to breathe before the Dreaming collapsed inward.

Light detonated through the room, a supernova of pure, unyielding power. The air warped, bent, screamed as the magic inside Arden twisted against itself. He gasped—choked--his body jerking, fighting against the inevitable.

He reached for something, for anything, but his fingers closed on nothing. His golden eyes, once burning with arrogance, went wide.

Fear. Real, desperate, helpless fear.

And then—he was gone.

Not a body. Not a corpse. Nothing left to burn or

bury. The Dreaming devoured him, shredded him into pieces too small for existence to remember. The last echoes of his stolen magic unraveled into the ether, consumed by the force he could never control.

Silence swallowed the throne room.

The Dreaming settled, the air rippling as if exhaling after a long, vicious hunt. The last shreds of Arden's stolen magic flickered, whirling into the ether, vanishing like he'd never been here at all.

The blood on the floor told another tale.

Standing in the center of it all, Vale was still as a statue. Shoulders squared, breathing steady—I could still see the way her hands trembled at her sides. The way the light beneath her skin hadn't dimmed.

This wasn't over.

Kian exhaled, rolling his shoulders, his fingers flexing like he needed to hit something. Someone. He cast a glance at Idris. "Well?"

Idris' golden eyes still burned. Still blazed. But his magic was already shifting—turning away from where Arden had fallen, toward something worse.

Zamarra.

He felt her before we did. His body stiffened. His breath came sharp, clipped. And then the castle trembled.

A pulse of raw, ancient power crashed through the walls, the stone groaning under the force of it. The banners that had survived Arden's attack ripped from the rafters. The torches guttered out.

A voice like cracked glass and dying embers slithered through the throne room, soft as breath, cold as death.

"You took my toy."

Vale's head snapped up.

That voice. That magic. That pull.

Zamarra knew Arden was gone.

A fracture split through the stone at our feet, thin at first, then growing. Spreading, the air darkened, the very fabric of the Dreaming twisting again —but this time, it wasn't Vale doing the tearing.

This time, something was coming for us.

Talek exhaled sharply, shifting into a ready stance. "So much for a breather."

Kian let out a slow, lethal breath, flexing his fingers as fire blazed through them. "Fucking finally."

Idris drew his sword.

Vale turned toward the encroaching darkness. The glow beneath her skin brightened, her magic coiling, shifting. Preparing.

The Dreaming shivered. The castle groaned,

stone grinding against stone as magic thickened in the air, pressing, pulling—*showing*.

Not here. Not anymore.

Wind cut across the flat stone over the sheer drop. The falls that had once run clear swirled with scarlet blood.

Kian's magic flared against my skin as my power rippled in protest.

But it was too late. The rift yawned wide.

And the Dreaming swallowed us whole.

The Dreaming spat us out.

Not gently—not like before. This time, it hurled us forward, slamming us into the battlefield like it wanted us broken before the fight even began.

I hit the ground hard, my knees skidding against rough stone, my breath stolen by the sudden impact. My fingers curled, digging into the dirt—

No. Not dirt. Not stone.

Bones.

The brittle snap of fractured remains crunched beneath my boots, the weight of my landing splintering through a field of skeletal debris. My stomach turned as I forced myself upright, my breath coming too fast, too shallow—

No. *No, no, no.*

I knew this place. I had bled here. I had fought here. I had nearly died here.

But it wasn't the same.

It was worse.

The air wasn't air. It was dense, suffocating, laced with magic so thick it felt like drowning. The wind howled like a living thing, curling against my skin, whispering, begging, warning.

The jagged cliffs that had once loomed over the battlefield were gone, as if something had crushed them from the inside out. The wind shrieked through the emptiness, sharp with the scent of blood and decay, a constant, hungry wail.

And the falls?

They ran red. Not water. Not mist.

Blood.

A slow, steady river of crimson poured from the broken cliffs, spilling into an abyss that had no bottom. The wind caught the spray, turning it into a fine mist that clung to my skin like a warning.

This was a graveyard. A killing field. And at the center of it was my baby sister.

Nyrah.

I stopped breathing.

She was kneeling. Too still. Too quiet.

Her arms were bound in coils of silver energy, her golden skin pale, drained, hollow. Her head lolled forward, her pale hair matted with blood, her body a fragile thing—

No.

I took a step forward, my legs numb, shaking. Another step. And another before I was caught in Idris' hold, his arm hooked around my middle, keeping me from my sister.

She wasn't moving. She wasn't breathing.

A jagged sob tore free from my throat. My vision blurred, the world narrowing, collapsing around the single, shattering fact that my sister—

No.

A shuddering inhale ripped through my lungs. Not again. Not her. I had fought too hard, had bled too much, had burned myself to nothing to get her back.

I wasn't losing her.

I wasn't fucking losing her.

"Nyrah." My voice broke. "Nyrah, look at me."

She didn't. She didn't fucking move. And beside her was a barely conscious Briar.

Zamarra had them both.

She stood atop the altar of bones, golden veins

pulsing beneath her skin, her body wreathed in twisting, shifting light.

Her once-fractured form had almost completely solidified, the hollowness in her face gone, the cracks in her body sealed.

She had been feeding.

And I was going to rip her apart.

Zamarra turned slowly, smiling. Her voice slithered through the heavy air, smooth as silk, sharp as shattered glass. "You're late."

Rage burned through my veins. I started to move, but the ground trembled beneath my feet.

The Dreaming was writhing. The sky was splitting. Fractures ripped reality apart as something vast, something hungry, twisted through the air.

And then the nightmares came.

They crawled from the fissures themselves, dragging free from the slashes in reality. Shadows with bodies, fangs that gleamed like shattered glass, claws dripping with the memory of every life they had ever taken.

These weren't like the others.

These were hers.

Zamarra lazily lifted a single hand, and with a flourish of her wrist, the creatures attacked.

We met them head-on.

Magic exploded outward as Kian, Xavier, and Idris shifted at once, their power colliding in a storm of fire, ice, and raw golden fury.

The impact shattered the ground, sending fissures racing toward the falls. The blood-red mist thickened, the air vibrating with so much raw power I could taste it.

Kian was the first to strike.

His onyx-scaled body twisted through the sky, illusions flickering in the air behind him—so many that the monsters didn't know what to attack. He was everywhere and nowhere, a storm of claws and deception.

Xavier cut through them like a blade. His iridescent-scaled form dove, talons flashing, fire streaming from his jaws as he ripped through the creatures with surgical precision.

And Idris. *Gods.* Idris.

He was power incarnate. His scarlet body lit the battlefield, magic roaring off him in waves so intense the very air warped. This—this was what Arden had tried to take from him. This was what Zamarra had feared. This was why she had cursed him.

A breath shuddered through me—a heartbeat before the sky shattered.

Lightning split the heavens.

Talek unleashed his own storm, the wind bending to his will. Electricity surged through the battlefield, the wind slamming into the creatures, hurling them off the edge of the falls.

But it wasn't enough.

The Dreaming itself fought against us.

Zamarra rose from her throne of the dead.

She barely lifted her hand before the world changed. The battlefield vanished—ripped away in a convergence of power.

I wasn't standing in the middle of a fight anymore. I was somewhere else.

The battlefield was gone—swallowed by something vast, something twisting, something wrong. And in its place, Nyrah.

Her body turned to dust in my hands.

No.

A strangled, wordless scream tore from my throat as she disintegrated, her face frozen in pain, her fingers stretching toward me, reaching, needing, and then she was gone.

Nothing but dust.

The wind carried her away, scattering her across the broken land.

I couldn't breathe. My hands were empty. My heart cracked open.

No—no—*this isn't real.*

It wasn't real. I forced myself to move, to turn, but then I saw my mates.

Dead. All dead.

Their bodies lay broken across the battlefield, blood slicking the stone, their scales cracked, their chests still.

Kian. His head lay at an unnatural angle, amber eyes staring sightless.

Xavier. His throat was torn open, his pale flesh marred with the ruin of a fatal blow.

Idris. His scarlet dragon scales had dulled to gray, his massive form sprawled in the wreckage, his wings crushed beneath his own weight.

I couldn't move. I couldn't breathe.

"No," I whispered. "*No.*" My voice barely carried over the silence.

I fell to my knees, the sharp bite of broken stone cutting into my skin, but I didn't feel it.

All I could see was them.

All I could hear was the howling roar of grief, the one clawing through my skin, through my throat, through my very soul.

This isn't real. This isn't real. This isn't—

Magic shivered in the air. A flicker of movement —too fast, too sharp—like a whisper against the edges of my senses.

Then there was a crack in the illusion. A ripple. A shift. Kian's magic—not gone. Not broken.

Fighting.

Illusion against illusion.

And suddenly, everything shuddered.

The battlefield blurred, twisted, fragmented. The stone beneath me trembled, and through the haze of my own breaking mind, I felt it.

This wasn't real. This was *her*.

Zamarra.

Her nightmare. Her trap.

And I was about to rip it apart.

Xavier saw the threads of it—saw the lie. And then he started severing them. The illusion rippled, twisted, fractured.

Idris—his rage burned hotter than the nightmare itself. His scarlet dragon form tore through the false world, wings beating against the illusion, power blazing, shaking the dream apart.

But it wasn't enough. The nightmare held. Zamarra was too deeply rooted in it.

It was up to me.

I turned toward her, toward the woman who

had done this. She stood at the heart of it all, her silver veins glowing with power, her face serene, her fingers woven into the fabric of the Dreaming itself.

She didn't look worried. She should have been.

"You can't fight me here," she murmured, her voice smooth as silk, cold as a blade.

And that was her first mistake. Because I wasn't going to fight her. I was going to tear her apart.

Light detonated from my palms. Not magic. Not a spell. The Dreaming itself answered me. The ground quaked beneath us. A pulse—deep and ancient—throbbed through the fabric of reality.

I didn't summon it. Didn't conjure it. It was given.

A blade of pure, white-hot energy formed in my grasp—light shaped into a weapon that had never existed before. A blade that wasn't forged—but born. I'd conjured many swords in my short time, but nothing like this.

Zamarra's eyes widened for the first time. "Impossible," she whispered.

I tightened my grip. "You should've never come back."

The Dreaming shuddered, and then it showed me.

The vision slammed into me like a tidal wave.

I saw her—as she had been in the temple. The golden stone cracked under the weight of the curse. The Luxa screamed, their light ripping from their bodies, veins of power siphoning into the spell, into her.

Zamarra stood at the center of it all, her hands outstretched, magic weaving like silk.

She was so sure. So precise. She had prepared for every possibility. Every possibility—except one.

She had stolen power that wasn't meant to be taken —magic not freely given.

I saw the moment it began to turn.

Her breath hitched. Her fingers trembled, just slightly. The power she had stolen wasn't settling. It was coiling. Shifting. Waiting.

But she didn't realize. Not yet.

Her eyes glittered with triumph as the final threads of the spell settled.

As Idris collapsed, broken and severed.

As Rune was ripped from him, roaring in agony.

As the Luxa fell, drained husks of what they had been.

The magic locked into place.

And for centuries, it slept.

Waiting.

Waiting for the moment she would dare to use it.

The temple fractured around me, and suddenly, I was somewhere else.

Direveil, but it was different than I'd ever seen it.

Zamarra stood on the cliffs, bathed in silver moonlight, magic thrumming beneath her skin.

She had waited. She had been patient. And now—she was ready.

Her hands lifted, silver veins glowing beneath her skin as she whispered the incantation. And for a moment, the magic obeyed. For a moment, she held all that power in her hands, bending it to her will.

Then it snapped. The stolen power fought back. She gasped—staggering—eyes wide in horror.

The Luxas' power was still alive inside her, but it wasn't hers. And it never would be.

I saw the exact moment she lost control. The night itself split apart, silver light slashing through the sky like claws. The power detonated inside her veins, magic writhing, turning, twisting against her.

Her scream tore through the cliffs.

And then the ground reached up to meet her. But it wasn't earth or stone. As the pale iridescent rocks wrapped around her, I knew exactly what they were.

Lumentium.

The unforgiving retaliation of the very magic she had tried to own. It buried her. Encased her in something harder than steel, something that had never existed before.

Magic forged into prison.

She clawed at it. She screamed. But the mountain did not move.

She had been sentenced.

Not by a king.

Not by a god.

But by the Dreaming itself.

The vision snapped. The battlefield roared back into focus. Zamarra's gaze locked onto mine—and for the first time, there was fear.

I knew her secret.

She had never been strong enough to control this magic, and now, the Dreaming knew it, too.

And I was about to show her exactly how much it hated her.

Kian's roar rattled the sky, Xavier's fire ignited the air, and Idris—his golden gaze locked onto Zamarra, unyielding, unforgiving.

And then I charged.

The blade in my hands seared through the illusions, slicing them apart like paper.

And I was on her.

Zamarra lifted her hands, power crackling between her fingers, shadows curling around her like armor. But it wouldn't save her.

She knew it. She saw it in my eyes. And she wasn't ready to lose.

She let out a sharp, hissing breath, her golden

eyes narrowing, and the ground beneath us split apart. Something crawled from the abyss. Not just a monster, a god's mistake. It dragged itself from the pit of the Dreaming, its form shifting, writhing, its bones snapping into place only to shatter and reform.

A creature born of broken nightmares and failed dreams, something that shouldn't exist, something that never should have been allowed to take shape.

And Zamarra fed it. Her magic latched onto the thing, pouring into its bones, its teeth, its too-many eyes.

It turned toward me. Its mouth split open in a jagged, unnatural way—too wide, too sharp, too wrong. And it lunged.

I barely had time to lift my blade before Kian crashed into it from the side, his massive claws raking across its shifting form. Illusions flickered in the air—dozens of Kians attacking at once.

The creature lashed out, jaws snapping as it tried to find the real one.

Xavier's blue flames tore through the sky, searing the monster's back, sending up an inhuman, fractured screech.

Talek's magic bent the air, lashing through the

battlefield like a storm, cracking the creature's bones.

Idris descended from above, his golden form streaking through the sky, power blazing from his wings as he dove.

But it was Freya who struck.

She didn't wait. She didn't hesitate. She darted beneath the beast's reaching claws, her fangs bared, her sword flashing in the blood-heavy air. Her blade sank deep into its side, carving through its impossible flesh, severing one of its many limbs.

The creature let out a guttural, ear-splitting shriek, the sound rippling through the Dreaming like a wound trying to heal but being shredded apart all over again.

And Zamarra moved. She wasn't running. She was waiting.

She thought I would be too distracted. That I would be too busy fighting her creation.

She thought wrong.

I saw the exact moment she realized it. That I wasn't going to stop. Her expression twisted.

She let out a sharp, desperate cry, "*No—*"

But I was already there.

I drove the sword of light—of Dreaming—into her chest.

She gasped. Not from pain—not yet.

The blade of light was buried in her chest, sinking past flesh and bone, burning through the core of her being. The Dreaming pulsed around us, a living thing. It had been waiting for this. For her to fall.

And she knew it.

Her silver eyes widened, shock flickering across her too-perfect face, but I didn't falter. I didn't hesitate.

I pressed deeper.

Zamarra didn't scream. She exhaled—a shuddering breath, a trace of disbelief. Then—her lips curled. Magic seared through the blade, dark tendrils wrapping around the light, twisting, shifting—trying to pull it into her.

My pulse slammed against my ribs.

She was trying to steal it. Her fingers trembled as she lifted a hand, gripping my wrist—not to push me away, but to drag me closer.

"You are mine now," she whispered.

The power that should have been devouring her was slowing. Sinking into her, bending to her will, folding into the void of her body.

She was trying to take everything.

My breath hitched. The Dreaming wavered. The

battlefield blurred at the edges as power began unraveling from me, twisting away, feeding her.

Zamarra was smiling.

I snapped, ripping the sword to the side, a brutal, fatal twist.

The light burned brighter, white-hot fire, searing through her body as I wrenched it deeper, twisting through muscle, through magic, through the stolen power she had hoarded for centuries.

Zamarra's eyes widened. Her lips parted. And this time, she did scream.

Magic exploded outward. Not hers—*mine*.

It recoiled, rejecting her. The Dreaming lashed against her touch, peeling away from her skin, severing, cutting, burning. She clutched at my arm, but her strength was already failing.

Her body began to fracture.

"You—" Her voice was raw, desperate. She still didn't understand.

I leaned in, my breath warm against her cheek. "The Dreaming doesn't belong to you."

The light pulsed, detonated, and Zamarra shattered.

Not a body. Not a death. The Dreaming ripped her apart.

Her form fractured into shards of raw magic,

splintering at the seams, peeling away from reality itself. The power she had stolen—the centuries of hoarded, twisted energy—turned against her.

She clawed at it, trying to hold herself together, trying to stay. But the Dreaming had decided it did not want her anymore. Her scream cut off, and then there was nothing but silence.

Not victory. Not yet. Just the Dreaming exhaling, releasing a breath it had been holding for far too long. For a single, weightless moment, everything was still. Like the world itself didn't believe she was truly gone.

Then, one by one, the monsters fell apart.

They screamed—raw, splintering sounds—as the power that had bound them together began to unravel. Shadowed limbs twisted. Claws curled into themselves. Their bodies convulsed, turning to nothing but dark mist and dying echoes.

The Dreaming did not let them linger.

A wind howled through the battlefield, sharp and final. The creatures writhed, fighting to stay, and then they were gone. The fractures in the sky shuddered. The jagged wounds of reality didn't close all at once, but silver light began to thread through the cracks, pulling them together.

The red mist that had tainted the air thinned,

fading into nothing. The heavy, suffocating weight pressing against my skin lightened, just slightly. The falls cleared of blood.

The Dreaming exhaled.

Not a sound. Not a word. But a pulse of something deep, something vast, something relieved.

And then, slowly, finally, the battlefield stilled.

The fight was over.

And I stood in the wreckage of what had been Zamarra, my sword of light still glowing in my palm. The magic beneath my skin burned, raw and untamed, but steady.

She was gone. But Nyrah—*Nyrah.*

I spun, nearly stumbling as I ran. Her light—her life—was flickering, dimming, fading.

"Nyrah!"

The sword vanished from my grip as I skidded across the stone, dropping to my knees beside her. She wasn't moving.

"Nyrah," I gasped, pressing my hands against her shoulders. "Hey. Hey, open your eyes."

Her skin was ashen, her golden glow flickering like dying embers. The magic that should have been hers—that should have been protecting her—was fading.

A tremor racked through her body. Her breath came in shallow, weakening gasps.

No. No, no, no.

The power that Zamarra had stolen—she had been draining Nyrah to rebuild herself. Now that she was gone, Nyrah was breaking apart.

Xavier dropped beside me, his hands hovering over her chest, his magic curling outward in silken threads—searching, testing—his breath caught.

"She's slipping," he murmured, voice tight.

No. No, I didn't just fight my way through the Dreaming to lose her now. My magic flared. I reached for her, trying to feed power into her, trying to force her body to hold on. It fought me. Or maybe —Nyrah was too weak to take it.

Panic clawed at my ribs.

"We have to do something," I choked. "I—I can't lose her. *Please.*"

Kian dropped to his knees beside me. "Then tell me what the fuck to do."

Xavier's jaw clenched, his hands glowing with the soft, iridescent shimmer of healing magic. But his voice was raw when he spoke. "She's too far gone."

I turned to him, my chest caving. "No."

Xavier's throat bobbed. His gaze flickered to

Nyrah, and something in his expression cracked. "We need more."

More magic. More strength. More of us.

Idris inhaled sharply. "Then we give it to her."

The words settled. Final. Certain. For a breath, no one moved.

Then Kian exhaled roughly. "Fine. But we do this together."

No hesitation. No doubt. Just all of us.

Xavier met my gaze, his hands tightened into a fist before he pressed his palm to Nyrah's chest. "On three."

We moved as one.

Xavier pressed against her sternum. I gripped her hands. Kian's fingers brushed her temple. Idris' golden power coiled between us as Rune looked through his eyes.

Talek hovered nearby, his hands flexing, the wind whipping around his body. "I don't do light magic," he muttered. "But I can hold her here."

A pulse of air settled over her like an anchor, keeping her tethered, keeping her from slipping further.

Freya limped toward us, her sword still slick with blackened blood. Her breath came sharp, but her voice was steady. "Move."

She pressed a bloodied hand to Nyrah's mouth, her magic surging forward, latching onto whatever thread of life was left.

Behind her, Briar staggered forward, her arms shaking, her face pale. But she knelt beside Nyrah, her own flickering power joining ours.

Xavier inhaled. "One."

Magic hummed.

"Two."

The bond flared, a surge of raw energy snapping between us.

"Three."

We let go.

Power flooded from our bodies. Not violently, not forcefully—but steady, controlled, unwavering. Nyrah jerked like she was being struck by lightning. Her back bowed. Her body shuddered.

And then she gasped.

Light burst from her chest, golden and warm, spreading outward like a breath of air after drowning. Her fingers tightened around mine. Her pulse throbbed back to life.

And I let out a ragged, shaking exhale.

"Nyrah?" My voice cracked.

She blinked, her blue eyes the most beautiful thing I'd ever seen. She was still weak, still barely holding on—but she was alive. Then her lips curved into a small, weak smirk.

"Took you long enough."

The breath left my lungs in a sharp, broken laugh.

Kian exhaled heavily, sitting back on his heels. "Fucking hell."

Xavier pressed a hand over his face, his shoulders slumping in relief. Idris let out a slow breath, his golden magic settling like embers in the air.

Talek, standing over us, huffed. "I would like to formally request that no one ever almost dies again. Thanks."

Freya let out a breathless chuckle, pressing a hand to her ribs before she collapsed to the ground, staring up at the starry night sky. "Agreed."

Briar shook her head, her voice hoarse. "Don't make me go through that again."

I let out another shaking breath, pressing my forehead to Nyrah's. "You're going to be okay."

She let out a weak, tired chuckle. "Damn right I am."

I squeezed her fingers.

It was over. But beyond the cliffs, beyond the scarred battlefield, the Dreaming wasn't quiet.

Not truly. Not ever.

It still whispered beneath my skin, shifting, breathing. Waiting. It had always been watching. It always would be.

I had fought my way through it, broken it apart, wielded it as a weapon. But now? Now it wasn't an enemy. It was a part of me.

And maybe it always had been.

CHAPTER 27

VALE

The castle was eerily quiet.

It wasn't the silence of peace. It was the silence of exhaustion.

Nyrah and Briar were already tucked into healing cots, their skin still too pale. The healers fluttered around them, hands glowing with soft, steady light as they worked to undo the damage Zamarra left behind.

Freya, however, was actively avoiding care.

"I'm fine," she snapped, batting away a healer's hands as she sat on the edge of a cot. "There are actual dying people here. Go bother them."

"You have at least three broken ribs and a bruised lung," the healer argued.

Freya snorted. "I need blood and a nap, not healing."

Talek, standing beside her, smirked. "She's not lying, by the way. You wheezed when you sat down."

Freya glared at him. "I'm not sure you even breathe, you storm-wielding asshole. Mind your business."

"I do breathe," Talek argued, arms crossed. "I just don't complain about it as much as you do."

Kian leaned toward me, whispering, "How long do we give them before we intervene?"

Xavier tilted his head. "I don't know. I kind of like the show."

I almost smiled—but the moment was too brief, too fragile. Because just past them, beyond the lines of healers, beyond the stretch of weary bodies, across the continent, the mountain was still standing.

The Guild.

A weight pressed against my ribs, tight and unfinished.

It wasn't over. Not yet.

Idris must have felt the turmoil bubbling in my gut because he turned to me, golden eyes sharp, reading me through the bond. "We're still going, aren't we?"

I nodded. "We have to."

Kian exhaled, running a hand through his hair. "Yeah, that's what I thought."

Freya, mid-argument with Talek, went rigid. "Wait—what?"

And then, before I could answer, a curtain snapped open.

Nyrah stood in the opening, barely upright, her hospital tunic askew as she braced herself on the wooden frame.

She was barely strong enough to stand. Her fingers trembled against the wood as Briar stirred beside her, eyes fluttering open in alarm.

"You're leaving," Nyrah said.

It wasn't a question.

I took a step forward, ready to catch her if she fell. "You need to rest. You've been through so much."

Her jaw clenched, blue eyes sparkling. "And you need to stop acting like I'm still a kid."

I softened, relief that she was alive and breathing, easing something in my chest that I never thought would be whole. But there was no fucking way she was coming with me.

"Nyrah."

She shook her head. "I know what you're doing. The mountain."

Xavier exhaled sharply, rubbing his temple. "Of course she heard."

Nyrah's fingers curled into a fist. "You can't just leave it there."

I swallowed. "No. We can't."

The room stilled.

Freya finally looked away from her healer. Talek went unnaturally quiet. Briar, still weak from the fight, gritted her teeth and forced herself upright in her cot.

The mountain was still standing. And none of us could live with that.

Nyrah's fingers twitched, like she wanted to move—wanted to follow.

I reached for her hands, gripping them tight. "You are my sister, and I love you more than anything in this world."

She stared at me, defiant and stubborn and so much stronger than she should have been.

"But I need you to stay here where it's safe."

Her throat bobbed. "This isn't my fight," she said quietly.

I shook my head. "It was never yours, but I love that you still want to fight it with me."

A long silence stretched between us as her gaze searched mine. Then she nodded—not a big nod. Just enough to let me go.

I pressed a kiss to her forehead, brushing her pale hair back from her face. "We'll be back soon."

Freya huffed, throwing herself back on the cot with a grunt. "Fine. Go knock over a mountain without me. But if you get crushed under it, I am not digging you out."

Kian grinned. "I knew you cared."

She flipped him off.

I turned back to my mates. "Let's go."

THE FLIGHT WAS EERILY QUIET.

Even Kian, usually the first to crack a joke, said nothing.

The mountain loomed ahead of us, its dark exterior scarred from centuries of greed, of cruelty, of sacrifice. As the morning sun bled across the sky, the Lumentium veins vibrated faintly, a lingering echo of the magic that had once imprisoned Zamarra.

A prison. A tomb. A graveyard.

Now, it was empty.

The Guild, the miners—gone. Whether they had fled or died with their cause, I didn't know. All that remained were the tunnels, carved deep into the earth—the only proof left of Arden's desperation, of centuries spent chasing a lie.

A frigid wind whipped around me. The Dreaming stirred beneath my skin, whispering through my bones, humming in the air.

This wasn't just a mountain. It was the past. It was everything we had been forced to endure. And it was time to let it go.

Idris stood beside me, his gaze hard, golden magic flickering at his fingertips. "You ready, my brave one?"

I nodded. "Together?"

Xavier's fingers threaded through mine as Kian hooked an arm around my waist, steadying me in the rising wind. Idris lifted his chin, his magic coiling through him, through us, as he took my other hand.

The bond flared, snapping taut between us.

And then the mountain trembled.

A deep, thundering *crack* split through the rock, spreading like veins, like fractures in time itself. The Lumentium shimmered, its unnatural glow flaring one last time—before shattering.

The once-impenetrable walls caved inward, the tunnels crumbling, the foundation giving way beneath the weight of its own sins.

Stone and bone and history collapsed—a kingdom of shadows swallowed whole.

The ground groaned, dust billowing into the sky like a dying breath, rising into the air, scattering into nothing.

And then all that was left was silence. Not just quiet. Not just stillness. But true, final silence.

The weight of it pressed against my shoulders, an absence so heavy it felt like the world itself had exhaled. A life's worth of pain, of ghosts, of curses— buried.

For real this time.

THE GIROVIAN ENVOY ARRIVED THREE DAYS LATER.

A stiff, pinched-looking man, his uniform too perfect, his shoulders too straight, his expression like he'd swallowed curdled milk.

But the worst part? He didn't bow.

Not when he entered the throne room. Not when his gaze locked on Idris and me, standing at the head of the chamber, his golden magic twisting through the air like something alive.

Not once did he bow.

The room seemed to hold its breath, a single ripple of tension coiling through the space. It was something deeper than silence, something waiting. My hands fisted at my sides, the weight of the crown on my head almost more than I could bear.

This man had come here to surrender, and yet, he acted as though he still had a choice. I didn't know what unsettled me more—the sheer arrogance of it, or the fact that Idris didn't so much as shift.

He simply stood, his presence filling the room like a storm waiting to break.

The envoy's breath hitched. He felt it. The power in the air, the force of a king restored, the quiet, coiled rage of a queen crowned.

And then—his knees hit the floor. Not gracefully. Not willingly. Like a body bowing under a weight too great to bear. His head lowered. His breath shallowed. And when he finally spoke, his voice was tight, strangled under the weight of the very air itself.

"The Province of Girovia recognizes King Idris' reign."

A long, suffocating pause stretched for far too long.

Say it.

My magic curled against my ribs, the pressure building behind my lungs as the envoy's jaw clenched, his throat bobbing.

"We... will honor the accords as written."

It was done. The war was over before it had really begun. They had hoped for a kingdom without a king. A land without power. They had counted on Idris being severed from himself forever.

They had been wrong.

Idris tilted his head, eyes bright with power, his expression unreadable. He studied the man, as if weighing something unseen.

Then, he spoke a single word. "Good."

That was it. No fanfare. No gloating. No long-winded speeches or demands for penance. Just a single, unshakable declaration. Like the fall of an empire was nothing more than a minor inconvenience.

The envoy stayed kneeling. He didn't dare to rise.

A sharp, amused snort broke the silence.

"Damn," Freya drawled from my left. "I was hoping they'd grovel or something, with all the headache they've been giving us for the last two centuries. You'd think an apology was in order."

The envoy barely looked at her. That was his second mistake.

Freya's grin widened, all sharp teeth and blood-stained humor. "I think I'm going to like keeping them in line."

Kian, lounging against one of the stone pillars like he was entirely too entertained, hummed thoughtfully. "Maybe next time we should make them grovel. Would that be undiplomatic?"

Xavier sighed, rubbing his temple. "Kian, you are not leading the council."

Kian sighed dramatically. "Freya and I would make an excellent team. Consider it."

Xavier stared at the domed ceiling, his patience wearing thin. "I think you'll be too busy being—I don't know—a fucking general?"

Kian's grin widened. "What? A guy can't multi-task around here?"

Idris finally—finally—laughed. A deep, satisfied sound, warm despite the tension in the room.

Kian grinned, looking far too pleased with himself. "See? The king approves."

Freya rolled her eyes but grabbed the envoy by his collar, yanking him upright. His eyes widened, his mouth opening in a strangled sound that wasn't quite a protest.

Freya leaned in, her voice all silk and steel. "And yet, here I am, doing all the dirty work while you fools argue about it."

I smothered a laugh at the envoy's shocked face while Freya bodily escorted him from the room. "We'll rebuild the council. But not today."

Freya tossed me a look over her shoulder. "Fine. But if any of them betray you, I call dibs on the execution."

Idris, still grinning, simply shrugged. "Fine by me."

I FOUND HER IN THE STABLES, STANDING BESIDE VETRA, brushing slow, even strokes down the mare's sleek coat. Sunlight streamed through the open doors, catching in the strands of her pale hair, turning them almost silver.

Briar stood nearby, her wings fluttering absently

as she handed Nyrah a softer brush. They weren't talking.

Just being.

When Nyrah had been well enough, she'd come with us to Idris' estate to bring back the warhorse that had carried me through battle.

She'd taken one look at Vetra, and I'd known. She wasn't just interested in the horse. She had claimed her. Before I could even blink, the two of them had bonded, as if something in Nyrah recognized the battle-hardened mare, and Vetra had recognized something in return.

A quiet strength. A shared survival.

I leaned against the stall door, crossing my arms. Waiting.

Nyrah didn't turn, but I felt the moment she sensed me. A tiny, almost imperceptible pause in the rhythmic drag of the brush.

"You're hovering."

I smirked, moving closer. "I'm the queen. I'm allowed."

She cast me a side-eyed glance before turning her attention back to Vetra, brushing out the mare's mane. "Abusing your power already?"

I grinned. "Absolutely."

For a moment, the only sound was the soft

rustling of hay, Vetra's slow exhales, the rhythmic strokes of the brush.

Then, Nyrah exhaled. "I'm not broken, you know."

I swallowed against the sudden knot in my throat. "I know."

She turned fully, meeting my gaze. Her eyes— once dulled by pain, by fear—were clear now. Steady. Stronger. Her body was gradually filling out, her cheeks not so hollow, her body finally getting what it needed.

"But I'm not whole, either."

A heartbeat of silence stretched between us.

"You will be," I murmured, the promise tasting like the truth.

Nyrah's fingers curled around the brush. Then, after a long moment, she murmured, "And if I never get magic?"

I stepped closer, covering her hand with mine. "Then you'll still be my sister." I squeezed gently. "You'll still be you."

Her throat bobbed. She nodded once, exhaling slowly. "Okay."

We stood there in the warm quiet of the stable.

The scent of sun-warmed hay, the steady breath

of a horse, the distant hum of the castle waking up wrapped around us.

Nyrah was still healing, but she would be okay.

And that was enough.

THE DREAMING WHISPERED BENEATH MY SKIN. A FAMILIAR hum. Not a threat. Not a burden. Just... *there.*

I stood at the massive windows of my bedchamber, overlooking the kingdom. The sky stretched beyond, endless and quiet.

She was waiting for me.

Lirael.

Her form shimmered in the reflection of the glass, golden light woven into something like a smile. "You did well."

I still found it odd that I didn't have to be asleep to see the Dreaming anymore. I exhaled, my chest aching with something like relief. "It's done."

"For now."

I met her gaze. "Will it ever really be over?"

Lirael tilted her head. "People seeking power? Never. But you mean *her.*"

I lifted my shoulder in a halfhearted shrug. "It's crossed my mind."

Her joy thrummed in my chest, a warmth I hadn't expected. "She is no more, my daughter."

"Then why—" I struggled to describe the feeling that lingered in my bones—not unease, but a kind of knowing. Like the Dreaming wasn't finished with me yet.

Lirael's expression softened. "The Dreaming will always exist, Vale. But now, it's yours to shape."

I hesitated. The weight of the last battle still set heavy on my chest. "If it was always your domain—why didn't you stop Zamarra? Why didn't you help?"

The question had been clawing at the edges of my mind. Not in anger. Not in resentment. Just in wonder.

Lirael's golden light pulsed like a heartbeat. "I was never meant to rule the Dreaming, Vale. I was simply its guardian. A keeper, not a wielder. Not like you."

A flicker of understanding eased through me. She could protect it. Preserve it. But she had never been able to command it.

"And I was bound," she continued. "Just as Idris was severed from himself, just as the Luxa were chained to their fate, I was trapped within my own realm, powerless to change what had already been set into motion."

"But I wasn't."

Her smile was knowing. "No, you weren't. You were the only way to break our fates."

It had always been me—not by prophecy. Not by fate. Not because anyone had chosen me for it. But because I had fought for it.

"You can always come to me when you need answers."

Her golden light pulsed once, the warmth of it brushing against my skin like a farewell. Then she was gone.

The Dreaming still hummed. It always would. But I didn't fear it now.

The door creaked open behind me. The warmth of their presence drifted through the bond before I even turned.

Idris. Kian. Xavier.

I turned as Idris crossed the room first, golden eyes searching mine. He didn't speak. He didn't have to. His hands found my waist, grounding me, steady as ever.

Kian leaned against the doorframe, arms

crossed, a slow smirk playing at his lips. "You keep sneaking off to talk to ghosts. Should I be jealous?"

I huffed out a laugh. "Maybe."

He pushed off the frame, closing the distance between us, slipping in beside me. "At least you always come back to us."

Xavier came next, warm and steady as always, his fingers trailing against my wrist before curling around my palm. "If you needed a distraction, all you have to do is ask."

I arched a brow, but his grin was already forming, his gaze dipping just slightly.

"That is not what I was thinking about," I muttered.

Xavier hummed, low and knowing. "No, but it should be."

I exhaled, letting the tension in my shoulders finally loosen. The past was over. The war was over.

Kian pressed a kiss to my temple, whispering, "Then let's start living."

Idris let out a slow, deep laugh—something rare, something real.

And as I looked at them—the three who had fought, bled, and stood beside me through it all—I knew the truth.

Our story wasn't ending.

It was just beginning.

This concludes The Severed Flames Series.
Thank you so much for reading. I can't express just how
much I have adored writing Vale, Kian, Xavier & Idris
along with their ragtag bunch of friends.

However, if you would love to see a special glimpse of
Vale & her men, turn the page for an epic Severed
Flames Bonus Scene. I hope you enjoy it!

BONUS SCENE

Dear Reader,

I hope you enjoyed The Severed Flames Series. Vale and her men have a very special place in my heart, and I am absolutely ecstatic for you to read more about them.

I have an extra special bonus scene for you as a thank you for reading. All you have to do is click the link below, sign up for my newsletter, and you'll get an email giving you access!

SIGN UP HERE:

https://geni.us/brokenfates-bonus

BOOKS BY ANNIE ANDERSON

SEVERED FLAMES

Ruined Wings

Stolen Embers

Broken Fates

IMMORTAL VICES & VIRTUES

HER MONSTROUS MATES

Bury Me

SHADOW SHIFTER BONDS

Shadow Me

THE ARCANE SOULS WORLD

GRAVE TALKER SERIES

Dead to Me

Dead & Gone

Dead Calm

Dead Shift

Dead Ahead

Dead Wrong

Dead & Buried

SOUL READER SERIES

Night Watch

Death Watch

Grave Watch

THE WRONG WITCH SERIES

Spells & Slip-ups

Magic & Mayhem

Errors & Exorcisms

THE LOST WITCH SERIES

Curses & Chaos

Hexes & Hijinx

THE ETHEREAL WORLD

ROGUE ETHEREAL SERIES

Woman of Blood & Bone

Daughter of Souls & Silence

Lady of Madness & Moonlight

Sister of Embers & Echoes

Priestess of Storms & Stone

Queen of Fate & Fire

PHOENIX RISING SERIES

(Formerly the Ashes to Ashes Series)

Flame Kissed

Death Kissed

Fate Kissed

Shade Kissed

Sight Kissed

EXCLUSIVE SNEAK PEEKS,
GIVEAWAYS, BOOK DISCUSSION.
COME FOR THE BOOKS.
STAY FOR THE MEMES.

To stay up to date on all things Annie Anderson, get exclusive access to ARCs and giveaways, and be a member of a fun, positive, drama-free space, join The Legion!

facebook.com/groups/ThePhoenixLegion

Acknowledgments

A huge, honking thank you to Shawn, Barb, Jade, and Angela. Thanks for the late-night calls, the endurance of my whining, the incessant plotting sessions, the wine runs... (*looking at you, Shawn.*)

Every single one of you rock and I couldn't have done it without you.

ABOUT THE AUTHOR

 Annie Anderson is the author of the international bestselling Rogue Ethereal series. A United States Air Force veteran, Annie pens fast-paced Paranormal Romance & Urban Fantasy novels filled with strong, snarky heroines and a boatload of magic. When she takes a break from writing, she can be found binge-watching The Magicians, flirting with her husband, wrangling children, or bribing her cantankerous dog to go on a walk.

To find out more about Annie and her books, visit www.annieande.com

facebook.com/AuthorAnnieAnderson

instagram.com/AnnieAnde

amazon.com/author/annieande

bookbub.com/authors/annie-anderson

goodreads.com/AnnieAnde

pinterest.com/annieande

tiktok.com/@authorannieanderson